# Lending a Paw

**Center Point
Large Print**

Also by Laurie Cass and available from
Center Point Large Print:

A Bookmobile Cat Mystery
  *Tailing a Tabby*

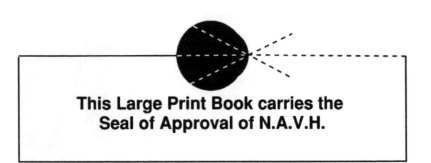

# Lending a Paw

## A Bookmobile Cat Mystery

# Laurie Cass

CENTER POINT LARGE PRINT
THORNDIKE, MAINE

This Center Point Large Print edition
is published in the year 2015 by arrangement with
NAL Signet, an imprint of Penguin Publishing Group,
a division of Penguin Random House LLC.

The text of this Large Print edition is unabridged.
In other aspects, this book may vary
from the original edition.
Printed in the United States of America on permanent paper.
Set in 16-point Times New Roman type.

ISBN: 978-1-62899-546-6

Library of Congress Cataloging-in-Publication Data

Cass, Laurie.
  Lending a paw : a bookmobile cat mystery / Laurie Cass. — Center
point large print edition.
     pages cm
  Summary: "With the help of her rescue cat, Eddie, librarian Minnie
Hamilton is driving a bookmobile based in the resort town of Chilson,
Michigan. After Eddie darts outside at the last stop and leads her to the
body of a local man, they work to help the police find the killer"
  —Provided by publisher.
  ISBN 978-1-62899-546-6 (library binding : alk. paper)
  1. Women librarians—Fiction. 2. Murder—Investigation—Fiction.
     I. Title.
PS3603.A86784L46 2015
813'.6—dc23
                                                           2015007640

For Jessica Wade, who asked for a cat book

# Acknowledgments

This is going to be a long set of acknowledgments, so please bear with me. Heartfelt thanks go to the following:

The bookmobile ladies of LaGrange County Public Library of Indiana. Not only did Kitty Helmkamp and her intrepid assistant let me tag along for a day of bookmobiling, but I got the insider's tour of their gorgeous library. Thanks so much to the entire staff!

All the bookmobile manufacturers I contacted were helpful, but Barb Ferne of OBS went over the top. Thanks for all your help, Barb.

The Association of Bookmobile and Outreach Services (ABOS). My membership with ABOS has been invaluable and I am constantly impressed by the dedication and commitment of bookmobile folks.

My fellow PlotHatchers, authors Janet Bolin, Peg Cochran (also writing as Meg London), Krista Davis, Kaye George (also writing as Janet Cantrell), Daryl Gerber (also writing as Avery Aames), and Marilyn Levinson. Having the support of people who understand the writing life is more precious than I have room to describe.

And Krista Davis deserves a special mention. Though she claims not to remember, it was during a conversation with her that I dreamed up the idea of a bookmobile cat series. Thanks, Krista!

Additional thanks go to:

Author Darlene Ryan, aka Sofie Kelly, aka Sofie Ryan, who has the magical ability to make me laugh at things that shouldn't be the least bit funny.

Author Peg Herring, who is always there when I need Thai food and/or information about Michigan schools.

The staffs at my local hangouts, the Central Lake District Library and the Bellaire Public Library.

Thanks always, always, always to my husband, who kept me fed and watered throughout the writing and editing of this book. You're the best, sweetie!

To my amazing agent, Jessica Faust, and the entire BookEnds staff.

A huge thank-you goes to my outstanding editor, Jessica Wade. Not only was she the impetus behind the book's entire concept, but she also took the mess that was the original manuscript and (oh-so-gently) helped me shape it into what you now hold in your hands. If you hear people say that books aren't edited these days, send them to me.

And last, but certainly not least, I'd like to thank the real-life Eddie for allowing me to write about him. While the fictional Eddie and the real version are not exactly the same, most days it's hard to tell the difference. Thanks, pal. You're the best Eddie ever.

# Chapter 1

When I was a little girl, I dreamed of growing up to be the president. Failing that, an astronaut or a ballerina.

My presidential aspirations were quashed when I found out that the president did not, in fact, get to do whatever he (or she) wanted. The astronaut idea faded when my mother told me that even people in space suits could get motion sickness, and my ballerina phase lasted only until I actually took a class and discovered that I had no aptitude whatsoever. Even at six, I knew what the ballet teacher's headshaking meant.

With those career paths closed off, I went to my alternative tier of professional choices, determined in large part because I'd had the great good fortune to grow up within walking distance of a public library. By the time I'd turned ten, I knew that I would be one of three things: a librarian in a big city, a librarian in a large town, or a librarian in a small town.

Big cities give me the heebie-jeebies, so that was out. A large town would have been okay, but a few short years after receiving my master's degree in library and information science and a few short weeks after the end of a long-term relationship, I found a posting for an assistant director position at the district library in Chilson, Michigan.

Chilson! I stared at the listing so long that my eyes dried out. Chilson was a small tourist town in northwest lower Michigan. It was where I'd spent childhood summers with my aunt. It was my favorite place in the whole world. Could I really be this lucky?

When the library board voted to hire me, I was deliriously happy. I was young, footloose, fancy-free, and, since I'd given up any hope of my height reaching five feet and had become resigned to the fact that my curly black hair was never going to straighten, things were working out just the way I'd crossed my fingers that they would.

But three years after my move to Chilson, not long past my thirty-third birthday, life took an abrupt turn.

I woke on that fateful Friday morning to the beeping of my alarm clock and a cat-shaped weight on my chest. Eyes closed, I thumped off the clock and spoke to the weight.

"Eddie, it's time to get up." I opened my eyes, then immediately shut them. "Why do you have to sleep so close to my face?" If I opened my eyes again, I'd see late-May sunshine streaming through the gap in the white curtains and illuminating my cat's furry face, which was maybe an inch from my chin. Soon after Eddie had followed me home last month, I'd learned his preferred mattress was a human one.

As there'd been no feline reply, I tried a second time.

"Eddie, get up."

A faint rumble spread into my chest.

"No purring." I gave him a gentle shove that was meant to instigate a move. It did nothing. "I have to go to work. Sorry, pal, but you have to get off." I rolled onto my left side. Eddie, still purring, slid off my chest and landed on my arm. "No," I told him. "Really off."

He opened one eye.

I pulled my arm out from underneath him. "What do you want me to do, stay in bed all day?"

He stopped purring and opened both eyes.

"Not a chance," I said. "I have to go out and make a living so I can support us in the style to which you've recently become accustomed."

He settled deep into the covers. With my freed arm I scratched his chin, earning more purrs. Then, grunting a little with the effort, I carefully moved him aside and got up to start the first day of the rest of my life.

Halfway to the bathroom I looked back at Eddie. My first cat. My first pet. My parents hadn't encouraged household animals—my dad was allergic to pet dander—and until I met Eddie I'd never felt the lack.

Eddie yawned wide, laying his ears back against the sides of his head and showing me far too much of his pink tongue.

"Cover your mouth when you do that, will you?" I asked.

"Mrr," he said sleepily.

"That's what you always say," I said. "You'd better learn some etiquette by October. Aunt Frances is a sweetheart, but she doesn't tolerate bad manners."

All winter I lived with my aunt in her old and large house, but come May she good-humoredly kicked me out to make room for guests who paid a lot more than I did. That was when I moved down the hill to the small houseboat I'd bought from an elderly couple when they'd moved to Florida. The month of April involved a lot of cleaning and prep before the guys at the marina moved the boat out of the warehouse and into the water, but I didn't mind the work.

Friends shook their heads at my living arrangements. I heard a lot of "Don't you want your own house?" and "You should be building up more equity," and "Your aunt is awesome, but isn't it a little like living with your parents?"

My reply was a smile and a shrug. It worked for me and it worked for Aunt Frances, who didn't like to live alone. Maybe someday I'd want my own lawn to mow, my own furnace to repair, roof to fix, and plumbing to worry about. Maybe. For now, I was happy. And so was Eddie.

Six weeks ago, on my last pre-Eddie day, I'd been spending a gloomy Sunday on the houseboat, scrubbing and washing. Come midafternoon, a slice of blue sky had appeared through the partially open warehouse doorway. I'd wandered outside to see. Not only had the low gray clouds vanished, but the temperature had gone from stay-home-with-a-book to I-need-to-get-outside-or-I'll-die.

I looked at the cloudless blue. At my boat. At the sky.

It'd be okay to take a short walk, I told myself. After the long winter we just had, it'd be criminal not to take advantage of this weather. A short walk, then I'd get the galley cleaned up, see that my neighbor Rafe hadn't passed out from paint fumes in the house he was rehabbing, meet my friend Kristen for dinner, and still have plenty of time to clean the bedroom before heading back up to Aunt Frances's place to sleep.

It didn't turn out that way.

My short stroll through the streets of Chilson turned into a long ramble through a nearby park, which became a wandering walk through an old cemetery.

No one knew that I like to spend time in cemeteries. Not my friends or relatives, and certainly not my coworkers. The single time I'd suggested walking through a cemetery to someone (my very-*ex*-fiancé), he'd made me feel like such a freak that I'd decided then and there to keep my cemetery inclinations to myself. I found cemeteries peaceful and calming in a poignant sort of way, and I always left from them eager to get things done.

The appropriately named Lakeview Cemetery was perched on the edge of a hill, overlooking the sparkling waters of the twenty-mile-long and two-mile-wide Janay Lake. That April afternoon I sat on a bench next to the headstone of Alonzo Tillotson (born 1847, died 1926) and enjoyed the pleasurable sensation that comes from skipping out on chores.

"I should get back," I said to the view, not meaning a word of it. "There's a lot to do." Which was true, but Aunt Frances wouldn't mind if I stayed in her house for another week. Her summer boarders wouldn't show up until after Memorial Day—there was plenty of time for me to move to the houseboat.

I slid down into a slouch and lifted my face to the sun. "Lots to do," I murmured lazily. "Finish the inside, wash down the deck, call the marina to schedule—"

*"MRR!"*

I leapt up. Small animal noises eeked out of me, little bleats of panic that made me sound pathetic and small and frightened. All true, but still. I grabbed on to an arm of the bench, sucked large amounts of air into my lungs, and tried to pretend that I was a fully functional adult.

The cat at my feet didn't look impressed.

"Did you make that awful noise?" I asked.

He—maybe it was a she, but the cat's attitude felt decidedly male—looked at me. Unblinking yellow eyes stared into my brown ones. His markings were black and white stripes with a chest and paws that probably would have been white if they'd been clean. A small pyramid of whitishness had its peak between his eyes, spreading down to touch the outside corners of his wide mouth. The pale triangle gave him a face so expressive I almost felt as if he were talking to me.

"Mrr."

Then again, maybe he was.

"Hello," I said. "My name is Minnie Hamilton. And before you ask, yes, it's short for Minerva, and no, I don't know what my parents were thinking."

"Mrr."

The cat was sitting up straight, studying me intently. I didn't care for the look. "Don't you have a home?" I asked. "Someone's looking for you, I'm sure."

Without visibly flexing a muscle, he moved forward three inches.

"Yup," I said, "there's someone coming, without a doubt. You stay here and wait, okay?" I nodded. "Nice talking to you."

I took one step away from the bench.

The cat didn't move.

I took another step.

He still didn't move.

Good. He wouldn't follow me home and beg to be fed and housed and cared for. Or was it only dogs that begged? Everything I knew about pets I'd learned from watching *America's Funniest Home Videos*.

I walked down the hill, not dawdling, but not hurrying, either, because being chased out of the cemetery by a cat was ridiculous.

So I headed back toward the marina with a light heart, thinking about the coming summer. My walk took me through the outskirts of town with its clapboard cottages, past the brick post office, past the stucco city hall, and through downtown with half its shops still closed for winter.

Throughout my journey, the sun shone and people smiled. I smiled back, happy to be alive, happy to be me. Then white-haired Mr. Goodwin, a regular library patron, said, "Hello, Minnie. Who's your little friend?" He pointed behind me.

I closed my eyes. "Don't tell me it's a cat."

The elderly man chuckled. "Okay, I won't. Hope you and your friend enjoy the rest of this fine day." He and his dapper cane moved off.

I kept my eyes closed for a moment longer. Mr. Goodwin had a vivid imagination; he was always telling shaggy-dog stories that kept you riveted until the final pointless ending. Sure, that was it. Another story. Just a really, really short one.

16

"Mrr."

I turned and there he was. The cat. Who looked remarkably proud of himself.

"Why did you follow me?" I asked, frowning. "And quit looking at me like that."

"Um, Minnie?" Another library patron was standing on the sidewalk, holding one small child by the hand and an even smaller one on her hip. "Cats don't like that tone of voice," she said. "If you keep talking to him like that, he's never going to answer."

"He followed me, that's all. He's not mine."

"Are you sure?" Laughing, she walked off.

I looked at the cat. He looked at me.

"You do have a home, don't you?" I asked.

He walked straight to me and gave me my first-ever fuzzy head butt, right on the boniest part of my shin.

"Ow! That hurt!"

He butted me again. This time it was gentler, almost a caress. Then he was winding around my ankles in figure eights, around and around and around.

I sank into a crouch and patted his head. He turned his face away, making my fingers slide under his chin. "You like that, do you?" I scratched his chin with one hand and petted his long back with the other.

His purrs were loud and rattling and . . . and comforting.

"Well," I said, "maybe you could stay with me until we find your real home."

"Mrr."

That day had been almost two months ago. I'd taken the cat to the town's veterinarian until the boat was ready, and the vet confirmed that the cat was a male, that he weighed thirteen pounds, had ear mites, needed to be wormed, was roughly two years old, and hadn't been reported as missing.

I'd run the obligatory ad in the paper and talked to the local animal shelter, but no one came to claim my little buddy. His name had been the inspiration of a bemused coworker. "Sounds like an Eddie kind of a cat," Josh had said after I'd told the story.

"What kind is that?" Holly, another coworker, had asked.

"Just . . . Eddie." Josh had shrugged. "You know what guys named Eddie are like."

And just like that, my cat had a name, because I knew exactly what Josh meant. Guys named Eddie spoke their minds, didn't waste time when they knew what they wanted, and were deeply loyal. They were the classic average good guys. At least that's what the Eddies I'd known were like, and the name fit my new friend as if it were tattooed on his furry forehead.

I looked at him now. He was squirreled into the covers of my bed, and he still looked like an

Eddie. And he still looked like he wanted me to stay home and nap with him all morning.

"Can't do it. It's the big day, remember?"

He half opened his eyes. "Mrr."

It was an invitation that had, more than once, tempted me to whack the snooze button on the alarm clock. Not this time. I ignored him and headed to the shower. Half an hour later I was dried, clothed, breakfasted, and had done my best to make the bed around the sleeping Eddie.

I also kept a promise I'd made to my mother and left a note on a whiteboard I'd tacked up in the kitchen about where I was going and when I was going to return. Mom worried—a lot—and my vow to always leave a note of my whereabouts comforted her. How leaving a note for myself would help anything, I didn't know, but she said it made her sleep easier.

So I scrawled a note and gathered up my backpack, but halfway out the door, I screeched to a halt. I'd forgotten to pack a lunch.

The panic of potential lateness seized me. I ran back inside, opened the tiny microwave that was now called the Eddie Safe, as it was one of the few places safe from the bread-loving Eddie, and pulled two pieces of bread from a loaf. In thirty seconds I'd slapped together a peanut butter and jelly sandwich and shoved it into a plastic bag. I found an apple in the back of the small refrigerator, grabbed a half-empty bag of tortilla chips, filled a plastic bottle with water, and dropped it all into my backpack.

"See you tonight, Eddie!" I ran out of the house and walked across the boat's deck, unlatched the railing door, hopped onto the marina's dock, and started trotting up the hill to the library.

Never once had I been late for work. Never. I always arrived on time for appointments and I'd developed such a reputation for arriving at the stated hour to parties that my friends routinely sent me invitations with a different starting time. Now, with so much riding on what happened today, there I was, skimming the edge of lateness.

I hurried up the hill and away from the marina, practically running through the narrow side streets. The library, a handsome L-shaped brick building, sat on the far side of downtown. To my left, I knew the majestic Lake Michigan would be an inviting horizon of blue, and behind me the adjacent Janay Lake would be glittering in the sunshine, but I didn't have time for my normal backward glances of appreciation.

"Morning, Minnie." The owner of the bakery was putting out his sidewalk sign. OPEN. FREE SMELLS. "Say, did you know—"

"Talk to you later, Tom, okay?" I waved as I went past. "Running late today."

After three blocks of antique stores, art galleries, clothing boutiques, and the occasional bookstore, fudge shop, and coffee shop, I reached the library. But instead of using my keys to let myself in the side door as per usual, I went around back. Then around the back of the back, past the employee parking and past the bins for cardboard recycling and trash. There, on the far side of the auxiliary parking lot, which was used only when famous authors came to speak, was the thing that was going to make or break my career.

The bookmobile.

Though it was inside a brand-new garage, I could almost see its wavy blue-painted graphics in the bright morning sun, its bright white letters emblazoned across its sides: CHILSON DISTRICT LIBRARY BOOKMOBILE. All fresh and spanking clean and waiting for me to . . . to what?

With a sudden and unwelcome rush, anxiety and dread darkened the shiny morning. Doubts assailed me from every direction. There was no way I'd be able to—

"Stop that." I took a firmer grip on the straps of my backpack. Hearing the words out loud made me feel better, and since there wasn't a soul around to hear, I kept going. "I haven't been carsick in years. I've taught myself how to read maps *and* bought a GPS, and since the bookmobile was my idea, I'm the one to run it. I can do this. And I'll do it right."

The night before, I'd slid the driver's daily checklist into my backpack. In ten minutes I was scheduled to be driving out of the parking lot and to my first stop on the opposite side of the county. It was time to hurry.

I unlocked the garage, climbed into the driver's seat, tossed my backpack onto the passenger's seat, started the engine, and backed the book-mobile out into the sun. Though the library director had grudgingly agreed to have a garage built for the bookmobile, it wasn't any bigger than it had to be. Doing the pretrip check outside would be much easier. I turned off the engine, pulled the hood release, and went outside. "Water level, oil level," I muttered, checking off the list as I went. "Good, and good." I hurried back inside and started the engine. Gauges, all good. No weird engine noises. Very good.

Back outside to check tire pressure, back in and back out to check the lights and turn signals. Back inside to check a dozen other things. Fellow drivers had assured me that it would get to be habit within a matter of days, that soon I wouldn't need the checklist. I almost, but not quite, believed this.

I ticked off the last item ("loose books secured"), shut the door, and slid into the driver's seat.

The bookmobile's dashboard clock stared at me accusingly. "Yes, I'm a minute late," I told it as I buckled myself in. "If you don't tell Stephen, I'll give you a good vacuuming tonight."

I could have sworn I heard a sniff.

First day as the bookmobile driver and I was already hearing things. Outstanding.

As I put my hand on the gearshift, a rush of excitement prickled my skin. It was actually happening. The bookmobile was real, and I was driving it. I was going to bring books back to the small towns who'd had their branch libraries closed. I was going to bring books to schools and senior centers and people who were homebound. This outreach program was going to make a difference. *I* was going to make a difference.

A happy grin spread wide across my face. It was a beautiful morning, the finest in months, maybe the finest ever, and this day was going to be one of the best ever and—

"Mrr."

# *Chapter 2*

I blinked. Had I heard what I thought I'd heard? No. Absolutely not. Insanity was far preferable. "Eddie?" I asked tentatively.

He sat up, yawning, revealing himself from where he'd been lying behind the backpack I'd tossed onto the passenger's seat.

"Eddie, what on earth are you doing here?" I was almost shouting. "How did you . . . ?" Then I remembered. I'd left the houseboat door open when I'd run back inside to make my lunch. And I remembered that Tom had been looking behind me when he'd tried to say hello. And that I'd left the bookmobile door open while I'd run through the preflight check, giving Eddie plenty of time to sneak aboard.

"You are a horrible cat," I told him. "What am I supposed to do with you? I don't have time to take you home."

The dashboard clock ticked forward. Now it was two minutes past eight.

Eddie and I glared at each other. At least I glared. He looked bored.

I glanced at the bookmobile's interior. Custom shelves and cabinets contained everything a miniature library could want. Two desktops, one front and one back, held laptop computers for checking out books. There was a wheelchair lift behind swinging bookshelves. A carpeted step that ran along the base of the shelves for stepping and sitting. An adorably cute refrigerator and even tinier microwave behind a fabric corkboard. Electric heaters. Roof-mounted air conditioners. Pop-up skylights for cross-ventilation. All that, but no room anywhere for an extraneous cat.

Three minutes past eight.

I scowled at Eddie. "You haven't left me much choice. But you'd better be good today."

He closed one eye and slowly opened it again. Though I'd been a cat caretaker less than two months, I knew what that wink meant. It meant he was a cat and he'd do whatever he pleased, when he pleased, and if I didn't like it, that was just too bad.

I dropped the gearshift into drive and put my foot on the accelerator. The Chilson District Library Bookmobile began its maiden voyage. Me, three thousand books, one hundred DVDs, a dozen jigsaw puzzles, two laptop computers—and one Eddie.

For forty-five minutes, as I drove to the east side of the county, I ignored the lake-filled and hilly countryside in favor of imagining what was going to happen to me when my boss found out I'd brought a cat along on the bookmobile. The most likely scenario was that Stephen would fire me for . . . for feline interference.

I mentioned this to Eddie, who was sleeping on the passenger seat, rounded into a big Eddie-ball. If his snores were any indication of his concern, he didn't seem to think it likely. I'd never known cats could snore, let alone snore as loud as Eddie. The first time his raspy breaths woke me up, I'd been sure there was an intruder in my bedroom, breathing hard through his face-covering ski mask. But, no. It was just Eddie.

"What happens, wise guy," I asked him now, "if I get demoted? What if I have to take a pay cut? What if I have to work longer hours?"

Eddie opened his eyes briefly.

"Sure, I already work weekends and lots of evenings, but that's because . . . because there are things to do."

Eddie started snoring again. It was easy to see why. There was no way his nasal passages could be happy in that position. How any creature could find it comfortable to be half upside down and half right side up with his face smushed into the side of my backpack, I had no idea, but what did I know about being a cat?

Then again, maybe I could learn a lot from cats. Eddie didn't seem to worry about anything and I hadn't come across anything that disturbed his sleep. There was a definite lesson here some- where, but if it required a diet of cat food, I wasn't sure I wanted to sign up for the course.

Eddie's snores faded to a dull roar. Four minutes

to nine and we were still miles from where I was supposed to be meeting Suzanne Slade, the library volunteer who'd gone all giddy at the chance of riding along with the bookmobile. "Oh, it'll be such *fun!*" Her white-blond curls had bobbed as she'd clapped. "Going on the first voyage. What a *treat!*"

I'd pushed aside my concerns of spending hours with that much perkiness in what was essentially a very small room, and we'd made arrangements to meet Friday morning in a church parking lot. Suzanne would get a ride back with a friend who worked in Chilson. "It'll work out wonderfully," she'd said.

I hoped Suzanne wasn't allergic to cats. For that matter, I hoped that no one who was going to board the bookmobile was allergic to cats. Or afraid of cats. Or mean to cats.

The GPS unit I'd bought came to life and said my destination was one quarter mile away. I could see the white steepled church, and I could also see an empty parking lot.

I steered into the large gravel space, which was big enough that it eliminated the need to back up the bookmobile. We were a little late. Could Suzanne have grown tired of waiting and gone home? I tapped the steering wheel, slid open the side window for some fresh air, and watched the clock tick away two more minutes.

"You know," I told Eddie, who, judging from

the way his ears were rotating, was at least partially awake, "I should check my phone and see if she's left a message. Excuse me, okay?" Gently, I rearranged parts of his black-and-white fuzziness—which started purring—and reached into the backpack for my cell phone. I'd been commanded by Stephen not to use it while driving upon pain of death (or words to that effect) and hadn't even turned it on that morning.

Just then a sedan sped into the parking lot and came to a sliding stop right in front of the bookmobile. Suzanne flung open the driver's door, jumped out, and came over to my open window.

"I'm so sorry I'm late." She sounded weepy and distraught. "Minnie, I hate letting you down like this, I'm so sorry."

"Well, we're only a few minutes late."

"No, no," she cried. "It's my mother. Downstate. A tree fell on her house. I have to go help sort things out—there's no one else. I'm so sorry—she called just half an hour ago and I had to pack and I'm so sorry to abandon you like this."

I hurried outside and came around to Suzanne. "We'll be fine," I said, giving her a big hug. "Don't worry about it. Your mom is what's important right now."

She sniffed and gave me a weak smile. "You'll manage?"

"Sure. Will you?"

"I'll be okay." She rubbed at her eyes. "I may look a mess, but I have a long drive to pull myself together."

I watched as she sped away and hoped she'd be all right. Another volunteer was scheduled to start next week, but still . . .

"Mrr!"

I whipped around. Eddie was poking his face out from where I'd opened the window. No, not just his face. A white foot was sneaking out, then the elbow. . . .

"Eddie!" I marched over to the window and stood on my tiptoes to push—in a nice way, of course—his various parts back inside. "Now stay there."

By the time I got in the bookmobile, he was half out the window again. I grabbed him by the midsection, pulled him inside, and shut the window. "What's with you, anyway?" I rubbed his fuzzy head and sat down with him on my lap. "I thought you were going to be a good cat today. And no purring. You know how that makes me forgive you anything."

He purred and snuggled his head into my armpit. I rubbed his ears. "You truly are a horrible cat." I picked him up, feet dangling, and deposited him onto the passenger seat. "If you stay at this level of horrible, we'll be fine. But if you—"

My phone rang. I looked at the screen. "It's Stephen," I told Eddie. "Think I should answer?"

Eddie had no opinion, so I took the call.

"Good morning, Minnie. How is it going so far?"

"Oh, not bad." Certainly things could be worse. I could have run out of gas. Or hit a deer. Or made a wrong turn that ended two miles later in a dead end with no way to turn around the thirty-one-foot bookmobile.

"I would have hoped that by now you'd be on the way to your first stop, but since you're answering the phone, I know the bookmobile is stationary."

"Just ready to leave this minute."

"And you have a volunteer with you?"

"Volunteer? Well, about that . . ."

"Minnie, you can't be out there by yourself," he said. "The library board was quite insistent that you not be alone on the bookmobile."

"I know." I knew all about the board's concerns, issues ranging from insurance costs to liability to maintenance responsibilities. I'd done the research on running a bookmobile; I'd found grant money to pay for the first year of operations; I'd even convinced one of the richest men in town to contribute money for the purchase of this grand vehicle.

Through it all, Stephen had been looking over my shoulder, quick to point out the smallest flaw in my plans. And through it all, I'd known perfectly well that a sizable minority of the library board supported each of his criticisms. If this maiden voyage went wrong in any way, the minority could become a majority and that didn't bear thinking about.

"Tell me you aren't alone on the bookmobile," Stephen said.

I looked at Eddie. "I'm not."

"Then why . . . ? Never mind. You'll tell me when you come in." He hung up and I turned off the phone. There wouldn't be decent coverage in most of the places I was going, anyway.

"Mrr." Eddie had draped himself over my backpack, his two front legs spread wide.

"Don't look so pleased with yourself," I said. "I would have figured a way out of the two-on-the-vehicle thing if you hadn't been here."

"Mrr."

"Would too."

"Mrr."

Cats. They always had to have the last word.

The morning sun sent shafts of sunlight between the maple leaves and onto the two-lane road. Driving through the dappled light, I kept my eyes moving, looking for wildlife, checking the mirrors to make sure I was staying in the middle of the lane, eyeing the dashboard gauges, trying to remember everything I'd been taught about driving the bookmobile.

Twenty minutes later I saw a cluster of homes

around a small school. The school's library budget had been slashed to the bone a few years ago. For a while they'd borrowed new books from a nearby branch of the Chilson District Library, but budget cuts had closed that down tight. It was the closing of that much-loved library that had spurred me to assemble an ad hoc committee, its purpose a feasibility study of a Chilson book-mobile. Which had ended up to be a committee of me, but everything had turned out just fine.

Mostly.

I flicked the turn signal and looked at Eddie. Though I couldn't tell for certain over the road noise, I was pretty sure he was snoring again. "First stop, coming up," I said loudly.

Slightly left we went, Eddie, the bookmobile, and me. Then a slow, wide sweeping right turn into the weed-infested gravel parking lot, a gentle braking to a soft stop, and we were there. The inaugural stop of the Chilson District Library Bookmobile had begun.

I slid open the side windows, then rotated the driver's seat to face the computer desk, and stood. I pushed the one-step stool from its home behind the passenger seat and stood on it to reach the fan installed into the ceiling. I'd turn on the air-conditioning if I had to, but that would mean turning on the generator and that was a dull roar I'd just as soon do without.

"And now what do I do with you?" I asked my

cat. After this stop we'd take a short break at a county park just down the road. I'd get him some water and a nice out-of-the-way, sandy spot for him to do anything he needed to do, but for now . . .

"Mrr." Eddie half closed his eyes and settled into a comfortable slouch.

For now, what was I going to do with him? In the time between leaving Chilson and arriving here, I'd come up with zero ideas. There was no cat carrier for him, I wasn't wearing a belt that might be turned into a leash, and I was not about to take off my bra and fashion it into an Eddie restraint.

*Knock knock.*

No time to think, no time for anything but action. "Just a minute!" I opened the cabinet door that held a tidy arrangement of filing and cleaning supplies, gathered them up, dropped them onto the floor in front of the passenger's seat, grabbed Eddie, shoved him in the cabinet, and shut the door. "Sorry, pal," I whispered. "I'll let you out as soon as they're gone."

I hurried down the length of the bookmobile, almost tripped in my rush to maneuver the steps, and pushed open the door.

A small group of children stood outside. "Hi, come on in. Welcome to the bookmobile!"

The six kids ranged from age five-ish to ten-ish, three boys and three girls. They stood there, glancing at one another, shifting from foot to foot. None of them made a move.

33

I grinned, made waving come-on-in motions, and did my best carnival barker imitation. "We have books, all sorts of books. We have Curious George, we have Hardy Boys, we have Amelia Bedelia, we have Indians in the cupboard, we have books about horses, we have books about baseball, we have books about cats and kittens. We have books with stories about far-off lands and castles and dragons and princesses and kings and queens and—"

"Princesses?" a girl asked, her eyes big and round. "You have princess books?"

I smiled at her. "We sure do. Come aboard and I'll show you."

She ran up the two outside steps, jumped onto the first stair on the bookmobile and turned around. "I'm going to get princess books," she told her compatriots. "I'm going to be first to get a bookmobile book." She whirled back around and bounced up to my side, her face bright and shiny. "Can I see them now? Where are they?"

"They're right over—"

My words were lost in the pandemonium of five children trying to get up into the bookmobile simultaneously. In no time at all, I'd guided the smallest to the picture books, and shown others the locations of biographies, nature books, and, of course, princess books. While I was guiding one of the girls to the Boxcar Children, a deep male voice boomed up into the bookmobile. "Hey, you kids! You were supposed to wait for me!"

They froze. Except for the princess-fixated girl. She was so focused on the golden-haired pictures on her lap that she probably wouldn't have heard lightning strike the ground next to her.

A big, bearded man came up the steps and glared at the kids one by one, starting with the oldest boy. "Trevor. Rose. Cara. Patrick. Emma. Ethan. What do you have to say for yourselves?"

"It was here, Dad," the smallest child said. "And you were going to be on the phone a long, long time."

Dad glanced at his watch. "Five whole minutes is indeed a long time." He sent me an amused look. "But you knew you were supposed to wait for me."

"It was *here*," the princess girl said. "And look!" She brandished the book at him, a cover of pinks and purples and gold.

"Again with the princesses." He shook his head. "Why am I not surprised?"

"It's *good!*" She pulled the book to her chest. "It's my favorite!"

He patted his daughter on the head and held out his hand to me. "Chad Engstrom. And, yes, they're all mine. Three sets of twins, what are the odds?"

"Minnie Hamilton," I said, shaking his hand. "They were hesitant to come on the bookmobile. Now I think I understand."

"Kids," he said, sighing. "Can't live with them, can't leave them out on the street for someone else to take."

"You're stuck with us," Trevor said, his nose buried in a biography of Thomas Edison.

Chad made a deep, menacing, growly noise. "And you're stuck with me. What do you think of that?"

"We think we love you," they chorused.

I laughed out loud. A scene like this would never have happened inside a library. If this was what driving a bookmobile was going to be like, I was hooked.

A hand tugged at the hem of my cropped pants. "Do you have a book about a puppy?" A girl— Cara? Or was it Emma?—looked up at me, her small face full of hope and expectation.

"You bet," I said promptly. For two months I'd done little except get ready for this day. I knew every inch of the bookmobile. I knew how many steps it was from front to back, I knew the mechanical systems inside and out, and I knew every single book on the shelves. "Right over here."

As soon as she was settled, another hand tugged at my pants. Big blue eyes filled with question marks looked up at me.

"Hi," I said. "I'm Miss Minnie. What's your name?"

"Ethan."

"Hi, Ethan. How can I help you?"

"My dad said you'd show me the bookmobile."

"Absolutely," I said just as a quiet *thump* came from inside Eddie's cabinet. "Why don't we start at the back?"

I showed Ethan and his father the wheelchair lift, spent some time over the strapped-in book carts that I'd soon be wheeling into senior centers and day cares, and told him how the books and DVDs and CDs and magazines were arranged. The top half of my brain was engaged with being a bookmobile librarian. The bottom half, however, was running around in frantic circles. How long could Eddie stay in the cabinet undetected? I knew he'd survive the day if he didn't eat anything, but by noon he'd start complaining that he was starving to death. Loudly.

"What's in there?" Ethan pointed at the critical cabinet.

"Storage," I said. "Paper towels. Glass cleaner. Nothing interesting."

Eddie gave the door a thump. I gave it a light whack, hoping the child would think I'd made the noise both times.

"Mrr," Eddie said.

"Shhh," I whispered.

"Sorry?" Chad asked.

"Shoot," I said quickly. "I forgot to bring a book your children might have enjoyed."

"Oh? What?"

Four years of undergraduate work in library science, two years of graduate school, nine years of working in libraries, college summers working in a children's bookstore, not to mention my own book-filled childhood, and my brain was dry of any suggestions. I gave a sheepish smile. "Afraid I can't remember the title. I'll try to—"

"Dad, look!" Ethan pointed. "The cabinet's moving!"

"Leveling," I said, putting my heel firmly against the door. "The bookmobile must not be completely level, so the door is opening on its own." Or it would have, if there hadn't been magnets holding the door closed, but there was no need to bother these nice people with that little point. I braced my heel against the bottom of the door, trying for a casual pose. "Do you have any other questions?"

His brother Trevor, sitting on the carpeted step at the base of the shelves, snorted. "Bet he has more than one."

"Answering questions is why I'm here," I said. "What do you want to know, Ethan?"

He pointed to the driver's seat. "Why does the library have a steering wheel?"

"Because this library is on wheels. You saw me drive up, remember? And if something has wheels, you need a way to steer it."

He nodded, then pointed to a shelf of books. "If the library moves, why don't those fall on the floor?"

"You have bookshelves at home, right? And I bet yours are flat, like this." I held my hands out in front of me. "If books on the bookmobile were like that, they would fall off when we hit bumps on the road." My hands made bouncing motions. "But these shelves are different. Do you see how?"

Ethan looked at my hands, looked at the shelves, and frowned deep enough to put crinkles in his forehead.

Trevor sighed heavily, but otherwise kept quiet.

Finally, Ethan pursed his lips and nodded firmly. "They tip."

His father clapped him on the shoulder. "Way to go, kiddo! You figured it out all by yourself."

But Ethan wasn't done asking questions. He pointed at the laptop computer on the counter behind the driver's seat. "What's that for?"

I moved away from the cabinet and showed him the RFID scanner and the wiring connecting it to the computer. "We use these to keep track of where all the books are."

Ethan was roaming, running his fingers over the shelves, his intelligent eyes hunting for things he didn't understand. More questions were clearly imminent.

Chad watched his son. "You've done a great

thing here." His other five children had piles of books at their feet.

"Thanks," I said. "We had a generous budget, but even a great big pile of money runs out at some point."

"That's right, you had a donation." Chad snapped his fingers. "I remember reading about it. Some guy who grew up around here?"

I nodded, smiling as I thought of my elderly friend. "Stan Larabee. He's about seventy now. He moved away after high school and got into Florida real estate development. When he retired a few years ago, he moved back up here and—"

There was a *click* that sounded a lot like the *click* the cabinet doors made when being opened. I looked up. Froze solid. Half a nanosecond later, my mouth started to open, but I was far, far too late.

"Hey, look!" Ethan said, pointing.

Princess jumped to her feet. "It's a kitty cat!"

"Mrr," said Eddie.

# Chapter 3

A cat?" Chad looked at me.

I sucked in a large breath and blew it out. "Your kids aren't allergic, are they?" Because now all six of them were sitting or standing or kneeling in front of the cabinet, giggling and pointing.

Chad snorted. "Those kids are so healthy, my wife and I have been tempted to inject them with a flu virus so they know what it's like to be sick."

"Can I pet him?" Ethan asked.

"Why do you have a cat in the cabinet?" Trevor asked.

"He's beautiful," Princess cooed.

The middle girl asked, "What's his name?"

"Eddie," I said, sighing. "His name is Eddie." I made my way through the children and crouched down. The troublesome one had retreated so far into the cabinet that his fur was sliding up against the back wall. "We've been discovered, pal. You might as well come on out." His yellow eyes stared at me. "Come on," I said, "the natives are friendly." I danced my fingers on the front edge of the shelf. He inched forward, sniffing, and finally came forward far enough to let me swoop him up.

I kissed the top of his head, then turned around to make the introductions. "Eddie, this is Ethan.

And Trevor. And Mr. Engstrom. And . . ." I looked at the other kids. "And what are your names?"

"Rose," said Princess Girl.

"Emma," said the youngest girl.

"I'm Patrick," said the middle boy, "and she's Cara."

"Hi, Eddie," Cara said in a voice so quiet I almost didn't hear her. "You're a pretty cat."

"Mrr," he said, and then the total and complete ham started purring. I rolled my eyes and the kids crowded closer, all reaching out to pet him. Eddie sighed and let them.

"I take it Eddie wasn't a planned feature?" Chad asked.

Maybe the world wouldn't end. At least not today. "He's a stowaway," I said, "and if word gets back to my boss that I let a cat on the bookmobile, my job will be toast."

Chad gave Eddie a head pat. "He's a friendly little guy. Why would your boss care?"

Reasons filled my brain so fast that my skull felt two sizes too small. Cat hair on the books. A distraction to driving. A disruption to the business of the bookmobile. Allergies. Unprofessional. Unclean.

Eddie was getting heavy, so I put him on the carpeted step. Five of the six kids surrounded him, oohing and aahing. Trevor went back to his book.

"My boss," I said, "is very concerned about the

library's image and I'm quite sure Eddie doesn't fit into that picture." I wasn't sure the bookmobile fit into Stephen's grand plan, either, but once Stan Larabee had written that lovely big check with "Bookmobile donation" written in the memo field, he hadn't had much choice.

Stephen was a big believer in a centralized library. He'd convinced the board that the availability of e-book lending made our small outlying libraries unnecessary and shut them all down in the name of fiscal responsibility. When I'd floated the idea of a bookmobile at a library board meeting, Stephen had asked in stentorian tones, "Is there anyone here who thinks a library should waste money on an expensive, high-maintenance operation like a bookmobile?"

Mine was the only hand that went up. It had been an awkward moment, but I'd kept my hand stubbornly high.

"Have any of you ever been on a bookmobile?" I'd asked, and rejoiced when a few heads nodded. "Do you think that maybe, just maybe, the thrill of being visited by a bookmobile is what helped give you a love of reading? Isn't that part of our mission as a library?" A few more heads had nodded, but then Stephen brought the topic back to dollars, specifically the library's lack thereof, and the nods stilled.

The single, solitary thing that had made our bookmobile possible was that lovely, large check.

I knew in my bones that if Stephen found any reason to shut down the bookmobile, he'd do so without a second thought. I'd be in disgrace, possibly fired, and the bookmobile would be sold as quickly as possible. A letter of apology would be written to Stan Larabee and that would be that.

I watched Eddie strut down the aisle, flicking his tail to touch the bare legs of each child. He ignored me, head-butted Chad, then, in one smooth leap, jumped to the passenger's seat headrest.

"Mrr," he said, surveying his human subjects.

The kids giggled. Chad chuckled. I sighed.

The Engstroms lugged away three milk crates full of books and made promise after promise that they'd return everything when the bookmobile came back.

"Bye, Eddie," they called. "See you next time."

"Or not," I said, closing the door behind them. I turned the dead bolt and went forward to the driver's seat, talking to Eddie all the way. "Because there isn't a chance in you-know-what that you're ever setting foot on this bookmobile again. This is a once-in-a-lifetime event that will never be repeated, and may my tongue turn black if I'm saying anything other than the total truth."

I stuck out my tongue and crossed my eyes.

"Still pink, see?" I pointed at my tongue. "I hope you're enjoying the ride because it'll be your one and only."

Eddie, of course, was paying no attention. At some point during my monologue, he'd slid into his dork position—all four legs spread out and draping over whatever object was the right shape. In some cases it was my backpack; at other times it was the back of the houseboat's dining booth. Any time he did it, he looked like a complete dork. In this case, he was doing it on the passenger's seat headrest. And looking like a dork.

I stood there, hands on hips, giving him my best Librarian Look. "You're not listening, are you?"

He turned his head. Looked me up and down. Opened his mouth in a silent "Mrr."

A laugh giggled up inside me. I shook my head and gave him a few pets. There wasn't much point in scolding a cat.

At each of the next four stops, it didn't take long for someone to notice that the bookmobile carried more than books.

"Look, Mommy, there's a kitty cat!"

"Sweetie, this is a bookmobile, there can't be a . . . oh. There is a cat."

I spent as much time explaining Eddie's presence and the need for secrecy as I did telling people where to find the Stephen King books.

"You mean Eddie won't be back?" a white-haired lady with hot pink glasses asked.

"This was a special day," I said, giving Eddie a pat and sending cat hair flying in four dimensions. "He really wanted to be here for the first trip, but he'll be happier at home."

"He looks really happy right here," the woman said.

I kept my smile pasted on. "Let me show you those Janet Evanovich books you were asking about."

The scene replayed itself at every stop, excluding the unscheduled halt at the lone gas station/convenience stop on the route. The closest thing to a Tupperware container in the entire place was a bowl of microwavable chicken soup. I bought it, took it into the bathroom, threw away the soup, washed out the plastic with hot water and soap, filled it with water, and carried it out to the bookmobile, ignoring the puzzled glances of the proprietor.

"No cat food," I told Eddie. "But they did have this." Unclipping the end of a loaf of bread, I said, "It's not the stuff I usually buy, but it's what they had." I pulled out the first inside piece of bread—Eddie didn't like the end slices—and tore it into cat-sized pieces.

He sniffed, then must have decided I'd suffered enough for the day and started eating. One bit went down, two, then parts of a third. He backed away, licking his lips, so I picked up the uneaten pieces and tossed them into a wastebasket. Bread wasn't part of a healthy cat's diet, but he liked it and it was better than nothing.

"Four stops down," I said, "and two to go. Ready, Eddie?"

"Mrr."

With food in his stomach, Eddie slept through the next stop, the parking lot of a small fieldstone church. He'd curled up with the paper towels on the floor and not one of the half dozen people who came on the bookmobile even knew he was there.

The last stop was at a township hall. I pushed the button to lower the stairs, unlocked the doors, and put my head out. No SUVs, no motorcycles, no bicycles, no kids. Huh. There was a single car, large and dark, but no one was in it. Probably a neighbor, using the lot for overflow parking.

"Are we early?" I asked Eddie.

He opened his eyes, closed them, and started a deep rumbling purr.

I patted his head as I reached inside my backpack for my cell phone. "Hey, look, there's reception out here. Go figure."

According to the phone, we were one full minute past the scheduled bookmobile arrival time. Aunt Frances couldn't understand how I didn't want to wear a watch, but I saw no need to strap something around my wrist when I had a cell phone.

I popped up the ceiling fan and went outside. Still nothing, still no one. We were in the bottom of a wide valley that ran between two hilly tree-covered ridges, and the fields between us and the hillsides were dotted with the occasional farmhouse and barn. Some of these farms, I'd been told, had been in the same family for more than a hundred years, handed down through the generations.

No one from any generation, however, seemed to be on their way to the bookmobile.

I climbed back aboard, pulled a file out of the rack I'd had installed above the desk behind the driver's seat, and found the list of today's stops. As I punched in the phone number, I mentally added "Phone each stop contact day before" to my ever-expanding prep list.

"Elaine? This is Minnie Hamilton with the bookmobile, and—"

"Oh, Minnie, I'm so glad it's you!" Elaine Parker said. "I called the library, but they couldn't find your cell number. I needed to tell you that our women's softball team is playing a Red Hat tournament series and we made it to the finals, isn't that great? Everyone is up at the field, so no one's going to visit the bookmobile." She paused, then said hesitantly, "You'll come back, won't you?"

"Of course we will," I said. "And congratulations on your softball team. I'll be back in three
weeks."

Elaine gushed her gratitude, and when I hung
up, I looked at my cat.

"Well, Mr. Eddie," I said, "now what?" Elaine
had said no one was going to show up, but the
bookmobile's published schedule clearly stated
that we'd be here for thirty minutes. On one
hand, there was little point in staying. On the
other, our schedule said "Williams Township Hall,
3:00 p.m.–3:30 p.m."

On the third hand, with a bookmobile full of
books, there was plenty to do. The half hour sped
by as I straightened and organized and when I
looked at my phone, it was past time to go. I
closed down the ceiling fan and went to shut the
back door I'd left open in hopes of attracting
patrons. It had been a dry stop, unless you wanted
to count the flies.

I stood on the bottom step and reached around
for the door handle. Just as the door was about to
click closed, a black-and-white streak bounded
over my foot and leapt into the outside air.

"Eddie! You get back here right now!"

He galloped across the parking lot.

"Eddie!" I yelled. "Don't go into the road!" I
pounded up to the front of the bookmobile,
grabbed the keys from the ignition, shoved my
cell into my pocket, ran down the steps, locked

the door, and pelted hell-for-leather after my cat.

If he heard my frantic calls, he gave no indication. I ran as fast as I could, but Eddie's four legs left me far behind. He hurtled across the gravel parking lot, went over the drainage ditch with a graceful leap, raced across the road—*The road! Oh, Eddie*—and over the opposite ditch, never looking left, never looking right.

By the grace of all that was holy, no cars showed up to hit either one of us. "Eddie!" I called as I labored behind him, more a pant now than a shout. "Come back!"

He ran down the far side of the road's ditch, then shot into a mass of small trees and overgrown shrubs and knee-high grass.

"Rot. Ten. Cat," I huffed as I ran. "Why. Do. I. Keep. You?" I made the same turn Eddie had and pushed my way through the vegetation. "Eddie? Eddie!"

Behind a row of shaggy bushes, I saw the roofline of a house. An old farmhouse, of one and a half stories, sagging clapboard siding, and no decorative frills whatsoever. "Eddie?" I heard a faint "Rrrowwr."

"Where are you, pal?" I pushed aside snagging branches and reached the side of the house. "Eddie? Are you okay?" Here, it was a little easier to forge through the jungle that might once have been landscaping. "Eddie?"

"Rrowr."

I heard him scratching his claws on something. "I'm getting closer, bud. Where are you?" More bushes, more shrubs . . . and then I burst out of the jungle and into a clearing bounded on one side by the house, on another by a decrepit barn, and on the other two sides by a view of the hills.

Eddie stood on his hind legs, scratching at the corner of the house. "What on earth are you doing?" I asked, looking around, and noted an old driveway. Huh. If I'd been smarter, I would have followed that instead of tracking Eddie through the wilderness.

"Rrrowwrr!" he yowled, scratching wildly.

"What is wrong with you?" I waded toward him through the tall grass. My voice took on the wheedling tone I used when I wanted him to do something he didn't want to. "Tell you what. You come here right now and I won't take away your PlayStation privileges. What do you say?"

He gave me a quick look over his shoulder. Went back to yowling and scratching.

So much for the wheedling tone. Not that it had ever worked before, but it didn't hurt to try.

I came within grabbing distance, but bided my time. If I reached for him now, he'd take off in a new direction. Surely, a nice monologue from Mother Minnie would calm him down. "What's the matter?" I looked down at my troublesome cat, who was continuing to scratch and was now making disturbing howling noises deep in his throat. "It's an abandoned farmhouse and no one has lived here in years. Mice and rats, maybe, but if it's mice you want, I'll take you up to the boardinghouse. Aunt Frances would love your help."

"Rrowr!"

I squatted down to scoop him up. He was a big cat and I'd learned the hard way to lift with my legs. "Here we go, let's—"

*"RROWR!"*

I jerked back. Eddie had never bitten me, never clawed me, never been anything but the lovable yet dorky cat that he was. But for a second there . . .

Fine.

Standing up out of my crouch, I tried to think what to do. My cat had gone berserk and I had no clue how to unberserk him. If only he could talk.

Or not. I might learn more than I wanted to know.

I watched him scratch. Obviously he wanted in the house, but what could possibly be in there? Through a side window I saw kitchen cabinets, their doors open and shelves as bare as Mother Hubbard's.

"There's nothing there, Edster."

"Mrrorwr!"

Again with the scary howly noise. If I showed him that the place was empty, maybe he'd come to his kitty senses and we could be on our way.

Since this was the kitchen, there must be a door just around the corner. "Let's go around the back, okay, Eddie?" I headed off in that direction. "C'mon, we'll—"

He bounded past me and streaked off.

Well.

"Must be you want to check out the backyard," I said, following him once again. Around the corner, I frowned. Why was the kitchen door open? And it looked broken. Strange . . .

"Mrr!"

"Okay, okay." I scanned the tall grass for signs of Eddie. "I can take a hint if I'm beaten over the head with it. I'm really pretty smart, you know. Did I ever tell you what I got on my SATs? Bet my score was a lot higher than yours, and—*oh!*"

For a brief, eternal second, I didn't move. Didn't think. Didn't breathe. Because Eddie was standing next to something completely unexpected—the figure of a man. He was lying on his back, one arm flung across his chest, his face turned away from me, so all I got was the impression of age, frailty, and the absence of any life. But maybe . . . maybe there was breath. Maybe there was a chance.

I rushed forward. "Hello? Hello? Can you hear me? Do you need help?" I was kneeling, checking for a pulse, feeling the cool skin, knowing I was far too late, but looking for life anyway. "Can you hear me? Can you—"

My hand, which had been on the man's wrist, came away slightly red and wet. Blood. What on . . . ?

I swallowed. The blood had come from a small hole in his shirt, right where his heart was. A small, bullet-sized hole. My gaze went from the wound upward to his face. Which was looking familiar, even in the slackness of death, even in this strange place.

Recognition clicked and on its heels came an instinctive reaction that, later, I would never be able to explain. But I'd had to try, couldn't not try.

"Stan! Can you hear me? I'm calling 911 right now." I reached into my pocket for my phone. The instant I heard the dial tone, I pushed the three numbers. "The EMT guys will be here before you know it. They'll take care of you, okay?"

I pushed the SEND button hard and leapt up to straddle Stan Larabee's midsection. My CPR class hadn't been that long ago. I could bring him back. I could. I had to.

"Nine-one-one," the dispatcher said. "What is your emergency?"

# Chapter 4

An infinitely long time later, Eddie and I were sitting in the bookmobile driver's seat, waiting for a deputy from the county sheriff's office to give us the okay to go home. Though my tears had dried up half an hour ago, sniffles remained.

"I couldn't save him, Eddie. I tried and tried but nothing I did mattered." I hugged Eddie tight and he didn't make even a squeak of protest. "I did everything they told me to in that class, but it wasn't enough." *Sniff.*

The EMT crew had arrived seventeen minutes after I made the 911 call. Amazing, really, considering the distances in this part of the county, but it hadn't been soon enough to bring Stan Larabee back.

"He's gone, Eddie, he's really gone." *Sniff.* "It seems so wrong. He was so full of life. There were so many things he wanted to do." During the planning phase of the bookmobile purchase, Stan and I had met on an almost daily basis. I'd learned enough about him to know that he deeply regretted some of the things he'd done while a wheeling and dealing real estate developer. I also knew that he'd divested himself of his third wife a decade earlier, had never had any children, and was working almost as hard at giving away his money as he had at making it.

"But no handouts," he'd told me. "I'm attaching strings to the checks I write. And no money for poor planning. If you can't use the money you have in a sensible way, why should I give, or even loan, you some of mine?"

Eddie bumped my chin with the top of his head.

Absently, I started petting him. "I don't even know who to call. I mean, sure, the police will notify the next of kin, but I feel that I should say something to one of his relatives." As far as I knew, though, there wasn't anyone. He lived alone in a great big house on a great big hill that had been designed to take advantage of the views of both Lake Michigan and Janay Lake.

A big fat raindrop splattered on the bookmobile's wide windshield. Then another, and another. The blue skies that had accompanied us through the morning and halfway through the afternoon were gone. A thick layer of low clouds, heavy with rain, had moved across the sun and now the bookmobile was getting its first shower.

"Hope it doesn't shrink," I murmured.

Eddie settled back down into my lap and turned on his purr.

"You're not so bad for an Eddie." I laid my hand on his back. His body heat seeped into my skin, warming me in more ways than one.

It had been my Florida-based brother who had

made me aware of Stan's existence. Matt, a Disney Imagineer, had run into "this older guy who said he'd just built a place in Chilson. He was down here to tidy up some business, sounded like. Anyway, I told him my sister was a librarian up there and he said for you to give him a call."

I'd demurred, but Matt had pressed me with all the pressure a big brother can bear. "Do it, Min. This guy is a big deal down here."

So I'd called. Stan invited me to lunch at the local diner and before we'd finished our burgers, it was clear that we were going to be friends. Despite the disparity in our ages, backgrounds, and life experiences, there was an instant rapport between us that defied all understanding.

But the more I'd gotten to know Stan, the more I didn't understand the difference between the man I knew and the Stan Larabee that everyone else seemed to have encountered. The comments I heard ranged from "He should have stayed in Florida" to "Stan Larabee never lifted a finger to help anyone in his whole life" to "Larabee wouldn't part with a dime unless he was guaranteed a quarter back."

Yet he'd written a check to the Chilson District Library with so many zeros I wasn't sure how he got them all to fit on the line.

"Here you are, Minnie," he'd said, ripping it out of his checkbook. "The only way this county is going to get a bookmobile is if someone pays for the whole dang thing. Give that shortsighted library board this check and my compliments."

I'd thanked him profusely and said something about the discrepancy in how I saw him and how the rest of Chilson saw him. He'd roared out a laugh that somehow held an edge of black. "You're not from a small town, are you? Stay here long enough and you'll see."

"See what?" I'd asked.

"That you can't live long enough to outlive a reputation."

Soon afterward, I'd stopped by to see my best friend, Kristen, owner and operator of the Three Seasons restaurant, and begun to see what he'd meant. Kristen had been horrified when I'd told her I'd gone to Stan and asked for money.

"You did what?" She'd looked down at me, every inch of her five-foot-eleven self vibrating with disapproval. "Stan Larabee doesn't hand out money. Everybody knows that."

"Everybody is wrong." I handed her the copy I'd made of the check.

Kristen pushed at a wisp of her blond hair that had escaped its tight ponytail and read the numbers out loud. "Two hundred and fifty thousand dollars?" Her voice squeaked. "Are you serious?"

"As your double chocolate cheesecake." I'd plucked the paper out of her hands. The way her mouth was staying open made me anxious about drool. I planned to frame the copy and hang it in my bedroom so I could see it first thing when I woke up in the morning and last thing before I went to sleep at night. A raised spot from Kristen-drool would ruin the effect completely.

She squinted as I tucked the copy away in a folder. "Did it cash?"

"Of course it cashed. Do you think Stan Larabee would write a bad check?"

"I'd believe anything about that man," she said darkly.

"Oh, pooh. I bet most of those stories are rumors made up at the bar at closing time. He was perfectly nice to me."

Kristen gave me one of those you've-only-lived-here-three-years looks, but said, "Maybe. I've never talked to him more than a couple of times, myself."

"Well, there you go. Makes you wonder what people say about you, doesn't it?" Grinning, I'd waved and toddled home, elation filling me so full I wouldn't have been surprised if I'd started floating. I'd bearded the lion in his den. Not only had I survived to tell the tale, but I'd been rewarded beyond anything I'd expected.

"Mrr."

Eddie brought me back from my year-old memory by bumping me on the chin. I'd stopped petting him. "Sorry about that." I scratched the top of his head and the purr machine restarted.

Outside, the high hills, now half-hidden by the driving rain, looked cold and empty and lonely. Tears threatened again and I bent down to put my face against Eddie's fur.

"Miss?"

I shrieked, Eddie yowled. I shrieked again as Eddie's claws sank into my thighs. He yowled again as I scrambled to my feet. He detached his claws from my skin and launched himself across the console, onto the passenger seat, and into the back corner of his cupboard.

The sheriff's deputy who had started the chain of unfortunate events stood there, dripping rainwater onto the carpet. "Minnie Hamilton?" he asked.

"Yes," I said as politely as I could while enduring level seven pain. The agony created by cat claws would drop soon, but there was going to be some teeth-gritting in the interim.

"I'm Deputy Wolverson. Sorry if you didn't hear me come in. I have a few questions for you."

What I minded was the water he was leaving on the new carpet. I reached for the roll of paper towels. "Would you like to dry off a little?"

"Thank you, ma'am, but I'm fine."

"No, you're not." I tossed the roll to him and he had little choice but to catch it. "You're dripping all over the inside of a very expensive bookmobile and the humidity's going up and it'll take forever for the carpet to dry and every wet spot will collect dirt like crazy and I'll have to hire someone to clean the carpet and I don't know where that money is going to come from, because we don't have anything like that in the budget for months and . . . and . . ." My mouth kept opening and shutting for a little while, but I'd run out of words.

"Ms. Hamilton, why don't you sit down?" he asked. "Is your cat okay?" He gestured at the cabinet.

"He likes it in there." I sat down with a thump. "Sorry. I didn't mean to scold you, it's just . . ." But I didn't know where to go from there. Fortunately, Deputy Wolverson did.

"Shock takes people different ways," he said, ripping a handful of paper towels off the roll. "Some cry, some get mad, some go quiet, others talk. Nothing to be ashamed of."

I studied him as he toweled off his hands and face. About my age, maybe a little older. Not movie star handsome, but appealing. No beer gut, seemed intelligent. And no wedding band.

Hmm.

He used a second handful of paper towels to dry off his hat and shoes. "Thanks," he said, and tossed the wads into the wastebasket. "I have a few questions to ask. Do you feel up to it?"

I nodded. "There's a chair in the back, if you want."

The chair had a bungee cord that held it in

place en route. Wolverson deftly unhooked the cord and rolled the chair forward. He sat down with an athletic grace and took a small notepad out of his front shirt pocket.

"Minnie Hamilton, employee of the Chilson District Library, right? Can I have your address and phone number? . . . Okay, thanks. So you found the gentleman in the house at what time?"

"About an hour and a half ago."

"You were parked here? Why did you go to the house?"

I glanced at Eddie's cabinet. "My cat. He ran out of the bookmobile. I followed him to that farmhouse and that's when I found Stan."

"Stan?" Wolverson glanced up. "You know the victim? What's his last name?"

Maybe he wasn't as intelligent as I'd thought. "You mean you don't know?"

The deputy's polite face suddenly didn't look quite so friendly. "We found no form of identification on the victim's body. If you have information, please share it."

The victim. A wave of spotted black filled my vision. I grabbed the edge of the seat and held on tight. No fainting. There weren't any smelling salts on board, and anyway, I'd read they were nasty. "It's Stan Larabee."

Deputy Wolverson's sudden intake of breath wasn't exactly a gasp, but it was close. "The Larabee Development Stan Larabee?"

And Larabee Enterprises and Larabee Realty and Larabee Limited. Before I'd gone to Stan with my proverbial hat in hand, I'd done my research to make sure he was as rich as everybody said. It turned out he had more money than anyone had guessed.

I nodded, and the deputy thumbed his shoulder microphone. "Dispatch, this is two eight seven. Victim was male and approximately seventy years old. Identification is . . ." He looked at me. "You're sure it's Stan Larabee?"

"Definitely."

He went back to his microphone. "Identification is confirmed. Cause of death is homicide, repeat, homicide."

The microphone popped and crackled. "Roger that, two eight seven."

Deputy Wolverson flipped his notebook shut and gave me a straight look. "Is there anything else we should know?"

Homicide. Stan was murdered. I'd known that as soon as I'd seen that small, horrible hole, but hearing the word spoken out loud was doing disturbing things to all sorts of emotions. "I can't think of anything," I said. "Do you know . . ." No, stupid question. The deputy had only been there a few minutes. Of course he didn't know who'd killed Stan.

The deputy waited for me to finish my sentence. When I didn't, he said, "The department's detectives will be investigating the incident." He tucked the notebook into one shirt pocket and pulled a business card from another. "But if you remember anything important before they contact you, here's my name and phone number."

I reached for the card and saw that my fingers were trembling. I made a quick open-and-shut-and-open fist, then took the card. DEPUTY ASH WOLVERSON, it read. "Um, I really don't have any idea what might or might not be important."

"Use your best judgment."

My fingers started quivering again. I sat on them. "Um, I'm sure you noticed that the back door on the house was broken open." He nodded. For some reason I nodded back. "And that car across the parking lot is probably his." Stan was a car collector. Every time I saw him driving, it seemed he was driving something different.

He turned, noted the location of the car, then took some notes. "Anything else? No? Well, thanks for your help, and you have my card if you remember more." He stood, opened the door, letting in the sound of pounding rain and the scent of wet earth, and left.

"Stan," I whispered. "Oh, Stan."

Eddie's head popped out of the cabinet. He sniffed left, sniffed right, then jumped down and made his way over to me. He stood directly in front of my toes and looked up at me, yellow cat eyes intent on mine.

I patted my thighs.

He continued to stare at me.

"Oh, fine." I leaned forward, scooped him up, and deposited him on my lap. He clunked the point of my chin with the top of his head and started purring.

"Murder," I said quietly. "Stan was murdered. That's so . . . wrong."

Eddie stomped around. Either he was working on a new dance step or he was trying to make my lap more comfortable for himself.

"How could it be murder? And why?" But even as I asked the second question, I knew the answer. Stan was rich. Incredibly rich. You didn't have to look very far to figure a motive for this one.

"But why here?" Sure, Tonedagana County had more remote places than this; there was a state forest not far away. And the next township south of here didn't have even a village inside its borders.

Eddie found whatever it was that he wanted in a lap and flopped down.

"Could Stan have been looking at the property, thinking about developing?"

"Mrr."

I nodded and started scratching his ears. "You're probably right. Developing anything out here would be nuts." The closest expressway was more than an hour away. Even the closest two-lane state highway was half an hour away. Not exactly easy access.

"Besides," I said, "that day I picked up the check, he said he was done with developing. Time to spend money instead of making it." He'd laughed as he'd said it, though. Where had his laughter come from?

"Well." I gave Eddie a squeeze and deposited him on the passenger's seat. "It's up to the police now. They'll figure out who killed Stan and—"

"Mrr!"

"What do you mean, 'mrr'? That's what the police do. They figure out who the bad guys are and put them in jail." While I'd never actually seen Eddie roll his eyes, he managed to give a good impression of doing so.

"Cut that out." I thumbed a lever on the driver's seat and rotated it around to face the front window. "I'm sure the sheriff's detectives are competent and experienced. They've probably investigated lots of deaths."

Eddie flopped himself lengthwise onto the seat and looked at me sideways.

"Don't look at me like that," I told him. "There are thousands of people in Tonedagana County. Tens of thousands." Almost forty thousand at the last census count. "Dozens, maybe hundreds of people in the county die each year." Eddie opened his mouth, but I jumped in fast. I didn't really think he understood what I said, but he gave such a good impression of doing so that I'd fallen into the habit of pretending that he did.

"Okay, sure, there aren't many murders here." The only one I could remember in the three years I'd lived in Chilson had started as a bar fight and had ended sadly with dozens of onlookers. Not much to investigate. "But they still have to have training. And maybe the detectives are former city detectives with twenty years of experience each and have solved hundreds of murders between them."

It was possible. Lots of people up here came from somewhere else. I did. Aunt Frances did. My boss did. Almost all of my summer neighbors did. Tom, the owner of the bakery, did. The guy who ran the hardware store did. It only followed that the county sheriff's office contained a lot of downstate transplants.

I started the engine. "It'll be okay, Ed. They'll find Stan's killer, I'm sure of it."

He looked at me as if I was the stupidest human in the universe.

"They will," I told him.

"Mrr," he said, and closed his eyes.

The roads were wet and strewn with sticks and leaves. I turned on the headlights. Used the brakes cautiously. Avoided deep puddles. Drove slowly.

As a result, it took forever to get back to Chilson. I came in the back way through town to avoid the burgeoning summer traffic, and around the back of the library. I hit the garage door opener and turned on the nifty remote-camera screen that was not only invaluable in helping me back up, but was also very helpful when edging into tight places.

Just as we were about to nose into the garage I checked the side mirrors . . . and saw a fiftyish man, feet standing wide, fists on his hips. The frown on his face was fierce enough to create deep creases around his mouth.

What was Stephen doing out here? To the best of my knowledge, he'd never come within spitting distance of the bookmobile. So why . . . ?

My boss made a come-out-and-talk-to-me gesture. If I grabbed Eddie, would I be able to put him in his cabinet without Stephen noticing? Not a chance, not with these big windows. I put on the air brakes, told Eddie to lay low, and scooted outside to where my boss was waiting.

"Hey, Stephen. What are—"

He cut into my greeting. "You're two and a half hours late."

Two hours and nineteen minutes, but who was counting?

"Don't tell me there's something wrong with the bookmobile." He squinted at the vehicle. "Mechanical breakdowns happen regularly, I understand."

And suddenly, I understood, too. Stephen

positively wanted the bookmobile to be too expensive for the library to run. If he could prove that it cost more than the operations budget had estimated, he'd find a politically palatable way of getting rid of it. *Find it a nice home somewhere else,* he'd say, smiling a very annoying smile. *We'll get only pennies on the dollar, but that's better than nothing.*

"The bookmobile is fine," I said. "It's—"

"How many people showed up at the first stop?"

The twins. The princess. Ethan and Eddie. So long ago, yet less than twelve hours in the past. It didn't seem possible. "We had a good turnout. Stephen, there's something I have to tell you."

He waved me off. "What I need is details. As this was the maiden voyage, I expect that things didn't go as smoothly as you'd hoped."

"Okay, but first I have to—"

Stephen held up a warning finger. "Am I or am I not your supervisor?"

"Yes, but—"

"Then give me the information I need." He sighed. "Minnie, you are a fine employee, but you have a bad habit of reprioritizing to your own satisfaction. When will you learn that you don't always know best? Not even I know best, not all the time, and I have almost thirty years of experience as a librarian. Experience counts, Minnie."

Uh-oh. Stephen had moved into Mentor Mode

and it would take drastic measures to get him out.

"Yes, experience." He nodded to himself. "Someday you'll know what I'm talking about. Having great promise is only that, a promise. It's up to you to learn as much as you can, pay attention as much as you can. Only then will it be possible for you to—"

"Stan Larabee is dead."

Stephen's mouth kept moving, but nothing came out.

"We . . . I found him in a farmhouse near my last stop. I called 911 right away, but it was too late."

"Stan Larabee? You're sure?"

I nodded, afraid to speak for fear I'd break down into wordless sobs.

"Larabee?" Stephen whispered, his eyes stretched wide. "Is dead?"

I looked at him. "Are you okay? Maybe you should sit down." I reached up for the door latch, opened it, and saw Eddie sitting at the top of the stairs. I slammed the door shut. "On second thought," I said brightly, "let's get you into the library. You'll be more comfortable there."

"Stan's gone?" Stephen's voice was tight. "He can't be dead. Can he?"

"Yes, and it's a little worse than that. He—"

"Worse?" Stephen's mouth twisted into a crooked smile. "Worse, she says." He barked out an odd choking kind of laugh and staggered

70

away, muttering to himself, "She thinks it could be worse. Worse!"

I followed him for a few steps, but he seemed strong enough, just not very steady. I watched as he made his way around the corner of the library, walking an erratic zigzag path bounded on one side by the building, bounded on the other by an invisible wall that he kept reaching up to touch. The last thing I heard before he went out of view was a final shout of frenetic laughter. "Worse!"

"Well," I said. "That was weird."

And I climbed back into the bookmobile to tuck it in for the night.

By the time I'd finished at the library and carried a squirming Eddie home in the backpack, I was ready to tuck myself in. After taking a quick shower, I fixed myself a comforting dinner of baked macaroni and cheese with bits of bacon tossed in, slapped together a salad so I'd be able to tell my mother I was eating vegetables, and ate in the houseboat's dining booth. The clouds had cleared off and it had turned into a beautiful, cool northern Michigan evening, but I didn't feel up to talking with my neighbors.

The marina crowd was a gregarious bunch, full of bonhomie and cheer, and on a normal Friday night I'd be joining in the fun. But tonight wasn't normal. Even Eddie was acting out of sorts. Eddie usually spent evenings perched on the flat dashboard above the boat's steering wheel, watching the boat traffic and the seagulls and whatever the neighbors might be doing, with occasional yowly commentary. Tonight, he stuck close to me.

When the dinner dishes were done and put away in the galley's cupboards, it was all of nine o'clock. "What do you think, pal?" I asked Eddie. "I could see what the boat rats are up to. Or I could drive out to Lake Michigan and watch the sunset." Neither of those suggestions appeared to interest Eddie. "I could walk up to Kristen's restaurant. I could call Mom. Or I could go up to the boardinghouse and talk to Aunt Frances." Those were all pretty good ideas. It would probably help to talk about the day.

But somehow I didn't want to talk. Didn't want to relive it all, didn't want to go back there, even in my head. Tomorrow. I'd talk to them tomorrow. I'd be ready in another day. Two at the most.

Eddie sauntered past me, trotted down the three stairs, past the bathroom, jumped up on the set of drawers I'd put in front of the back door, then leapt onto the bed.

Or I could go to bed. It suddenly seemed like an excellent idea.

Ten minutes later, clad in old shorts and a tank top and teeth brushed, I slid into bed. I picked up a copy of Karin Slaughter's latest thriller. Two pages in, I put it down in favor of the next book on my To Be Read stack: *Gravity's Rainbow*. That lasted two paragraphs. Then I tried Lorraine Bartlett's most recent cozy mystery. But even that mostly happy little world didn't keep me from reliving the events of the day.

Sighing, I sat up and hugged my knees. Sounds of boater revelry wafted in through the open window. A flickering of lights glinted on the ceiling, lights that seemed as if they were coming from the big boat next door. Which didn't make sense, because the Olsons never came up before July, a fact for which everyone at the marina was grateful. I was watching the lights, trying to figure out their source, but somehow I saw only the flashing red beacon of the ambulance.

*Oh, Stan.* Of all the people in the county, how could it have been me that had found him?

Eddie chirped and rearranged himself. I petted his fur smooth. "Whatever it was that sent you running to that farmhouse, I guess I'm glad." Did cats have ultragood eyesight? Some birds did. And some dogs had super-duper smelling powers. And there was hearing. What animals were good at hearing? Maybe Eddie had a special combination of all three?

I looked at him. Nah. If Eddie's sensory powers were anything special, I wouldn't startle him into a four-legged leap every other time I opened the nonlatching closet door, against which he'd started taking his afternoon naps.

"Poor Stan," I said quietly. Then, all at once grief rose up in me. *Oh, Stan.* I swallowed down the sobs and tried to think. What would Stan want right now? What would he want me to do?

Eddie twisted his head around and looked at me upside down. "Sorry, big guy." I patted him gently and he closed his eyes.

"It was murder," I said softly. "Someone killed Stan. Maybe I could . . . ?" I shook my head before finishing the sentence. I was a librarian, for crying out loud. I could classify, alphabetize, plan outreach programs, sort staff schedules, and make sense of service contracts, but putting murderers in jail was outside my job description. "That's what the police do," I said, stroking Eddie's back.

He twitched, as if my touch were ticklish.

"Sorry." I smoothed down the fur he'd ruffled up. "I told that deputy everything. It wasn't much, but what else can I do? I can't go poking around doing the job of the detectives. They know what they're doing, and I'm a librarian."

Then again, I knew Stan and they didn't. Maybe I didn't know much, but I knew the things he laughed over. I knew what he liked to eat for lunch and what clothes he wore. I knew that he liked buying cars and I knew that he hated buying clothes. I knew that he liked chocolate and I knew that he liked to take long drives.

Eddie picked up his head and stared straight at me.

"But still . . ." I thought out loud. "What was he doing in the other side of the county? Why was he in that particular farmhouse?"

"Mrrorrw!" Eddie jumped onto my lap, thumped my chin with the top of his head, and started purring.

"Well, finally." I slid back down into the sheets, rolled on my side, and fell asleep with my arm around a rumbling cat. But even Eddie's purrs couldn't chase away my dreams, dreams that were haunted with sights I didn't want to see and sounds I didn't want to hear.

# *Chapter 5*

The next day was Saturday, the day I had a standing invitation for breakfast at my aunt Frances's house. It was also the only morning Aunt Frances didn't cook breakfast for her summer boarders. Instead, a boarder cooked for everyone else. It was part of the deal when you stayed there, and learning of the duty had scared off more than one prospective boarder.

"You want me to cook breakfast for seven people?" the shocked inquirer would ask.

"Eight," Aunt Frances would say. "My niece usually shows up."

Every summer the niece quickly learned whose cooking was good, whose was awesome, and whose should be avoided at all costs. Since another one of Aunt Frances's rules was that you ate heartily and complimented the cook no matter what, I'd found it was easier to skip the Saturdays likely to include burned bacon and flat pancakes.

This summer, however, Aunt Frances had hit the breakfast mother lode. Everyone from seventy-year-old Zofia down to twenty-two-year-old Harris seemed to have kitchen skills in abundance. The week before, sixty-five-year-old Leo had wowed us with sour cream and blueberry pancakes accompanied by buttery pecan maple syrup. The week before that, fifty-three-year-old Paulette had us begging for more breakfast burritos.

This particular Saturday, having left Eddie on the houseboat sleeping on the floor in a square of sunshine, I walked through downtown, up the hill overlooking Janay Lake, down a street lined with maple trees, and up the wide steps of the porch that ran across the front of Aunt Frances's century-old home.

The wooden screen door banged shut behind me. The entry, stairway, and spacious living room were all empty, but laughter drifted in from the kitchen. Wooden floorboards creaked under my weight as I passed through the living room, admiring yet again the pine-paneled walls and ceiling, the end tables and coffee tables built from driftwood, the maps thumbtacked to the walls, and the fieldstone fireplace big enough for cooking a side of beef. It was a room full of calm and ease and I always felt that nothing bad could possibly happen here.

A tall, angular woman appeared in the doorway to the dining room. She smiled. "Thought I heard someone. Good morning, bright eyes. You must have had a long day yesterday with your book-mobile. I thought you'd call and tell me all about it."

I stood on my tiptoes to kiss her cheek. She'd recently turned sixty, but I'd yet to spy a single wrinkle. "Morning, Aunt Frances." It was a good time to tell her about the events of yesterday. An ideal time, really, but I couldn't find the words to start the sad story. After breakfast. I'd be ready by then. "I'll tell you everything after we eat. Who's cooking this morning?"

"Dena and Quincy. Everyone else has been banished from the kitchen."

I raised my eyebrows. "Dena and Quincy? But I thought Harris was being matched up with Dena."

She sighed. "I know, dear, I know. I'm sure it'll work out in the end."

Fine words, but she looked a little concerned. And for good reason: Dena was twenty-five and Quincy had recently hit fifty. My aunt had a secret that I'd sworn on a tall stack of paperback mysteries to never reveal unless doing so would save at least ten lives. Aunt Frances only took boarders who were single and in need of a mate. Her extensive interviewing process, ostensibly to determine compatibility for the unusual environment and living arrangements, was in reality a way for Aunt Frances to start the matchmaking process. None of the boarders ever knew they were being set up, and in her fifteen years of taking in boarders she'd never had a failure.

If a pair she hadn't intended was forming, all her plans would be toast. "Well, you haven't missed yet, have you?"

"There's always a first time," she muttered.

"You said the same thing last year and that turned out fine by the end of the summer," I said. "You can't expect August endings in June. Especially early June. Don't you always say that building a lasting love is like building Rome? That it can't be done in a day?"

She *hmm*ed a little, thinking it over. "You're right," she said. "You're so right that I think I'll stop worrying." She winked, grinning. "No point in it, anyway."

It was impossible not to smile back; my aunt had a very contagious grin. "There's lots of time," I said.

"Time for what?"

I jumped. Aunt Frances turned to Paulette, the boarder who'd been matched with Quincy, and said, "I was wondering if there was time to have another cup of coffee before breakfast. Do you have any idea what those two are cooking up for us?"

The pleasantly plump, tawny-haired woman scowled. "Nobody tells me anything around here." She stomped off, her pink flip-flops popping loudly with each stomp.

"Bugger," Aunt Frances muttered.

"No, it's good," I said softly. "Paulette is already in love with Quincy. She's nuts with jealousy."

"But how does that help with Dena and Harris? And how does it get Quincy to quit pretending he's twenty-five when he's fifty?"

"You'll figure it out. You always do."

A bell rang, clear and bright. Years upon years ago, the bell from an old train engine had been hauled up into a maple tree outside the kitchen porch. One end of a rope was tied to the top of the bell; the other end was attached to the porch. The sound of the bell meant summer, blue skies, and food.

A dark-haired woman poked her head through the dining room doorway. "Ah. There you are. Good morning, Minnie. Come on in, breakfast is ready."

"Hi, Zofia," I said. Seventy, spry, and widowed for five years, Zofia had finally loosed herself from her children's clutches long enough to scamper north for the summer. "I'll be staying with an old friend," she'd told them, lying through her teeth.

"Coffee's fresh." Zofia waved us into the dining room and gestured at the wide-planked pine sideboard. "Tea water is hot, orange juice is cold."

Aunt Frances took her seat at the head of the table. "Zofia, you haven't been helping, have you? You'll get your turn next week."

"What, me, be useful?" Zofia put her palms flat against her collarbone and opened her eyes wide.

With a name like Zofia and her tendency to flowing skirts and dangling earrings, anyone would have guessed her to have been an actress, a Gypsy fortune-teller in a carnival, or at the very least a high school drama teacher. In reality, Zofia had married her childhood sweetheart, stayed home to raise their four children, and supported her husband in his career as a vice president for a major car company.

I took Aunt Frances a cup of coffee and greeted the others as they came in through various doors. Harris, the just-graduated college kid, from the back porch. Leo, whom Aunt Frances had matched with Zofia, came in through the living room, the morning newspaper in his hand. Paulette followed Leo, still stomping.

"And heeeeeere we come!" Quincy pushed open the swinging door between the kitchen and dining room. His mostly bald head was red with heat. "Ready or not!" He held the door open for a willowy young woman who was the triple threat of thin, beautiful, and smart. It was a combination that made me long to hate her, but I hadn't figured out how to. She was too nice.

Dena smiled up at Quincy. "Thanks," she said, maneuvering around him. He beamed and I started to share some of Aunt Frances's worry. Dena was carrying a plate in each hand and another up each arm. She'd learned the trick, she'd told me, while waitressing in college. "Hash browns, bacon baked with maple syrup, fried eggs, and melon slices." She gave Aunt Frances the first plate. "Nothing burned and nothing raw except what should be."

After a few moments of pleasurable eating, Aunt Frances turned to Leo. "Did you get the newspaper?"

His mouth full, he nodded.

The paper! I'd forgotten all about it. News of Stan's death was bound to be on the front page. I had no idea if my name would be in print or not, but it very well could be. I mentally kicked myself for not calling Aunt Frances last night. And Kristen. I really should have told Kristen. And my . . . well, not my mom. I wasn't ready to deal with her concern. I loved my parents dearly, but Mom's mothering method involved a lot of what, in my teenage years, I'd called smothering. There was more than one reason I lived a five-hour drive away from my parents.

My aunt piled her fork full of hash browns. "Anything important in the paper this morning? These are outstanding, Dena, by the way."

"Um, Aunt Frances? Could I talk to you a minute in the kitchen?" The breakfast table didn't seem like the best place to discuss finding a dead body.

"Hang on, kiddo." She was watching Leo, who'd picked up the newspaper and was waving it at her.

"A guy was killed out in the east part of the county."

"Oh?" Aunt Frances's eyes were going up and down, matching the flapping of the newspaper as she tried to read the headline. "What was his name?"

"Don't remember," Leo said. "But he was murdered."

Surprised murmurs ran around the table.

"Bar fight?" Zofia asked.

"Bet there was a girl involved." Paulette sniffed.

"Um," I said.

Leo shook his head and held the newspaper out at arm's length so he could read it. "He was some rich guy, born and raised here." He scanned the article. "Says here that he was found by—" He stopped. "By the bookmobile librarian."

Everyone suddenly focused on me. The silence was so sudden that I thought my ears had stopped working.

"Minnie?" my aunt asked softly. "Is this true? Are you all right?"

Her kindness almost undid me. I nodded and gripped my coffee cup tight. "Ed . . . we'd . . . I'd stopped by that old township hall . . . and . . . and heard something. It was at an old farmhouse. I called 911, but it was too late."

"Poor Minnie." Aunt Frances put her hand over mine. "How horrible for you."

"Yes. And Stan . . ." I swallowed. "I knew him."

The boarders murmured sympathy. The pressure from Aunt Frances's hand grew intense. "You knew him? Stan . . . ?"

"Stan Larabee. He's the one who donated the

money for the bookmobile, remember? You said you didn't know him, last fall when we started planning everything."

"Yes, I remember saying that." She released my hand. I stared at my skin, where a white mark showed how her hand had lain.

"You poor thing," Paulette said, "having to see something like that."

The others chimed in, asking questions that ranged from who, to how, to why, to when, and to where. All of them asked something, all of them except Aunt Frances, who sat through the remainder of the meal without eating another bite of breakfast.

I spent the rest of Saturday in the library and barely noticed the passing hours. This was easy to do since the bookmobile's circulation was separate from the main library and had been shoehorned into a windowless space that had once been the newspaper archives.

My idea had been to get the newspapers microfilmed and donate the print copies to the local historical society to free up the space. Stephen's objection had been predictable. "Who's going to pay for the microfilming? It's not a cheap endeavor, Minnie. Not cheap at all."

After I'd found, applied for, and been awarded a grant that covered a majority of the costs, Stephen had said, "Even if it's empty, that room isn't big enough to house a bookmobile collection." After I'd found a system of shelving that went floor to ceiling, Stephen had sighed. "Now, Minnie, please don't take this the wrong way, but height is not one of your sterling qualities." But I'd been ready for that objection and handed over a catalog of library ladders before he finished his sentence.

The room was high and stark and I loved every inch of it. A few weeks back I'd convinced the janitor—with the help of some fresh doughnuts—to install a tiny drop leaf desk for one of the bookmobile's laptop computers. I puttered away the rest of Saturday morning, the afternoon, and half the evening, moving from desk to shelves to desk, comparing the main library's top circulating items against what was checked out on the book-mobile, comparing the checkouts against the lists of top bookmobile books other librarians had sent me, poking around, researching, thinking, and poking some more.

Early on, I tried to call Kristen, but was dumped into her voice mail. I sat there, gripping my cell phone, surprised at the depth of my disappoint-ment. Until that moment, I hadn't realized how much I'd wanted to talk to my best friend. I left a short message to call and went back to work.

The huge breakfast I'd eaten lasted me until midafternoon, and I ignored the gnawing in my stomach until I got a headache. By the time I walked home, took some ibuprofen, and ate cold cereal for supper, I was tired enough to crawl into bed with a book and an Eddie. I drifted to sleep so fast that I didn't have time to wonder why I'd worked so hard all day.

Sunday morning, I woke to darkness and rain dripping off the eaves of the houseboat. A morning made for sleeping in. I rolled over, vaguely heard an Eddie-squawk, and closed my eyes.

Bright sunlight in my face woke me. I squinted at the clock. "Half past ten?" I grabbed the clock and pulled it closer. Sure enough, most of the morning was gone. By the time I was showered, dressed, and full of another bowl of cereal, the sky was so blue it was hard to believe it had been pouring rain three hours earlier.

My left-hand neighbor, Louisa Axford, nodded at me as I came out on deck. "Rain before seven, done by eleven," she said from the comfort of her chaise lounge. "You must be busy up there at your library. I haven't seen you in days, seems like."

"Friday was the first bookmobile run."

"That's right." She smiled. Everybody did when you mentioned the bookmobile. "Shakedown cruise. How did it go? Any problems?"

And to think I'd ever bemoaned the fact that people didn't read the local newspaper. "The bookmobile ran fine," I said. "No scratches, no dings, no generator issues, no engine problems."

"Good for you." She pushed back a strand of her long, gloriously white hair. Louisa and her husband, Ted, had owned some sort of manufacturing business downstate before they sold it and retired. Their houseboat was bigger and newer than mine, but not by much. I'd never figured out exactly what the business had been, but they affectionately referred to it as the cash cow. It had taken me some time to realize that they could have afforded Stan Larabee's aerie. Could have afforded it, but didn't want it. They preferred to travel, and did, at great length from September through May, all over the world. "Stop on by for a drink later on," she said, "and we'll celebrate."

"I will, thanks."

What Louisa and Ted didn't do, however, was read. When I first met them and learned of their lifestyle, I'd assumed they were readers. All those airport waits, all those hotels. Perfect for lots of reading. But they'd smiled and demurred when I'd recommended Lee Child's books. "No, thanks, hon. We're not readers."

I'd blinked. Not readers? They were smart and funny and had plenty of time—how could they not want to read? In spite of this, we got along fine as neighbors, to the point where we'd exchanged front-door keys, because you never knew what could happen. My right-hand neighbors, though . . .

"Have you seen the Olsons?" I asked.

Louisa laughed. "Have you seen the calendar?"

"I know they hardly ever come up until the end of June, but—"

"Try never." Louisa picked up a glass of ice water. A wedge of lemon was perched prettily on its rim. "In the ten years we've owned this boat, they've never once been up before the Fourth. And am I complaining? No, I am not. Gunnar Olson is a horrible excuse for a human being and I will be forever grateful to you for occupying that boat slip. We see far too much of him, otherwise."

She made a face. "Before you leased that slip, he made our lives miserable. Did I tell you he complained to the city that our boat's engine violated the noise ordinance? And every time my Ted went on deck to smoke his pipe, Gunnar made sure to stand on his deck and make a show of coughing and wheezing. And that fuss he made over Holton's dog, remember?" She cast a malevolent glance Olson-ward. "The man is a menace. Happily, he bothers you these days instead of us." She toasted me with her water. "Thank you, dear. Thank you, thank you."

Remember the low price of your boat slip, I told myself. Cheap is good. And Gunnar wasn't up north all that often. "But if the Olsons haven't been up, then . . ." I frowned.

"Then what, hon?"

"Nothing." The boat lights I'd thought I'd seen

on Friday night must have been the product of my weary and troubled mind.

Not that I wanted to see the Olsons. Mrs. wasn't so bad, as far as I could tell from what little I saw of her. Mr., though, was as bad as Louisa said. There'd been a reason the lease for my boat slip was so cheap; I just hadn't known what it was until Gunnar Olson showed up. Full of bluster and condescension, he'd spent his sixty years being sure that his opinions were the correct ones.

The day Gunnar berated me for not coiling my ropes properly—"They're lines, little miss, *lines!*"—I went to talk to Chris Ballou, the marina's second-generation owner, manager, maintenance guy, and boat repair guy.

He'd grinned, his teeth bright white against his sun-worn skin. "Piece of work, ain't he? But you can handle him, Min. That's why I let you take that slip."

I'd looked at him sourly. "And why you leased it to me at a discount? You could have warned me."

"And ruin the surprise?" He'd laughed and gone away whistling.

Now Louisa tipped her ice water in my direction. "Mr. Ballou was here earlier, looking like he was ready to burst. Said he needed to talk to you." She took a sip and made a face. "Isn't it five o'clock yet?"

"Did Chris say what he wanted?" Maybe he'd

finally tracked down a used bilge pump for me. Chris was many things, but speedy wasn't one of them. My boat's bilge pump had been wonky since the end of last summer and I'd rather have the thing replaced cheaply before it died than expensively after the fact.

Louisa shook her head and turned her face up to the sun, closing her eyes. "Get some SPF fifty on, young lady, or you'll end up like me, wrinkled as an old prune."

"Good idea," I said, and went to hunt down Chris. I found him behind the counter in the marina's dusty parts shop, sitting in an ancient canvas director's chair, his feet up on an equally ancient cardboard box. He was deep in a conversation about fishing lures with Rafe Niswander, a mutual friend and neighbor from up the road, and a boat owner who went by the name Skeeter. Whether that was a nickname or his given name I had no idea and had never asked. Some questions are best left unanswered.

Since Skeeter and I were both the same age and were both single, half the marina had been trying to get us together since last summer when he'd first rented a slip. We'd even made a desultory attempt at a date, but there'd been no spark of interest flaring up, no flame of romantic heat, no nothing. We'd ended the evening as we'd begun: friends.

"Hey, Min Tin Tin." Chris toasted me with a

bottle of motor treatment. "What's doing, girl?"

If I had to make a guess, I'd have said Chris was in his early forties, but he had that whippet-thin body that meant he'd look forty when he was sixty. From his speech patterns, however, you'd think he was twenty.

"Louisa said you were looking for me." I nodded hellos to Skeeter and Rafe.

"Oh, yeah." Chris dropped his feet to the concrete floor and half stood to reach for something underneath the counter. "Before I spread any more rumors, I got to find out if they're true." He held up the newspaper and stabbed a finger at the article about Stan. "Says here the bookmobile person found old Stan Larabee. Was that you? My money's on it."

I stared at the article. Why did Chilson have to have the only newspaper in the area that still ran a weekend edition? Was there really enough news in the county to print a paper six times a week? Once a week would surely be enough.

"Leave her alone, Ballou," Skeeter said quietly.

Chris stabbed the paper again. "I knew it, I just knew it. Everybody was saying so, right, Rafe?"

"What do you mean, everybody?" I asked.

"You know." Rafe shrugged. "Everybody."

I crossed my eyes at him. For a smart man, Rafe could be exceedingly inarticulate when he chose, and outside of his working hours, he typically chose the path of inarticulateness.

"At the bar last night," Chris said. "Larabee being killed was all anyone talked about. Well, that and who's going to get all his money."

Of course Stan's death was the hot topic. How could it not be? The hometown boy had made good, come home to retire, and was murdered by person or persons unknown. Every occupant of every barstool in town had probably laid claim to knowing Stan and having an opinion on the murder. "Your buddies figure out who killed him?"

Rafe shot me a half grin, but my sarcasm was lost on Chris.

"Could have been a lot of people." Chris dropped back into the director's chair. "You better watch out. Killer's going to be after you, next."

I snorted. "Really."

"Well, sure. It's all over town. Stan was beat up real bad and then shot, right? And you're the one who found him, so he must have told you who did it before he died. Bound to have."

"Uh-huh," I said. "And does everybody also know why the police haven't arrested the killer?"

"Well, sure, there're a couple reasons." Chris's feet went back up on the cardboard box. "The guy's in hiding, for one. I mean, who kills somebody and goes to work the next day? And maybe all Stan gave you was a first name and it'll take some time to figure out which one it is. Some names are real common, you know."

"Like 'Chris'?"

"Nah. There aren't that many . . . hey! You ain't saying I killed Stan Larabee. No way are you saying that. He didn't really say a Chris killed him, did he? Hey, Minnie, don't walk away like that. You got to tell me!"

Out of sight of Chris, I winked at Rafe and Skeeter. "It'll take some time to figure it out," I said, deadpan. "You might want to come up with an alibi."

"An alibi? For when? Minnie . . . hey, Minnie!"

But I was already out the door.

The rest of Sunday I spent taking care of the mundane details of life. Balanced the checkbook, hauled a pillowcase full of dirty clothes over to the marina's coin laundry, cleaned the kitchen, and wiped down the houseboat's many railings. Eddie followed me around, criticizing my efforts as only a cat is able to do. His unwavering stare clearly meant *That's as clean as you can get it? Please.*

"If you think you can do better, go ahead," I told him.

He sat down and licked his chest.

I popped my cleaning rag in his direction, but he didn't flinch. "Why is it that I clean the whole place and get nothing but grief, but the only chore you have is cleaning yourself and if I comment on that, I get ignored?"

Since the answer to that was obvious—*I'm a cat*—I didn't expect a response. And that's exactly what I got.

I made the standard Sunday call to my mom and dad, stumbling a little over Mom's question of "Did anything fun and exciting happen to you this week?" but recovered quickly enough that she didn't sound suspicious when I said the guy who'd donated the money for the bookmobile was dead.

"Oh, Minerva, I'm so sorry. Did you send a note to his wife? He was elderly, as I recall. Cancer, was it? So many people get cancer these days—it's all this plastic, I just know it. The other day I was reading about this woman who—"

From long experience, I knew the only way to get a word in edgewise was to interrupt. "It wasn't cancer, Mom."

"It wasn't? Are you sure?"

"Absolutely." The word "murder" hovered on my lips, but I brushed it away because I knew what would happen if I said it out loud. Mom would say, "Minerva Joy, are you sure you're all right?" and escalate rapidly to "You're not fine, I can hear it in your voice. Bob? Get the luggage, we're driving up to Chilson right now."

After they got here, it would take me days to reassure my mother that, yes, I was fine, that, no, I didn't need therapy, and that I wasn't going to fall on their necks weeping with anxiety and sorrow and loss and beg to be taken home with them for an extended stay.

So I didn't say that Stan had been murdered. I dealt with the guilt by vowing that I'd tell Dad all about it. And I would. One of these days.

"Just because he didn't have cancer," Mom said now, "is no reason not to stay away from pesticides. Speaking of toxic chemicals, how is Kristen doing with getting organic pork?"

The conversation stayed permanently diverted. The call came to a close with Mom's typical "I worry about you, honey. Are you eating enough vegetables? And are you still writing the notes? Please tell me you are."

I reassured her on both counts. As soon as we said good-bye, I made a quick call to Aunt Frances and asked her not to tell her sister-in-law and her brother, aka my dad, anything about the end of Friday's bookmobile trip. Since Aunt Frances had known my mother longer than I had, it didn't take much persuading.

Somehow, it was inevitable that Kristen would call when I was on the phone. I picked up her message: "Sorry I didn't call earlier, had to take a fast trip down to Traverse to test a new cheese. Stop by tonight, okay? See ya!"

I stowed my cell phone in my purse, patted a sleeping Eddie on the head, scrawled a note on the whiteboard, and headed out.

• • •

The name of Kristen's restaurant, Three Seasons, was a direct result of her vow to specialize in serving locally grown foods. When she was working up her business plan, she decided to draw up sample menus from each season. Spring was full of greens, asparagus, lamb, and fish. Summer ranged from cherries to corn to peaches to tomatoes to pork and fish. Fall was apples and squash and potatoes, beef, and fish. It was when she started work on the winter menus that she ran into problems.

"I can't serve frozen vegetables!" She'd thrown her arms in the air, making her tall self even taller. "What am I going to do?"

We'd been at the sideboard in Aunt Frances's dining room, our backs to a winterscape of white lawns and naked trees, our fronts facing Kristen's pages and pages of spread-out scribbles. "Shut down in the winter," I said. "Go somewhere warm. You don't like snow that much, anyway."

"What?" She'd put her hands to her sleek hair. "I can't do that! How can I be closed four months out of the year?"

"Okay, close after New Year's, open on April Fools' Day."

"How can I be closed three months of the year?"

"Who's going to eat there in February?" I'd asked. "Besides me and Aunt Frances, I mean.

The snowbirds are all gone after the holidays and we're too far from most of the ski resorts to be a destination."

"I can't be closed three months of the year," she'd said, but it was almost a question.

"Why not? Lots of restaurants around here are closed in winter." I ran roughshod over the objections she was starting to think up. "Interview the people you want to hire and tell them right off what you're thinking. If they shy away, well, maybe you'll have to stay open to keep your core staff. Why not at least try? But this way you'll only need to come up with menus from three seasons."

By then she was starting to think about it. "Three seasons," she'd said. "I can do three, easy."

Thus the restaurant's name was born. The location, after weeks of searching for a perfect place that I was convinced existed only in Kristen's head, was locked in when a rambling bed-and-breakfast that had once been a family cottage went on the market. "Cottage" being a loose term, since in this case it referred to a mammoth five-thousand-square-foot structure.

Kristen's bank had kicked loose the loan when she barged into the bank president's office and served him chicken piccata, asparagus with morel mushrooms, and an apple tart. Four months later the restaurant opened to great acclaim.

This Sunday evening, I walked in through the

back door, simultaneously greeting and staying out of the way of the sous chef. I nodded at various staff members and wound my way through the pantry to Kristen's office, where she was working away at her computer.

"Hey." I sat in the chair opposite her desk. Now that the time had come to tell her all about Friday, I didn't know how to begin. "How's the new chef working out? He's been here two or three weeks now, right?"

Kristen kept clicking keyboard keys. "Why can't I get a steady supply of strawberries? It's June, for crying out loud." She ranted on about her supplier, calling dire threats upon his head, his children's heads, and his children's children's heads.

When she took a breath before making a new threat, I asked again. "New chef?"

She squinted at the computer, then pushed herself away from it. "The jury is still out, but I think he'll be fine."

"How was the cheese?" I asked. "Wasn't that why you went down to Traverse City?"

Sighing, she shook her head. "Why is it so hard to find exactly what I want?"

I'd been Kristen's personal search engine for years due to her need to use both hands while cooking, but this wasn't a question that took any research. "Because you're a prima donna restaurateur who is so persnickety that you can't be satisfied with anything less than the absolute best?"

She considered my question. "Sure, that could be it."

"Or it could be that you're a persnickety grouch who won't be satisfied with anything, even if it is the best."

This, too, she considered. Then she grinned. "Nah. I don't see it."

"And I don't see why anyone would want to run a restaurant."

"No?" Still smiling, she picked up her phone. "Hey, Harvey, bring me a couple of specials." She shut down her laptop and crossed her arms. "Before we eat, I want to clear up one or two small points. And get that puzzled look off your face. You know what I'm talking about."

I hung my head. "Yes, I do, and I don't know what came over me, but I promise never to eat processed cheese ever again."

She smothered a laugh. "Do it one more time and I'll feed you goat cheese for a month." A real look of terror must have shown on my face because she laughed outright, then said, "Small points. Are we or are we not best friends?"

"We are." Kristen had grown up in Chilson and I'd been a regular summer visitor as soon as I'd been old enough to be put on a bus headed north. Since my mom's job as a guide at Dearborn's Greenfield Village was busiest in the summer, it hadn't taken much whining to get sent up to Aunt Frances. Kristen and I had discovered each other at the city beach the summer I'd turned twelve and we'd been friends ever since.

"Okay, then." She leaned back and draped her long legs over the corner of her garage sale desk. "Do we or do we not share all the important events in our lives?"

"No."

She sat up a little, frowning. "What do you mean, 'no'?"

"You never did tell me about what happened between you and Danny Stevens behind the high school gym."

"And I never will. Larger point. Are you planning to tell me about finding Stan Larabee before hell freezes over, or after? You've been here five minutes already, Minnie. Start talking."

"I . . . don't know how." There were no words, no way to express what I needed to say, nothing that would help, nothing that would change what had happened, nothing that would change the pictures in my head. *Oh, Stan . . .*

"Minnie," she said gently. "Talk to me."

A large silence dropped down between us. I watched it expand and grow to fill all the space in the room, to take up all the air. I was starting to struggle for breath when the office door opened and Harvey, the sous chef, bustled in with a plate in each hand.

"Ladies," he said. Behind him rushed a waiter carrying a small table. The table went down next to me. The waiter, who'd had a white tablecloth over one arm, flung it out and over the table. Out of one apron pocket came linen napkins; out of the other came flatware. He backed away and Harvey set the plates on the table gently, turning the entrée so it would be closest to the edge of the table. He whisked a small vase of flowers out of his back pocket and centered it on the table-cloth. "Is there anything else I can get you?" He looked expectant.

"No, thanks. That's it." After hovering a moment, Harvey shuffled out, and Kristen pushed her rolling chair back from her desk and came around to a stop in front of the other plate.

I'd already bellied up to the table. "That guy is so in love with you he can hardly see straight." I stuck my fork into the lightly browned lake trout.

"Huh. Does that explain why he dropped a tray of dinner rolls the other night?"

I stuffed my mouth full. "Oh, man, do you know how good this is?"

"It's my creation, isn't it?"

"Yeah, but . . ." I waved my empty fork in the air before I plunged it once again into the entrée. "But you get jaded, eating this kind of stuff every day. It's only people like me, who only get to eat like this on rare occasions, who can truly appreciate it."

"It wouldn't be rare if you'd let me feed you more often."

"Let's not go there," I said.

"You can eat here every day for free. Twice a day. Three times, if we had breakfast." She put her arms flat on the table and looked at me hard. "I know how much I owe you, don't think I don't."

"You don't owe me anything," I said in a low voice.

"Yes, I do." Kristen banged the table with her fist, making the flatware bounce and the plates rattle. "You're the only one who believed in me. My parents didn't, my former fiancé didn't, and for sure my former evil corporate employer thought I was nuts. Only you believed. Not only that, but you did all the research on—"

I cut her off. "You don't owe me a thing. You're my friend. That's what friends do."

"There are friends and there are friends." She sat back. "But since you obviously don't want the fun of an argument, I'll say you don't owe me anything, either. Except for one thing."

I picked up my fork again. At age twelve, she'd welcomed a downstate stranger into her life and had never once turned her back on me. She was wrong. I owed her far more than I could ever repay. "Okay, one."

"Tell me what happened with Stan Larabee. Tell me the truth, the whole truth, and nothing but the truth, and I'll never ask you about it again."

"Never?"

"Well, I'll *try* not to ask you about it again." She smiled the half smile that always made me giggle. "And this isn't idle curiosity—it's simple clarification of what the grapevine has already told me."

"Which is . . . ?"

She flittered her fingers. "Oh, the usual. Stan had been beaten up something horrible, half the bones in his body were broken, one of his kidneys had been removed, and he wrote the name of his killer on the floor in his own blood, but when you were trying to save him, you stepped on the blood and messed up the writing."

"The grapevine is batting zero."

Something in my voice must have given away the emotions I was trying to hold in, because Kristen moved to my side and put a hand on my shoulder. "Was it bad?" she asked gently.

"I really don't . . ."

Don't want to talk about it, don't want to think about it, don't want to see Stan's limp body again, don't want it to have happened. What I wanted was Stan to be alive. I just wanted him back.

"Oh, Minnie." Kristen's arms went all the way around me, and it was there, in the comfort of my best friend's embrace, that the tears came.

"Bawled my eyes out," I told Eddie. "Cried like a little kid who'd dropped her ice-cream cone in the dirt. And before you ask, yes, that happened to me once. Chocolate soft-serve. It was a harsh lesson. Would you like to hear about it?"

Eddie's eyes remained closed.

"I didn't think so."

We were cozied up in bed, me sitting up with my arms around my legs, Eddie lying like a meat loaf in the middle of the comforter. If he'd brought a tape measure to bed, I don't think he could have centered himself more accurately.

"I ended up telling her everything," I told Eddie. "About you stowing away, then you being the one to run over to that farmhouse. She thinks it was fate. I'm not a big believer in that kind of stuff. What do you think?"

Eddie didn't move.

"Yeah, you're right. Fate, shmate. Things don't always happen for a reason; sometimes they just happen." I smiled. "Zofia would agree with Kristen, I bet. She said it was fate that brought her to Aunt Frances this summer." I put my chin on my knees. "You know, Aunt Frances took the news about Stan a little weird."

I thought back to breakfast, how her hand had left a mark on mine, how she'd eaten hardly a bite of food. "Maybe she's just worried about me." It didn't fit, though. "Well, I'm out of ideas. What do you think, Edster?" No response. "Eddie?"

A low buzzing noise came from my furry friend.

Eddie was sound asleep. And snoring.

# Chapter 6

The next morning was bright and sunshiny. "The perfect summer morning," I told Eddie as I got dressed for work. "Too bad you'll have to spend it inside." He opened one eye, then closed it. I wasn't sure if he'd been saying, "Yeah, and where will you be?" or "I'll be inside? That's what you think."

Though not likely, it was certainly possible that Eddie had found a way to get out. My houseboat was of wooden construction, lovingly assembled in a Chilson backyard years ago, in the days when I was putting freshly loosened baby teeth under my pillow. The only fiberglass on the entire boat was in the shower. I had a feeling my homemade status was what irritated my right-hand neighbor, Gunnar Olson, so much. Why he didn't get a slip at the marina up by the point for his sleek forty-two-foot cruiser was a great mystery to many.

"You didn't, did you?" I asked the unmoving curl of black-and-white fur. "Find a way outside?"

He didn't answer. Of course, if he had figured a way out, I would be the last person he'd tell. I kissed the top of his head, did the whiteboard thing, and headed to work.

The marina where I was moored, Uncle Chip's Marina (now owned by Chris, Chip's nephew), was on the southeast side of town. If there'd still been a set of railroad tracks that went through Chilson, Uncle Chip's would have been on the wrong side of them. Relatively speaking, of course. This was an old resort town, one of those places where the same families had been summering for more than a hundred years, and even the dumpy parts of town were more tired than unkempt.

Back in the late eighteen hundreds, the summer people came up by train or steamer in June and left in early September. In the last few decades, though, most cottages had been retrofitted with insulation and central heating. People came up for the fall colors, for Thanksgiving, for Christmas, stayed through New Year's, and braved the snow and wind to come up skiing over the Martin Luther King and Presidents' Day weekends.

Then again, some things hadn't changed a lick in eons. The Round Table was still the local diner. There was still a Joe running Joe's Fish Market, and the movie theater, the Grand, was still showing second-run movies and their popcorn was still being popped by Penelope the Popcorn Lady.

I walked to the library trying to think of all the changes someone Stan Larabee's age had seen. The art galleries and antique stores must have housed other businesses in the forties, but the bank had a 1901 date on its cornerstone. The brick county courthouse had celebrated its hundredth anniversary a couple of years ago, and judging from the dust heaps in the corners of the auto parts store, that particular business had been in existence since the days of Henry Ford and the Model T.

Then there was the library.

Smiling, I trotted up the steps to the side entrance. The two-story L-shaped building had started life as the local school. The town had grown, more kids had enrolled, and the town fathers had decided to erect a new building to house the older students. Time passed, technology changed, and it was time to build a new elementary school. The old building, filled with Craftsman-style details, had been abandoned.

Just before the roof was about to fall in, the library board put a bond proposal on the ballot. "The current library is stuffed to the rafters," they said. "No room to expand. Let's take the old school and renovate it into a library that will serve Tonedagana County for the next hundred years."

And that's exactly what happened. The millage passed handily, an architect was hired, renovation commenced, and two months after I was hired, the Chilson District Library moved into its new home.

I used my key to unlock the side door. My low heels clicked on the large square tiles of the wide hallways as I walked past the reading room with its fireplace and window seats, past the broad switchback stairs that led to the upper levels of meeting rooms, Friends of the Library book-sale room, and offices.

Or, rather, office. Stephen's lair was the only office on the second floor. It was a large space with a view of Janay Lake, and when the leaves were off the trees, the view included Lake Michigan. There'd been much muttering when Stephen had staked claim to the space. Let him, I'd thought. Who except Stephen would want to be up there all alone in January when the wind was howling and the snow was blowing? Double-paned windows or not, that corner office was bound to be a cold place to work.

Only it turned out that Stephen had convinced someone to donate insulated curtains and some-one else to donate a high-efficiency space heater. November through April, Stephen's office was the warmest in the building.

I pushed open the hinged solid slab of wood that served as the gate separating the public space from the employee area. My Saturday stint in the bookmobile collection had been productive, but there were a few things I needed to do in here. I'd originally been thrilled at the title of assistant director, but I'd quickly learned what it really meant.

"Minnie."

I jumped. "Stephen! When did you get here?"

He had the rumpled, harried look of someone who'd been working hard for hours. Which was difficult to fathom. While Stephen was organized, effective, and politically connected, he was also of the firm belief that nothing important got done before ten in the morning, and planned his arrival at the library accordingly.

Stephen took off his glasses and rubbed his eyes. "I need you to put together a staff meeting for this morning. Ten o'clock in the conference room. I want everyone there." He replaced his glasses. "Everyone. Call them all in."

A comprehensive staff meeting two hours from now? It couldn't be done. He knew that. He had to know that.

"Everyone," he repeated, and this time the command was delivered with steel.

I watched him go. What being assistant director meant, at least in this library, was that I did whatever the director wanted me to do. I went straight to my office, riffled through my desk drawers for a staff directory, and picked up the phone.

It took a fair amount of cajoling and some outright bribery to get everyone to come in. Most of our staff was part-time, and many had young children who needed watching, or a second job, or both. I promised doughnuts, tracked down a high school kid to babysit in the children's section, and swore that the meeting wouldn't take longer than an hour.

At ten o'clock I taped signs to the exterior doors that the library would be open by eleven and shooed everyone upstairs.

Stephen had seated himself at the head of the long conference room table. He was in a pensive pose, elbows on the polished wood, fingers interlaced, brow furrowed. The chatter and laughter that had accompanied us on the climb up the stairs fell away as we entered the high-ceilinged room. The signs of pending doom were all too easy to recognize.

I came in last, closing the door behind me.

Stephen glanced around. "Is this everyone?" At my nod, he positioned his glasses on the table and rubbed at his face. Which, I noted with something akin to shock, was stubbly. Stephen was always dressed impeccably. Shoes shined, pants ironed to a crease, button-down collars buttoned firmly. I felt a twinge of misgiving.

"I've called you together this morning," he said, "because I have news that could drastically change the Chilson District Library."

The twinge became a tremor. I clasped my hands together and leaned against the wall. A chair would have been better, but the only empty one was next to Stephen, so I decided the wall was perfectly comfortable.

Stephen cleared his throat. "I assume everyone

has heard the news that Stan Larabee is dead."

Heads nodded.

"In the last two years, I've had many discussions with Mr. Larabee. Matter of fact, I had the privilege of getting to know him quite well." Stephen fingered his glasses. "In his youth, Mr. Larabee was mentored by a Chilson librarian. He always felt the books he'd been encouraged to read had much to do with his financial success."

If Stephen had called this meeting to tell us how libraries and librarians could be a power for good, I was going to—

"Which is why Mr. Larabee left a generous portion of his large fortune to our library."

There was a short, stunned silence, which quickly erupted into a conversational babble that filled the room.

"Sweet! Can we get new computers?"

"But I thought his family would get all the money."

"Someone told me he was going to set up a foundation, you know, one of those places that gives away a little money to lots of people."

"I heard he was leaving everything to some university."

Stephen thumped the table. When everyone quieted, he said, "I have no idea of the size of Mr. Larabee's estate, or who the other beneficiaries might be. Frankly, it's none of our business. But there is the serious matter of Mr. Larabee's murder.

Before anything else, the killer must be found. I expect the police will be questioning each of you. I also expect each of you to cooperate fully."

And with that, he left.

The buzzing started before he'd even closed the door.

"Generous? What does that mean?"

"Did you see Stephen's eyes? Bloodshot red, all through. Man, I've never seen him look like that."

"The police? But we didn't do anything. Why do they want to talk to us?"

"But I heard they already found Larabee's killer. One of the EMTs knew sign language, and Larabee spelled out the name of his killer right before . . . you know."

"No, Minnie found him, right before he died."

"Minnie found Stan Larabee?"

"Yeah, when she was out in the bookmobile."

One by one, all the employees turned to look at me. But since that happened on a regular basis, I'd been expecting it. It had turned out that another part of my job was asking Stephen the questions the rest of the staff was too afraid to ask. Our employees ranged in age from fresh out of high school to pie-baking grandmothers, with a hefty core in the twentysomething to fortysomething range, and every single one of them came to me if they needed to ask the library director a question.

Time and time again, I told them to ask him

themselves, that he wasn't so bad, not really. Time and time again, I was moved to pity by the looks of abject fear. "You do it, Minnie. You know how to get around him."

What I knew was that by aiding and abetting I was making a bad situation worse. I was being an enabler. And one of these days I'd figure out a solution.

"Don't ask me," I said to the questioning eyes. "Whatever you want to know, I don't have the answer."

Josh, our IT guy, said, "You got to know something."

"I do," I said. Everybody leaned forward. "I know that it's time to open the library."

"Aw, Minnie . . ."

"Doughnuts are downstairs in the break room. Thanks for playing and better luck next time."

That got me a few laughs. I hurried out of the room and down the stairs to unlock the doors. Not even half past ten. It wasn't uncommon for summer mornings to be slow. Maybe we hadn't turned anyone away, maybe—

I spotted a shape at the tall window next to the front door. A large human shape, with hands cupped around its face, peering into the library with its forehead against the glass. Which would leave a mark high enough that I'd have to stand on my tiptoes to clean it off.

The dead bolt made a *snick* noise as I turned it.

I opened the door and put my head out. "Mitchell, what are you doing?"

"Huh?"

Mitchell Koyne was about my age and I had no idea how he made a living, because he spent more time hanging out at the library than he did working at his various seasonal jobs. From our conversations, I knew he'd worked on his share of construction crews, that he did snowplowing and was a ski lift operator, but what he did to fill the gaps between seasonal jobs was another of life's little question marks.

My friend Holly, one of the clerks, insisted that he smuggled drugs from Canada. When I'd pointed out that he didn't have a boat, she said, "Not that we know of." But I couldn't see it. Mitchell was many things, but a good liar was not one of them, and it takes lies to be a criminal.

Now Mitchell unstuck his forehead from the window, turned his baseball cap around, and grinned at me. "Waiting for you guys to open. What's the deal?"

I looked up, way up. Mitchell was one of the tallest men I'd ever met. I much preferred to talk to him when he was seated. "Staff meeting." I untaped my note. "What brings you here so early?"

"Would you believe I've turned over a new leaf?"

I headed back inside and he kept step with me.

Sort of. "Does this new leaf include paying your overdue fines?"

"Funny, Min. You're really funny today."

"I thought I was funny every day."

"Every other, maybe."

We walked a few steps; then Mitchell blurted out, "What did you do this weekend?"

That was when I knew it wasn't the pursuit of abstract knowledge that had Mitchell here before the crack of noon. He was intelligent, computer savvy, and read a wide range of books and magazines (heavy on the science fiction), but the only other time we'd seen him in the morning was the Monday after the time change. He'd forgotten to move his clocks back and come in at a quarter to noon.

No, this morning Mitchell was after gossip about Stan, just like everyone else.

I stopped in front of the checkout counter. "I'll say this once and only once." I looked around. Half the staff was still mingling, eating doughnuts and dropping crumbs into the carpet. "You guys might as well listen, too. Yes, I found Stan Larabee. Since he was already dead, he told me nothing about his killer and he left no clues about his killer. And I didn't know about his will. I didn't even know he *had* a will."

"What will?" Mitchell asked. "Did he leave you a bunch of money or something?"

"If you'll excuse me," I said, swallowing down

the sniffs that were suddenly coming, "I have work to do." Then, like Stephen, I left. Only I doubted that after his speech he hurried down to the bookmobile's circulation room and bawled his eyes out.

My unexpected crying attack didn't last long, but by the time I'd washed my face and made my way back upstairs, two representatives from the sheriff's office were at the circulation desk getting a list of employees from Holly. One was tall and thin, the other short and stout. Both looked close to retirement age. Mr. and Mr. Sprat.

Holly Terpening was my best library friend in spite of the many differences between us. She was about my age, but was happily married, loved to cook, had two small children, a dog, and straight brown hair, and was average in height, which meant she was six inches taller than I was. Though the only commonality we shared was the love of the same books, it turns out that's enough for a strong friendship.

"Are you going to want to talk to all of us?" Holly stared at the officers. "Why? I mean, none of us knew anything about the will before this morning."

The officers exchanged a quick glance. Hmm. Had Stephen committed a faux pas in giving us that information?

I shook my head. Too many television plots

were rattling around inside my skull. I didn't know the first thing about the real-life behavior of law enforcement officers and wished it could have stayed that way.

"This one." The tall officer pointed at a name. "That's who we want to talk to first. Minerva Hamilton."

I rubbed at my eyes. Dry this time. Excellent. I pasted on a smile and went to talk to the officers.

Come midafternoon, Holly and Josh and I found ourselves in the break room at the same time. Josh shoved dollar bills into the soda pop machine and pushed buttons. "What'd they ask you?" The machine clunked out three cans of diet cola. One can went into the left side pocket of his baggy cargo shorts, another went into the right side pocket, and he popped the top on the third and started drinking.

I shrugged. "The same questions the deputy asked on Friday afternoon. Why was I there, what did I see, that kind of stuff." Over and over and over again. The only things I'd gleaned from the recent conversation was that the weapon had been a rifle and the uncomfortable knowledge that the killer had been waiting in the farmhouse for Stan to approach. This was why the back door had been open. Broken open, they'd said, with scuff marks from a boot and a fist to prove it. My hesitant question about getting prints or DNA from a fist had earned me polite smiles and what felt like a pat on the head. "Sorry, Ms. Hamilton. There was nothing to get off that door."

Josh lowered his soda can. "Did they ask if you knew about Larabee's will?"

"I said up front that I didn't know about it."

"Jeez, Minnie, you're not supposed to volunteer information. Everybody knows that."

Josh, as the only male on full-time staff under the age of fifty, sometimes took on the persona of Man of the World. The fact that he'd never set foot outside of Michigan's borders didn't dent his attitude at all.

"They were going to ask me anyway. What difference does it make?"

He shook his head and took another drink.

"What did they ask you, Josh?" Holly looked at the vending machine that was filled with chips and candy bars and turned away. "It didn't seem like you were in there very long."

"Nah." Josh leaned back against the table I'd talked Stephen into buying. "Did you know they were detectives, not deputies?"

I had, actually, and I was sure Holly knew, too. That is, unless the officers had been misrepresenting themselves when they'd introduced themselves as Detectives Devereaux and Inwood.

Holly pressed Josh. "What did they ask you?"

"Not much." He glugged down more soda. "Did I know Larabee? No. Did I know about the will? No. Do I have any idea who'd want to kill him? No, not unless Stephen wanted to get his hands on that money sooner rather than later."

"Josh Hadden!" I cried. "You didn't!"

He smirked. "Would have been fun if I had. Just think of it, Stephen considered a person of interest, his reputation shattered. The board loses confidence, and—"

"Stop it," I commanded. "That's not funny at all."

"Sure it is," he said, laughing.

I glanced at Holly. She'd slumped into a chair. "What's the matter? Are you okay?"

"They asked me a lot of questions," she said dully. "Lots more than they asked either of you."

That was weird. "Why would they have more questions for you?"

She fiddled with the collar of her pale pink polo shirt. "I'm not sure. Say, the Tigers won last night, did you hear? Ten innings."

Josh looked at me. I looked at him. Holly was not a sports fan.

"What were they asking, Holly?" Josh pulled one of his sodas out of his pants and pushed it in her direction. "What did they want to know?"

"Oh, nothing."

I popped the top of the can and turned the opening in her direction. Holly always talked when she had a drink. Didn't matter if it was coffee, tea, water, soda, or an adult beverage. To

Holly, a fluid in her hand meant she was supposed to be talking. "Here you go," I said. "Drink up."

One sip was all it took. "Stan Larabee was my cousin," she said.

I frowned. "What kind of cousin?" Couldn't be a first cousin—the age gap was too wide.

"No, no. Second cousin, twice removed. Something like that."

A muscle at the back of my neck loosened. "He must have had lots of distant cousins. Everybody does. Six degrees of cousins, right?"

Which I thought was fairly funny, but Holly wasn't listening. "It's not that, well, not directly. It's because . . ." She took another drink. "It's because I asked him . . ." Another gulp. "I asked him to lend me some money."

Josh went still. "You did what?"

Holly clutched the can. "You know how Brian and I want to buy our own house. That's why he's out in Wyoming working at that mine. He's making good money, really good, but there's this house I just fell in love with and we don't have enough for a down payment and I thought . . . I thought maybe . . ."

"Everybody knows that Stan Larabee doesn't lend money," Josh said. "Not to anyone."

Didn't lend money, I thought. Past tense. So very, very past tense.

"Yeah," Holly said. "But since we were cousins, I thought maybe this time it'd be different."

Josh made a rude noise. "No wonder the police were asking you questions. Bet old Stan kept that begging letter in a file." He grinned. "Does Brian know you asked Larabee for money?"

Her eyes went wide. "No! He'd hit the roof. He's coming home for the Fourth of July. Don't you tell him, Josh. Don't you dare! It'll ruin his whole trip home."

"It's going to cost you," Josh said, his grin going wider. "There's this whole stack of data entry I've been putting off, and—"

"Time to get back to work," I said. "See you two later."

I left them to their wrangling. If past experience was any guide, Josh would try to get a little too much out of Holly, she'd retaliate by reminding him that she was a neighbor to the attractive young woman he was thinking hard about dating, and they'd call it a draw.

So Holly had tried to get a loan from Stan and failed. Who else, I wondered, had done the same thing?

After work I stopped to pick up some fresh whitefish for dinner. The moment I unwrapped the white butcher paper, Eddie was on the back of the dining area's bench seat, sniffing and twitching his whiskers.

"Pulled out of Lake Michigan a few hours ago," I told him, "so quit criticizing. It's not going to get any fresher unless you go get it yourself, and I really don't see that happening. It would require a little too much exertion on your part. And it's for me, not you, anyway."

Eddie sat down and looked at me.

"Okay, that was a little harsh." I kissed his head. "Sorry. It's just been a weird day."

"Mrr?"

It sounded like a question, so I started talking as I dipped the fish into an egg wash. "For one thing, Stephen's a mess. He's never a mess, and I'm wondering if Josh was right, that the police think maybe Stephen killed Stan to get the money. But why would he do that? The library could use more money, sure, but we're doing okay."

Eddie started digging at the upholstery with his claws.

"Hey, quit." Since my hands were all fishy, I pushed at him with my forearm. "And Holly's a mess, too," I said, laying the fish into a bowl of breading Kristen had sent me home with the previous night. "I wish she wasn't so nervous about telling her husband she asked Stan for a loan. Maybe Brian will be mad for a minute, but he's a good guy. He'll understand." Or . . . would he? He seemed nice, but how well did I really know him?

"How well does anyone know anybody?" I quietly asked the fish. "Can anyone really depend on someone else?" I felt a flash of longing for a love long gone, a love I'd once thought would last to the end of time. Most days, most weeks, I was happy with the places my choices had taken me, but every so often, every once in a while . . .

A flash of black and white went past my left shoulder and landed on the counter.

"Eddie!" Laughing, I elbowed him away from my dinner and encouraged him onto the floor. "You are a horrible cat."

His four paws hit the linoleum with a quadruple thump and he gave me a look that, if the universe had been created by cats, would have instantly frozen the blood in my veins.

"Oh, here." I gave him a small piece of fish.

"Mrr," he said, and slurped it down.

# Chapter 7

The next morning, Eddie did his best to accompany me throughout my showering, dressing, and breakfasting. He blinked at me all the way through the assemblage of my peanut butter and jelly sandwich, the bagging of a handful of potato chips, the shoving of food and a jug of water into my backpack, and the writing of a note on the whiteboard.

When I zipped the backpack closed, he bounced into action. Off the bench, across the floor, and up against the door before I'd taken more than a step in that direction.

"Oh, no, you don't." I picked him up, gave him a small noogie, and put him back on the bench. "It may be Bookmobile Day, but you're not coming with me. That was a onetime deal. I'll see you tonight. Have a good day." Not that Eddie could understand what I said, of course. Still, it was kind of like wearing your favorite underwear to a job interview. You knew it didn't make any difference, but why take the risk?

I opened the door. A fraction of a second later I heard Eddie's front and back feet double-thump the floor. The sound of elephant feet raced toward me and I slammed the door shut before either of us got out. "Not a chance, pal."

He slid to a stop. Stood on his hind legs. Pawed at the door.

I blew out a breath. "Listen, buddy. Remember that long talk we had? Cats don't belong on a bookmobile. And no bringing up Dewey. He was in a library. Different situation altogether."

Still scratching, he looked over his shoulder. "Mrr?"

"You are pathetic. Adorable, but pathetic. And now, if you don't mind, I'm going to work." I picked him up again, put him on the bench again, gave him the gentlest of shoves to send him off-balance, and raced to the door. By dint of sliding out sideways like one of those skinny fish, I got safely outside before Eddie could get a paw in the doorway.

I heard his yowls as I walked off the dock and across the marina's dewy grass. Even halfway to downtown I thought I could hear poor Eddie calling to me. My steps slowed . . . but, no. It wouldn't work.

I put my fingers in my ears and walked on.


"Where is she?" A portly, gray-haired man looked around the bookmobile.

"I'm sorry?" Thessie, my seventeen-year-old volunteer, looked puzzled. "Minnie is the book-mobile librarian." She pointed to where I was standing, maybe ten feet away from the man, working with a six-year-old boy to find a book about butterflies.

"No, no." The man brushed away her gesture. "The cat. I heard there's a cat on the bookmobile. I like cats. Where are you hiding her?"

"A cat?" Thessie's eyes went big. My stomach instantly clumped together in a tight mass. "There's no cat here," she said.

"Sure, toe the party line, I get it." He winked broadly. "So where is she?"

I handed the kid a book on snakes—"Try this"— and moved to intervene. "Sorry," I said, putting on my most gracious and helpful smile. "There's no cat here today."

"Why not?" He frowned. "It's a great idea."

"Thanks, but . . ." I tipped my head to the side and we adjourned to the back of the bus. "It was a onetime deal," I told him quietly. "Eddie was a stowaway last Friday. He wasn't supposed to be here, and I'd appreciate it if you didn't spread the word."

"Stowaway Eddie?" His lips twitched.

I looked at Thessie. She was engrossed in explaining rattlesnakes to the six-year-old. In a low voice I asked the man, "Who told you the bookmobile had a cat?" Forget the consequences, full cover-up ahead!

"Well, now." He rubbed his chin. "Seems like I heard it Sunday morning at church." More rubbing. "Or was it yesterday at the Rotary meeting? Sorry." He shrugged. "Can't say for sure."

Yes, life as I knew it was over. But Stephen

couldn't fire me; only the library board could and they wouldn't meet for another three weeks. Timing is everything. I could polish up my résumé and send it out . . . where? There wasn't anywhere else I wanted to be.

The man read my expression of woe. "Ah, don't worry about Stevie." He slapped me on the shoulder. "He's so stuck in that ivory tower he built for himself that he'll never hear a word about Eddie."

"You know Stephen?" A small hope beat in my heart.

"He's the same now as when he was a kid. Smart, but not really seeing anything."

I blinked and tried to imagine a young Stephen. Somehow he looked just like he did now, only shorter, buttoned-down shirts and all.

"Downstate," the man said, "he and his folks lived on the next block. And here I end up retiring practically down the street from him. Funny old world, eh?"

Life up north was full of odd coincidences like this. On a ferry ride to Mackinac Island last summer I'd sat in front of my high school biology teacher. And two winters ago I'd been skiing at the nearby Nub's Nob, and ridden up the ski lift next to a guy I'd had a class with in graduate school. Things like that happened when the region's major industry was tourism on a grand scale. Up here, the odds of running into your grade school crush were about the same as running into the latest *American Idol* idol.

Stephen's old neighbor asked, "So, you going to bring Eddie around next time, right?"

I smiled. "Not a chance."

During the drive to the next stop, I kept the conversation tight on the complexity of tasks involved in being a librarian. Thessie was a high school senior and considering library science as a major. Ergo, her volunteering on the bookmobile. "There's a lot more to being a librarian than most people realize," I said.

"Yes, I know. Um, that man? What did—"

"Dealing with odd questions is one of those things they don't tell you about in college." I tossed off a careless laugh. "Another thing they don't tell you about is working with library boards. Chilson's board is wonderful, but I could tell you stories." And I did, on and on without a break until we came to the next stop. "Well, here we are," I sang out. "And we have people waiting for us already. Isn't that great?"

Thessie may have been only seventeen, but she was no slouch in the brains department.

"So if anyone asks about the cat, what do I say?"

"There is no cat," I said firmly.

"Yeah, but maybe there could be." She gave me a sidelong look. "I mean, if there was a cat, it might be fun having it around."

I rotated the driver's seat and brought the laptop to life. "Will you pop the roof vents? Thanks." Thessie, at least eight inches taller than me, could reach the ceiling easily. "No cat. There's no way Stephen would allow a fuzzy, furry feline on the bookmobile."

"Not a cat guy, is he?" Thessie asked.

"He's not an animal person." Neither cat nor dog nor feathered friend was held in esteem by the library director. "Says all pets do is eat and make messes that other people have to clean up."

It was easy to see the gears whirling around in Thessie's pretty dark-haired head. I shook mine. "There's no use bringing it up. Even if we get around his dislike of pets, he'll say that people are allergic and we can't possibly run the risk of exposing anyone."

"Okay, but the bookstore downtown has a cat and they don't have any problems. And wasn't there a library in Iowa or somewhere that had a cat living there?" She glanced around. "A bookmobile's smaller, I guess, but if we vacuumed every time to get the hair and dander out—"

I was shaking my head. "Not going to happen." I unlocked the back door and pushed it open. "Good morning! Come up and into the bookmobile."

Up the stairs first was a young man of about twelve. Red springing curls, bright blue eyes, and braces on his teeth. "Do you have anything about fishing? There's this bass in the lake I want to catch and my grandpop said you might have something."

Thessie took him under her wing and escorted him to the high shelves at the rear end of the bus.

Next up the stairs was an elderly couple, hand in hand, looking for books on gardening. After I got them settled, I noticed a young woman coming aboard. Twentyish, long sun-washed blond hair, tan, wearing flip-flops, shorts, and a tank top covered by a flowered-print short-sleeved shirt, she looked the image of a California surfer girl.

I watched as she ran a finger over the books, scanning the titles, her head tilted to one side. She went through half a dozen shelves like that. Hunting for something, but not asking for help. Hmm. "Are you looking for something special?"

She jumped. "Oh! Um, no, thanks. I'm just looking. Is . . . that okay?"

A shy surfer girl? I didn't know that was possible. Then again, I'd only been to California once, and that was when I was six and we took a family trip to San Francisco, so what did I know?

"Absolutely it's okay," I said. "If you have any questions, just ask." I turned away, then had a thought. "If you're looking for something in particular, I can get it from the main library and bring it out on the next trip."

"Oh . . ." She opened her mouth, shut it, glanced around. "Um, no, thanks." She scurried down the stairs.

I stared after her. What had that been all about?

"What did you say to her?" Thessie asked. "She looked . . . well, scared."

Frightened as a rabbit had been my thought. "All I said was we could pull a book from the main library and bring it out to her."

"Well, there you go," Thessie said comfortably. "That's pretty scary, for sure."

I stared at her, then started laughing. Which is a good way to end a bookmobile stop.

The last stop of the morning was the rutted gravel parking lot of a middle-of-nowhere gas station and what you might have called a convenience store except that it didn't stock anything that travelers might have found it convenient to purchase. Bottled water? Soda? "Nah, we don't carry that crap." Snacks? "Got some beef jerky the wife made last fall." Map of the area? The grizzled proprietor would nod at a map stuck on the wall in 1949, long before paved roads reached this part of Tonedagana County.

The points in the location's favor were a tolerably clean bathroom, the large amount of shade cast by a huge oak tree, and that it was a nexus point for a number of homeschooling families. As soon as the bookmobile's purchase had been publicly announced, a representative mother had called me and begged for a stop.

We drove into the shaded parking lot, which had more cars in it than I'd ever seen.

"Are all these people here for the bookmobile?" Thessie's gaze was stuck on the group of adults and children milling about.

I studied the adults, trying to see if anyone looked familiar. One mother, two . . . "All of them," I said. "There are six families around here who homeschool."

"Lots more than six kids." She sounded apprehensive.

"It'll be fun," I said, stopping the bookmobile in front of a knot of cheering children. "What's the matter?"

"Kids I like just fine. It's tight spaces I'm not good with."

I stared at her, then stared at the aisle that would soon be filled with youngsters and moms and a dad or two. Houston, we have a problem. "Tell you what," I said, flipping the driver's seat around. "You sit here and run the computer. I'll take care of all the questions and send them your way to do checkout. It'll be fine."

"I'm so sorry," she said in a small voice. "I just never thought . . ."

"It'll be fine," I repeated, patting her on the shoulder.

When I pushed open the back door and let the

kids run up and inside, the noise level instantly went from calm to ear-damaging. I shot a glance at Thessie. She'd wedged herself into the gap between the seat and the bookmobile's outer wall, a feat I wouldn't have thought possible for any creature larger than Eddie. But though she was pale, she'd put on a bright smile and was chatting with a round-cheeked youngster.

I felt a tug on the hem of my crop pants.

"Miss Minnie? Miss Minnie?"

I looked down into eyes so brown they looked almost black. "Well, hello there, Brynn." Brynn and her mother and brothers came to the library as often as they could, which wasn't as often as any of them would have liked because of their ancient and undependable station wagon. The children's father had a high-level position with a boat-building manufacturer, but he had to travel on a regular basis.

While no one in the family liked his absences, he had to keep the job for the sake of top-quality health insurance. For Brynn's sake, for the sake of treating the leukemia she'd been diagnosed with two years ago, for the sake of this cheerful, clever little girl. Though I would have gone to the stake rather than publicly name a favorite library patron, Brynn was high up on the list. And if there was a Kids Only list, she'd be—

"Where's the kitty cat?" she asked.

She'd be sliding down toward the bottom.

I crouched down and spoke in a quiet, low voice, the kind of voice no one would overhear. "What cat?"

"You know." Brynn's gaze darted around the bookmobile. "Eddie the bookmobile cat."

Not only did she know there'd been a cat on board, but she knew his name. "What makes you think there's a cat?"

She stomped one small foot. "Rosie Engstrom told me so. She said his name is Eddie and he's black and white and real fuzzy and that I'd be able to pet him and he'd purr."

Rose. The Princess Girl. Naturally, she'd be the one to rat me out. Just like high school, the princesses always win. "Brynn, I'm sorry, but Eddie can't come on the bookmobile. He—"

"But I want to see the kitty," she said, her lower lip trembling. "I want the kitty!"

"Brynn—"

"I want to pet Eddie." Tears gushed out of her eyes and down her face. "I want to make him purr. Why can't I see Eddie? Rosie wasn't making things up, was she? There is really an Eddie, isn't there? She said he was so nice."

What had I done to this poor, sick little girl? Unintentionally, sure, but that didn't matter. Not to her and not to me. This lovely child had already dealt with more pain in her life than most people would ever endure and I was not going to add to her burden. "There is most definitely an

Eddie." I leaned down and kissed the top of her head. "He'll be on the very next bookmobile trip. I promise."

Thessie looked at me sideways the rest of the afternoon. Her comments, dropped every ten miles or so, ranged from "You have a cat named Eddie?" to "In the cabinet?" to "I can't believe you have a cat named Eddie," to a sad look and a slow headshake that said, *Gee, it was nice knowing you and I hope you find a new job soon.*

When we reached the Chilson city limits, I swore her to secrecy.

"But Mr. Rangel's going to find out," she said. "You know he will."

I shook my head. Not in disagreement, but in denial. "I told Brynn I'd bring Eddie to her." Michelle, Brynn's mom, had the schedule and we'd figured out the next stop closest to their house. "I said I would and I will."

Thessie sighed as she unbuckled her seat belt. "I hope you know what you're doing."

I did, too.

After putting the bookmobile away for the night, I hauled a milk crate full of books to the book-mobile room. The light switch, like most light switches in the world, was too high for me to turn on with my elbow, so I turned toward the wall and pushed it up with my shoulder. Which is why I didn't see the person huddled at my desk until I turned back around.

"Holly! What are you doing?" I put the milk crate down and leaned backward, stretching. "Hiding from Stephen?" I chuckled, but she didn't say anything. "Are you okay?"

She gave a muted sniff. "Kind of."

" 'Kind of' means no, not really." I walked to the desk and saw her face. Her puffy, red-eyed face. "Hey," I said softly. "What's the matter?"

"It's . . . it's . . ." She buried her face in her hands. "The police. I couldn't go back to the front desk, I just couldn't."

"The police talked to you again?"

She nodded and swallowed a sob. "Just now. They asked all these questions and . . . and they think I killed Stan Larabee, I just know it. What am I going to do?"

I wanted to give her comforting platitudes, tell her that since she didn't have anything to do with the murder, there was no way she'd ever be arrested. That everything would be fine. But the police had talked to her twice. They hadn't talked to anyone else at the library twice. Or . . . had they? I didn't know, so I asked her.

"Only me." She sniffed. Sniffed again. Hung her head. "Minnie, I'm in so much trouble," she whispered.

"No, you're not," I said. "The police are talking

to lots of other people." They had to be. "They'll find the killer and—"

"But what if they don't!" she wailed. "I look like a good suspect—I asked Stan Larabee for that loan and sent him a nasty note when he wouldn't do it and what if the police decide I'm the killer and don't find the real one? What will happen to my kids?"

"Holly—"

She seized my hands. "Minnie. Will you help me? Please say yes. The real killer is out there somewhere and the police are going to arrest me instead and I need your help. You *notice* things. You know you do. You were the only one to notice old Mr. Wednesday—I can never remember his real name—that he didn't come that one Wednesday and you went to his house and found him lying on the floor with a broken hip. And you were the only one to smell how hot that printer was and saved the library from burning down. You'll find something that'll prove I'm innocent. Please say you'll help me. Please."

The naked need in her eyes was too painful to see. I drew her to me in a hug. "Of course I'll help." And then, for the second time that day, I said, "I promise."

Kristen sighed. "I can't believe your mother lets you go out alone."

Though part of me wanted to roll my eyes at her statement, part of me agreed with it.

"I mean, honestly." Kristen pushed aside the paperwork in front of her, parting it like the Red Sea, and thumped her elbows on her desk's scratched surface. She put her chin in her hands. "Two career-killing moves in one day. I'd say it's a new record."

"At least I've never told my boss he was an addlepated nincompoop."

She grinned. "We're discussing you, not me. Why didn't you tell Brynn you'd drive Eddie out to see her in your car?"

"She wants to see the bookmobile cat, and he wouldn't be a bookmobile cat that way, would he?"

She squinted at me, then nodded. "True enough. But what on earth made you promise Holly Terpening you'd help find Stan's killer? You know what's going to happen. By 'help,' Holly means 'You go do this while I sit here and feel sorry for myself. Pooooor me.'" Kristen clasped her hands to her chest and batted her eyelashes.

"She's not the same person you knew in high school," I said. "And what makes you think helping Holly has anything to do with my career?"

"Because I know how she works. She'll whine and moan and be on you to help poor little her every second of every day, and you won't get any work done and Stephen will fire your skinny little butt because it'll take you more than ten minutes to reply to his e-mails since you're spending too much time helping Holly."

I'd never understood the raw antagonism that existed between Kristen and Holly and I probably never would. "Well, anyway. What I really wanted to talk to you about was Stan Larabee."

She glanced at the wall clock. "I don't have time."

"Yes, you do. You said you'd talked to him a few times. Did he come in here?"

She sat back in her chair, her long arms dangling. "You're serious about this."

"Did he or didn't he?"

The silence between us lengthened to a thin strand. "Okay," she said, breaking it. "Okay. Most of what I know about him is rumor and gossip and innuendo and I'm guessing you don't want to hear any of that." At my nod, she went on. "So the only thing I know for honest-to-goodness sure is that he and Caroline Grice have been in here a couple of times looking very friendly."

I blinked. "No kidding."

"Yep." Kristen smiled, obviously pleased at my nonplussed status. "Very cozy they were."

"You think they were on a date?"

"Bottle of expensive wine, dinner, coffee and dessert. Not sure what else it could have been."

Stan dining with the most elegant and cultured widow in town. Who would have thunk it?

There was a knock on Kristen's door. A white-hatted male head poked in. "Hey, Kristen. The guy from that new organic farm is here. You want me to send him back here?"

Kristen stood. "No, I'll see him in the kitchen. Minnie, if you want some dinner, we have some portabella mushrooms I'm trying to finish off. If you ask nice, this guy will whip up something interesting for you. He's the new one I told you about." And in three leggy strides, she was out the door and gone.

The chef looked at me. "Do you want mushrooms for dinner?"

"I'd rather eat road salt."

He grinned. "I'm not a big fan, myself." His white jacket was embroidered with the name "Larry." He might have been thirty, but his round face had that cherubic look that aged slowly. He also had a thick elastic brace around his left hand and wrist.

I nodded at it. "Can't be easy doing chef stuff with that on."

"Fact." He cradled it on the opposite hand. "Keep it elevated, they say. Like that's going to happen."

"What did you do?"

He looked over his shoulder, then at me. "I told the boss I sprained it playing softball."

"But . . . ?"

"You promise not to tell?"

What was one more promise? "Don't see why I would." The words hung in the air and I made a fast amendment. "Unless it hurts Kristen. She's my friend."

"Yeah, I get that." He made a slicing motion with his good hand. "The other night I stayed late, practicing with the knives. I'm saving up to buy my own Wüsthofs, but Kristen got a new set and I wanted to work with them a little."

My eyes went wide. "You cut yourself?"

"Ah, just nicked the tendon a little. It was late, I was still nervous about starting this new job, you know how it goes. No big deal. I'll be fine in a week." He grinned and I grinned back, thinking that Kristen might have herself a winner this time.

"What do you think of Three Seasons?" I asked.

"This place is great." He nodded eagerly. "It's a lot like the place I'm going to have. Someday, I mean. I'd want to build a brand-new building, though. You never know what's going on inside old walls, right?"

He was right, but building new wasn't cheap. When I said so, he nodded. "Yeah, but you got to do like they say, dream your dream and live into it, so that's what I'm doing. And it's just money. They print more every day. I have a spot all picked out—"

"Thought so!" Kristen's voice rang out, and I don't know who jumped higher, me or Larry. "Here." She slapped a full plate on her desk.

"Yeah, yeah, I know you think you don't like mushrooms. Just try it."

I looked at the plate, looked at Kristen, looked at Larry. He grinned. "Nice meeting you," he said. "Have a good dinner."

"Mrr?"

"Of course I didn't try them," I told Eddie. "Fungus among us. Eww." Ever since a childhood bout of stomach flu had coincided with my mother's dinner offering of sautéed mushrooms on Swiss steak, I hadn't been able to eat a mushroom nausea-free. I wasn't fond of Swiss steak, either.

Eddie and I were sitting on the front end of the houseboat with a pizza from Fat Boys between us. Sausage, green peppers, and bacon. Pre-cat, I used to get anchovies, but Eddie liked them too much.

"So." I wiped my face with a paper napkin. "Caroline Grice. Go figure."

A white paw reached out for the pizza box.

"Hey, that's tomorrow's lunch." I tossed my napkin in the box and flipped the top shut. "My lunch, not yours. You get cat food."

He stared at the pizza box, then flopped down on the chaise lounge.

"I mean, Caroline Grice? Sure, she and Stan were about the same age, but other than that . . ." I shook my head.

Stan had been a farm boy who'd made his fortune through smarts, timing, savvy, and incredible chutzpah. Caroline had been born into wealth, had married wealth, and was now an extremely wealthy widow.

Caroline was an alumna of Smith College; Stan was a Chilson High School graduate. Caroline was a patron of the arts; Stan had been a NASCAR fan. Caroline wore clothes purchased from stores that didn't advertise. I'd heard Stan say that a thousand dollars spent on a suit was a thousand dollars wasted. Caroline's world was curved edges and calm voices; Stan's had been full of hard knocks and braying laughter.

I looked at Eddie. "They say opposites attract. Do you think that's true?"

He made a pointless swipe at the pizza box.

"Don't waste your energy," I told him. "Save it for tomorrow when you'll need to sleep all day."

He ignored me and I went back to thinking about Stan and Caroline Grice.

Though Stan had been stratospherically rich, he'd been accessible. If you'd wanted to run the risk of hearing him tell you his canoe joke for the forty-second time, all you had to do was find LARABEE, STAN in the phone book and dial.

The Grices were different. Grices had lived in splendid isolation out on the point, a couple of miles from town, since before Chilson was Chilson. Grice children attended private schools;

Grice adults spent their leisure hours at the country club or tootling around in boats that cost more than the bookmobile. No Grice had ever checked a book out of the public library and no Grice (rumor said) had ever set foot in the Round Table.

I spent a moment wondering how they'd even met, then shook my head at myself. Of course they knew each other. Even if they didn't have common interests, Chilson was still a small town, and people in their economic stratosphere would inevitably meet.

"You know," I said to Eddie, "maybe Caroline had a reason to kill Stan. Jealous rage, maybe? They say murders are almost always committed by someone you know." I could give Caroline's name to the police, but I didn't see that going anywhere. I could just imagine the response if I called and suggested that one of the detectives talk to Caroline Grice. "Thank you, Ms. Hamilton. We're investigating all possibilities." *Click.*

"I guess I'll just have to find a way to talk to her myself."

Eddie opened his mouth in a yawn so big and wide that I had time to count the ridges on the roof of his mouth.

Cats.

# Chapter 8

A t noon the next day I shut myself in my office and tried to make a plan. Most of what I knew about Caroline Grice had come from Stephen. A few months after I'd been hired, he'd handed me a list of names and her name was halfway down the page.

"We need new blood," he'd said. "Our most loyal donors are in their seventies and we need to freshen up the pool."

At the time I'd been appalled at his heartlessness, but now I was beginning to understand the need. I didn't like it, but I understood. If you're not growing, thanks to natural attrition you're shrinking, and having a community's financial support is a critical part of a library's success.

Back then, thanks to letters, phone calls, and face-to-face visits, I'd drawn a few new regular donors into the fold. Caroline Grice had not been one of them.

Now I leaned back in my chair and tried to go at the situation in a manner of which Stephen would approve. Action items. You must distill a project into action items. I pictured the agenda.

Goal: Talk to Caroline about Stan, face-to-face if possible.

Proposed Methodology: none.

And the meeting is adjourned. Thanks for coming, folks.

"Research," I said to myself. "It's time for research."

I opened up my computer's browser and typed Caroline's name into the search engine: 178,000 results. Huh. I put quotes around her name: 4,658 results. Better, but more than I could drill through during my lunch break. I added "Michigan" to the string and found her husband's obituary, a press release announcing her husband's retirement, and her daughter's wedding announcement.

All the people in the world to research and I managed to pick the only one who wasn't on Facebook.

I flexed my hands and cracked my knuckles. There had to be some way to find a connection that would give me an excuse, some way to find common ground, some . . . "Got it." I searched for genealogy Web sites, found one that looked serious, dithered a little about the ethics of what I was about to do, then signed up for a free two-week membership.

Twenty minutes later I found what I needed. And here I'd thought the only benefit to having an extremely common last name was never needing to spell it for other people.

I printed out my brand-new data and opened my phone book to the *G*s. There it was: GRICE,

BRANSON. Ten years after her husband died and she still had the phone in his name.

I punched in the numbers and waited. "Grice residence," a polite voice said.

"I'd like to speak to Caroline Grice, please."

"This is she."

"Really?" I blurted, then winced at myself. Even the Grice staff must get a day off once in a while.

"I'm quite certain, yes. How may I help you?"

"This is Minnie Hamilton. We spoke a couple of years ago when the Friends of the Library were working on a fund-raiser."

"Yes, I remember." Still the polite voice. "Stephen Rangel's work, if I recall correctly. The man is tireless."

"Yes, ma'am. But I'm calling you regarding a different matter. I've been doing some genealogy research and I've come across an ancestor we might have in common. Would it be possible to meet with you?"

"How interesting." So polite. "But I'm afraid I must disappoint you. The only relations about which I know anything are my parents and my children. My cousin Richard, however, has been doing extensive research into the family. Shall I give you his number?"

I dumped my backpack on the kitchen counter. "Hi, honey, I'm home!"

No Eddie came running to greet me. I wandered around, looking.

A faint snore came rattling out of the closet. I slid open the door and found a black-and-white cat nestled in among my shoes. His body lay across my hiking boots and his front paws were wrapped around a blue flip-flop. The right one.

"You are the weirdest cat ever," I told him.

He opened his eyes to thin slits and opened his mouth in a soundless "Mrr."

I picked him up. "Come hang out with me, okay?"

We went to the kitchen and I deposited him on the back of the bench seat. I pulled the stack of mail I'd picked up from my post office box out of my backpack. "Junk mail, more junk mail, and a reminder from my mother that Thanksgiving isn't far away." Mom was nothing if not aggressive when it came to holiday plans. "Cool note card, though." I propped the reprint of what the card said was a Diego Rivera mural up on the kitchen counter. "Maybe if you wrote letters, you'd get some mail."

Eddie's nose twitched.

"No fish tonight," I said. "You're probably smelling the salmon Skeeter gave to Louisa."

Louisa was, once again, harboring matchmaking tendencies. "There's plenty for four," she'd said when I'd seen her at the post office. Though I'd begged off, citing bills to pay and a report to write for work, she had that glint in her eye. She'd had it last summer, too, when she'd tried to pair me up with Rafe Niswander. Great guy, and now a good friend, but no sparks, same as Skeeter, no matter how cute a couple Louisa thought we'd make.

"Where do you think Skeeter got his nickname?" I asked Eddie.

He yawned and starting licking his chest.

"And my first attempt at investigating was a complete failure, by the way." I leaned against the kitchen counter and explained my brilliant idea of trying to talk to Caroline about mutual Hamilton ancestors. Somehow saying it out loud helped me think it over. "But she's not into genealogy. So now I'm back to having no ideas."

Eddie sent me a look that clearly said, *You are so stupid,* and went back to work, now licking his right paw.

I opened the refrigerator door, didn't see anything worth cooking, and shut it. "Tell me I'm dumb, but when's the last time you had a good idea?" I opened kitchen cabinets, looking for dinner inspiration. "Maybe eating that salmon would have been a good idea—hey!" I yelped because Eddie had launched himself across the space from bench to kitchen counter, skidded across the plastic laminate, and knocked my mail to the floor.

"What's the matter with you?" I picked him up, dumped him onto the floor, and stooped down to pick up the mess. "You know you don't belong up there. If Kristen saw that, she'd . . . oh."

In my hand was the card from my mother.

And suddenly I knew how to arrange a meeting with Caroline Grice.

The rest of the week was busy with covering for vacationing library staff and last-minute reshuffling of the bookmobile schedule. On Saturday, the paperwork on my desk had piled so high that I skipped Saturday's boardinghouse breakfast and went in to work early.

Happily, by Sunday noon I caught up with life in general and left the houseboat with a clear conscience.

I bought a small bag of cookies from Tom, probably the last time I'd do so until after Labor Day when the summer crowds left for home, and headed for the Lakeview Art Gallery.

A couple of blocks later, I walked into the gallery for the first time ever. My mom's card had reminded me of Caroline's long-running support for the arts. Thanks to the reporting of the local newspaper, I knew that it was mainly Caroline's money that had allowed the nonprofit arts association to rent this side street store-front.

Inside, artwork of all shapes and sizes hung on walls painted a light blue-gray. Large landscapes, small portraits, wall sculpture, photographs.

Acrylics, watercolors, oils, pastels. The sheer variety made me blink in surprise.

"Welcome to the gallery," a young woman chirped from behind a jewelry showcase. "I'm Lina. Let me know if you have any questions, okay?" Lina had long flowing honey brown hair and wore a loose top that looked like something hauled out of the back of my mother's closet, circa Mom's high school graduation class of 1969.

"Busy today?" I asked.

"Let's see." She plopped her elbows on the glass. "The first person who came in wanted directions to the fudge shop, the second person who came in wanted to use our bathroom, and you're the third person."

"Sounds a little boring."

"Dull as fifth-grade math class, some days. Other days it's pretty cool." Her thin face grew animated. "Last week? On Tuesday? You'll never guess who came in that door." With an index fingernail painted with daisies, she pointed at the door I'd just walked through. "That hot guy from that new show? Everyone's talking about it."

She named a cop show I'd heard Josh and Holly discuss, but since I didn't have a television on the houseboat and watched very little at the boardinghouse, I couldn't offer a sound opinion on the actor's hotness.

"That must have been exciting," I said.

"Yeah, I keep hoping somebody else famous will walk in." She looked at me hopefully. "I don't suppose . . ."

"Sorry. I live here in town."

"Oh." She deflated. "Have you ever met anybody?"

"Nope. Famous people don't hang out at libraries very often."

"You work at the library? That's pretty cool."

She didn't sound sarcastic. "I think so. And I just started driving the bookmobile."

"The bookmobile?" Her enthusiasm was back, better than ever. "That's really cool! You really drive it?"

"Forward *and* backward."

Lina giggled. "I can hardly back up our Mini Cooper without hitting something. You must be a really good . . ." She stopped and looked at me with a changed expression. "Hey, wasn't it someone on the bookmobile who found that dead guy? Was that you?"

This wasn't how I'd expected to lead into a conversation about Caroline, but hey, I could adjust. I nodded.

"Wow, that must have been awful."

"Yes, it was." Then, "Thank you for saying that. Most people are just curious."

"Oh, I'm curious." She grinned. "I just have really good manners."

I laughed. "My mother always said manners

will take you places you can't get to any other way."

"Sounds like my mom. So do the police know who killed him?"

"As far as I know, they don't have any suspects."

"That's too bad." She sighed. "Mrs. Grice is pretty upset about it."

"I heard they'd been seeing each other."

"Yeah, for a little while now, but not—" She came to a screeching halt.

"Not what?"

"I shouldn't say, I really shouldn't." She bit at her lower lip.

It was time to bring out my big gun. The Librarian Voice. "Lina," I said sternly. "If you know something, you have a duty to share it."

"Yes, but—"

"This is murder. There's nothing worse."

She gripped her hands tight. "Okay. Okay, you're right. It's just . . ."

"I know," I said much more softly. "It can be hard doing the right thing."

"Yeah." She sighed. "This was like the week before Mr. Larabee died, right? Mrs. Grice stopped by to check out some new art. She's standing right there"—Lina gestured at a spot on the wood floor in front of a large abstract painting—"and Mr. Larabee comes in the door, all loud and big."

That was Stan.

"He walked real fast over to Mrs. Grice and started saying something about how she needed to listen to him. Mrs. Grice, she's always so nice? But she went all cold. She said, 'If you wish to discuss a personal matter, I prefer that we do it in private.' So they went in the office and shut the door behind them."

"So you didn't hear what they were talking about?"

Lina colored. "I did kind of walk over that way. I mean, Mr. Larabee's nice and all, but he was so much bigger than Mrs. Grice and I thought if he got mad and she got scared, that I could . . . do something."

As good a justification for eavesdropping as there could be. "But you didn't hear anything."

"Just that Mrs. Grice was talking a lot and Mr. Larabee hardly got a word in." Lina half smiled. "It was kind of funny until . . ." Her smile fell away.

"What?"

She looked at the office door. "Until they came out. The door opened and Mr. Larabee said something I couldn't hear. Then Mrs. Grice said, clear as anything, 'Not if you were the last man on earth. I daresay the next time I see you will be at your funeral.' And she left. Mr. Larabee stood there a minute; then he left, too."

Lina hugged herself. "But she didn't mean it. I

mean, that's just something people say. You never mean something like that. You just don't." She looked at me, fear on her face. "Right?"

I spent most of Sunday night trying to figure out what to do about Lina's story. The girl flat-out refused to go to the police. "I can't do that, not to Mrs. Grice. She's so nice. I'm an art major and working in a gallery is going to look great on my résumé. I mean, if the police go to her, she'd know I told and she'd fire me for sure." So if the police were going to find out about the incident, they'd have to find out from me.

Monday morning, the air of the public entry to the Tonedagana County Sheriff's Office smelled stale and confined and vaguely threatening. I knew it was all in my head, but even still, in the short time I stood there, waiting for someone to come to the window, I decided that if no one showed up in the next ten seconds, I was out of there.

I counted down fast to two and was turning to leave when a woman's square face appeared in the window and gave me a quick once-over before the glass slid open. "Can I help you?"

"Hi. I'd like to talk to Detective Devereaux or Detective Inwood." She made no move, so I added, "It's about the murder of Stan Larabee. I have some information that might be useful." Or

155

not. Since they were the trained professionals, they were the ones who would be able to figure it out.

"Your name?"

"Minnie Hamilton."

"I'll see if one of them is available."

I hummed the *Jeopardy!* song to myself a few times and eventually the tall and thin detective came out into the entryway. Devereaux or Inwood? I couldn't remember.

"Miss Hamilton. You have something for us?"

"Hi, Detective. I heard a story yesterday that I think you should know about." I looked around. There wasn't anyone else in the small lobby; there also weren't any chairs. Not even a bench. "Should we go somewhere else?"

"A story," he said flatly.

"Not a made-up story. Something I heard."

"Secondhand knowledge, then."

Irritation started to climb up the back of my neck. "A young woman overheard a conversation between Stan Larabee and a woman. The woman made a statement that could be construed as a threat."

"Uh-huh. Construed as a threat. So it wasn't really a threat."

"She said, and I quote, 'Not if you were the last man on earth. I daresay the next time I see you will be at your funeral.'"

"So you're quoting the girl who was eaves-

156

dropping on the woman who was talking to Larabee?"

Said like that, it sounded lame. Still. "Yes," I said.

He looked at me. Down at me, since he was more than a foot taller. "Their names?"

"The young woman's name is Lina. I don't know her last name, but she works at the Lakeview Art Gallery."

"Uh-huh." He made no move to take out the notepad I could see sticking out of his shirt pocket. I itched to yank it free and write the information down myself. "And the woman's name who made the purported threat?" he asked.

"Caroline," I said. "Caroline Grice."

He blinked once, then said, with zero inflection, "You think Caroline Grice killed Stan Larabee."

The irritation zoomed up into my skull and exploded in my brain. "What I think is that last week I was told to pass on any information about Stan's murder. So I'm passing along what I heard. What you choose to do with it is up to you."

He sighed. "Miss Hamilton, thank you for coming in. But we hear stories like this all the time. Sometimes they're true, sometimes they're not. We'll sort it out, though, don't you worry about that."

"I'm not worried. I'm just trying to help."

157

"And we appreciate it. Now if you'll excuse me, I have an appointment."

He nodded and left, abandoning me to wrestle with my irritation all by myself. I felt head-patted and . . . and managed. I hated that feeling. Just because I was young and female and short didn't mean I was brainless.

"Or clueless," I added, walking out of the building with fast yard-swallowing strides, thinking furious thoughts.

What a waste of time that had been. He hadn't taken anything I said seriously. Maybe—I smiled a cruel smile—maybe I should send him a copy of *Little Girls Can Be Mean*. You'd think police officers would be glad to listen. You'd think they'd be happy to hear anything that might help an investigation. You'd think—

I stopped short.

An appointment, he'd said. Some appointment.

I watched the tall, thin detective get out of his car and walk through the front doorway of the most popular diner in town.

# Chapter 9

It was almost nine p.m. when I left the library, but thanks to the time of year and the combined geographic facts of being north of the forty-fifth parallel and being at the western edge of the Eastern time zone, there was still almost an hour of daylight left to me.

I walked home through the backstreets of Chilson, avoiding the busy main downtown blocks, thinking about dinner. There might, just might, be some spaghetti sauce in the freezer, and I was pretty sure there was a box of spaghetti in the cupboard. Yesterday I'd picked up salad-type items, so the only thing I needed would be—

*Thud!*

A man's voice called out. "Ow!" (Pause.) "That freaking hurt!" (Pause.) "A lot!"

I was close to the marina, just outside Rafe's house. Or what would be a house when he finished redoing the roof, siding, wiring, HVAC, and plumbing of his century-old fixer-upper. I stepped gingerly onto the warped porch floorboards, wood creaking underneath me, went up to the front door, and knocked. "Rafe? It's Minnie."

"I'd rather suffer without an audience," came a strained voice. "Go away."

"You know I'm not going to." With that as

warning, I opened the door. One quick glance was all it took. "I'm getting my car," I said. "And then we're going to the hospital."

The lovely little town of Chilson had many things—outstanding views, a fine school system, a wide variety of stores and restaurants, and a top-notch library—but it did not have a hospital. Or an urgent care clinic. At first Rafe had pushed for me to take him to his doctor's house. "It's Monday, right? He'll be out golfing, but he'll be home by dark. A few beers in him isn't going to hurt his sewing skills any."

But as we argued, the wad of paper towels I'd made Rafe hold to his forearm started turning red. "We're not waiting," I said. "Pick a hospital."

"Lots of choices." He shifted to let me buckle his seat belt around him. "The Traverse City hospital is sweet, but it'll take an hour to get there. Last time I got stitches, I went to Kalkaska and they did a good job, but my buddy Carl works at the Gaylord hospital and I haven't seen him in a while. Then again, they say Petoskey has really hot nurses."

By this time I'd started the car and pointed its nose north.

"I thought I got to pick," Rafe said.

"You took too long, so we're going to Charlevoix. It's closest."

"Oh." He made a "huh" noise. "I didn't think

about that. Charlevoix will be okay, I guess. The view's not as good as Petoskey. View of the bay is half the pay, you know?"

"Keep pressing on the paper towels," I said.

Both the Charlevoix and Petoskey hospitals were built next to Lake Michigan. How you could rate one as having a view better than the other, I wasn't sure, but since there was no lake view from the emergency room of either hospital, there wasn't much point in starting a comparison chart.

"Nice slice," the ER doctor said. He'd lifted the reddened paper towels and was studying Rafe's forearm. "How did this happen?"

Rafe grinned at the doctor. "Little problem with the reciprocating saw. It wanted to go left when I wanted it to go right."

"The saw won," I muttered.

"Saws usually do," the doctor said. "A few stitches and you'll be good to go."

Rafe glanced at the doctor's name tag. "Tucker Kleinow," he said out loud. "You new here?"

"I'm going to clean your wound," Dr. Kleinow said. "This will sting a little. . . . Yes, I just moved up here last month."

"Yeah?" Rafe asked. "Where you from?"

Rafe would pick at the guy until he found a connection of some sort. With Rafe there were maybe three degrees of separation. "Let the doctor work," I said. "It's not his job to satisfy your curiosity."

"Oh, I don't mind," Dr. Kleinow said, giving me a brief smile.

It was a very nice smile and, I suddenly realized, it was on a very good-looking face that was about my own age. He had that blond hair that would turn white in the summer, and wasn't so tall that I'd get neck pains looking up at him. A definite bonus. I glanced at his left hand. No ring.

Rafe caught my look and winked. "So, Doc, what does your wife think of life up north?"

"No wife," he said absently, dabbing at the wound. "Haven't found anyone who can live with the hours I work."

"Weeeell," Rafe drawled. "Isn't that a coincidence? Minnie here is—"

"Is thinking you should be quiet and let the doctor stitch you up." Rafe was kind, honest, intelligent, hardworking, and often funny, but the word "subtle" wasn't in his vocabulary.

The doctor glanced from me to Rafe, reached a conclusion I couldn't interpret, and went on with his work.

Rafe waggled his eyebrows. "Come on, Min, you got to—"

"Keep quiet."

"You're the killjoy of the century."

"That's me. Now hush."

"Not even—"

I put my index finger to my lips in the classic librarian gesture. "Shhh."

This time, with the needle approaching his skin, he shushed.

Rafe wedged himself against the passenger door and put his feet up on the dash. "That doctor caught your eye, huh, Min?"

I slapped at his ankles until he moved his feet. "None of your business, Mr. Niswander."

"Yeah?" He snorted. "Bet you come asking about him inside of a week."

The paternal side of Rafe's family had lived in the area for thousands of years and the maternal side had homesteaded outside Chilson right after the Civil War. What Rafe couldn't find out about someone wasn't worth knowing. Speaking of which . . . "What are people saying about Stan Larabee's murder?"

Rafe picked at the bandage on his arm until I growled at him to quit. "Larabee? Most are saying that he got what he deserved, that he was a cruel dude, and it's a shock no one knocked him off before now."

"Cruel?"

He shrugged. "Rich people don't have a rep for being nice."

Irritation flared. "That's stupid. Money doesn't have anything to do with being nice. Anyone from any socioeconomic group can be cruel. Matter of fact—"

"Hey, hey." Rafe held up his good hand. "I'm just saying what they're saying. You asked, remember? Don't yell at me."

"Sorry," I muttered.

"Want to know what people are saying about you?"

Like I wanted a hole in my boat's hull. "No."

"About you and Stan's death, I mean."

That was different. "Sure."

He settled back against the door. "The best one I heard is you killed Stan yourself because he tried to take advantage of you."

I stared at him until the car's tires hit the rumble strip on the edge of the two-lane highway. "That's . . . that's . . . ," I spluttered, steering the car back to the middle of the lane.

"Yeah, I know." Rafe grinned. "Nutso. I'm just saying what they're saying. Ready for the next one?"

"Not yet." I sucked in a few breaths, blew them out. "Okay, I'm good."

"I heard someone say you saw Stan hiding something in the farmhouse, that some mob guy killed him for it, and now you're scared they're after you."

"Somebody's been watching too much TV."

"Way." Rafe nodded. "I heard that one at the diner."

The diner. My anger at the detective went bright red all over again. He hadn't taken anything I said seriously, not one thing. Was he even taking this investigation seriously? Maybe Holly was right; maybe they were pegging her for Stan's murder and not looking for anyone else.

The back of my throat tightened and it took me a couple of swallows before I could say, "Anything else?"

"Normal stuff. There's a ghost in the farmhouse who killed Stan. That no one killed him, that Stan set it up himself to look like a murder so he could make the ultimate payback."

"Payback against who?"

Rafe shrugged. "Dunno. I heard that one at the auto parts store."

"If Stan set it up to look like a murder, he would have set it up so someone would be framed for the murder."

"Never said those boys were brilliant." He grinned.

"So who are they saying killed Stan?"

"Besides you? Well . . ." He held up the index finger on his good hand. "There's your boss. Doesn't look right, the library getting all that money. And there's Cookie Tom." Rafe put up a second finger. "He hated Stan's guts because of some boat deal. Stan sold him an old Century and the motor died on Tom first time he took it out." Rafe smirked. "And there's Otis what's-his-name."

"Rahn?"

"Yeah. Ran where?" Rafe laughed. "Word is old Otis was dating one of Stan's sisters way back when and Stan dumped a bucket of pig feed on him right before he made the big move." He looked at his fingers. "What was that, three? Yeah. Next is Bill D'Arcy."

"Who's he?"

"Nobody. He's new in town. Hangs out at the Round Table and never talks to anyone. Which is pretty suspicious. So he's four. And there's that Holly you work with. The cops have been talking to her. And there's Lloyd Goodwin."

I frowned. "Mr. Goodwin? How could he kill anyone? He can't even walk without a cane."

"Maybe that's what he used before he got out his gun." Rafe twirled an imaginary cane and whacked it on the dashboard. "Yah! Gotcha!"

"Why would Mr. Goodwin kill Stan?"

Rafe got in one more whack. "Wouldn't. Neither would you or old Otis or Holly or Stephen or Tom. I figure it was one of his relatives. He had a ton of sisters and all of them had a passel of kids. Bound to be one of them, hoping they'd get money. Everybody says they'll challenge the will. Or maybe there's some old family feud and it ended up in murder. Like the Hatfields and the McCoys, only with Larabees and former Larabees." He laughed.

"I didn't know Stan had so many relatives."

"Oh, sure. He didn't like them, is all." Rafe grinned. "Can't say I blame him. You ever met any of his sisters?"

"How many does he have?"

"Three?" He squinted, peering through the front windshield as if the view of the rolling countryside would jog his memory. "Four, maybe."

"You're no help."

"Get what you pay for."

"I'm paying for gas money to Charlevoix and back. Plus I spent my whole night on you. Doesn't that count for something?"

"Almost makes up for the time I spent fixing the roof of your houseboat last September."

Point to Rafe. A big one. "And I still owe you for that." Fall was the busiest time for his job, and he'd spent two straight weekends helping me repair my rotting roof. "I can't believe anyone thinks I killed Stan."

"Yeah, well, you know people. Some of them will say anything just so they can say something."

I glanced at him. "Rafe Niswander, I'm not sure if you're the smartest person I know or the dumbest."

"Smartest," he said, and put his feet up on the dashboard.

I pushed them down. "How many stitches did you just get? Dumbest."

"Oh, yeah? Bet I can tell you something about Stan Larabee you don't know."

"You're on." I slid a five-dollar bill out of my front pocket and laid it on the console. Time spent with Rafe almost always resulted in a five-dollar bet and I'd prepared myself while he was getting sewn up. "Let's see yours."

Rafe *oof*ed and grunted and eventually got his wallet out of his back pocket. He put his five on top of mine. "That farmhouse where you found Larabee? He owned it."

"He . . . what?"

"Paid cash for it a couple weeks ago." Rafe nodded. "Heard it firsthand from a guy who used to work with the brother of the guy Larabee bought it off of." He swiped the fives off the dashboard and shoved them in his front pocket. "Not much of a mystery, then, why he was out there. He was checking out his new digs."

So, one question answered. But a bigger one remained. Why had Stan bought a decrepit farmhouse in the middle of nowhere? I opened my mouth to ask, but Rafe jumped in.

"But I got no idea why he bought it. Eighty acres in the middle of east county flatland?" He snorted. "Hardly anyone wanted to live there fifty years ago and no one wants to live there now. Real estate in that part of the county moves slower than my hair grows."

He was right, and I said so.

"See?" He preened. "Smart."

I pointed at his bandage. "Or not."

He gave me a hurt look. "Hey, these things happen. I can't be careful all the time, you know. No one can."

Which was truth itself. I smiled at him. "Let's go see what Kristen has for leftovers."

"If she has steak to get rid of, will you cut it for me and not make fun?"

I held up my hand in the three-fingered Scout salute. "I promise."

The next morning I walked a different route to work and passed the Lakeview Art Gallery. Closed, of course, that time of day, but I stopped and looked in through the wide windows at the paintings. Charcoal portraits, abstract acrylics, watercolors of water views.

Hmm.

The rest of my walk to work, my thoughts went from art to music to literature to libraries and back to art. By late morning, I'd come up with an idea, so I went upstairs and tugged on the lion's beard.

"You want to do what?" Stephen asked.

His hair had a rumpled look and . . . I took a quick count of buttonholes. Yes, Stephen's shirt was one button off. If he'd been anyone else, I would have smiled and made a shirt-buttoning gesture, but this was Stephen, and there were lines one was not invited to cross.

Lots of lines, in fact. Stephen wasn't one to socialize with us minions, and no one was absolutely certain if he was even married. Holly said there was a Rangel child in the middle school and one in high school. Josh said there was no way Stephen had ever fathered children, not with that haircut. They'd looked at me to cast the deciding vote and I'd claimed noncombatant status.

All of which meant that though Stephen was practically wearing a sign that said, "I'm upset," there was no crossing that big fat boundary line he drew over and over again.

I averted my eyes from his shirt. "I'd like to have a display of local art here in the library. A temporary exhibit for a month."

"We're not going to sell art," Stephen said. "Not our purview."

"Agreed. The artist's contact information will be printed on a card underneath. We could use the main hallway. It'll bring people into the library and give our regulars something new."

He made a "hmm" noise. Wavering. Definitely wavering.

"After all," I said, "our mission statement mentions cultural enrichment. What better way for patrons to be introduced to art than to see the work of local artists displayed at their library? At the old library, there wasn't room, but we could use the entire main hallway."

"The long-term benefits could be significant," Stephen said slowly.

*Yes!* I kept my smile small and my fist-thrust in my pants pocket.

"However, the work involved could overshadow those benefits." He toyed with his glasses. "Your hours have increased substantially over the last year due to your efforts to champion the bookmobile."

"But I'm salaried," I said quickly. "It doesn't cost the library any extra. And I'm glad to do it, I really am."

He made another "hmm" noise. This one was harder to decipher.

"What if I talk to some of the gallery owners in town," I offered. "See if they're willing to help. They select the art, I check to make sure the art's suitable, the galleries get agreements from the artists to be part of the show, they move the art up here, and I help them hang it. Hardly any work at all."

Stephen rubbed his eyes. "I don't have the energy to argue. Keep me informed, is all I ask."

"I . . . are you sure?"

He was already back to studying his computer monitor. "Check about insurance. And don't hand out any front-door keys."

"No, of course not." I went to the door and turned. "Stephen?"

"Yes?"

I wanted to ask him what was bothering him, wanted to say if he needed to talk about something, about anything, that I could be trusted. That I could be his friend. "Is there anything I can do for you?" I finally asked.

"No, thank you," he said, chiseling the boundary line into stone.

There was nothing to do but leave. So I did.

I spent the next couple of hours shuffling spreadsheets and databases, printing reports, and checking bookmobile projections against reality. Far too early to tell, of course, but it did my heart good to see that, on a per-stop basis, my plucked-out-of-thin-air estimates of patrons and materials checked out were low.

I smiled at the nice numbers, then pulled out the phone book and picked up the phone.

"Grice residence."

This time the female voice had a French accent. Or what I thought was a French accent. Could have been Swiss, for all I knew. Or Belgian. Not that it mattered; I needed to get through her to Caroline. "I'd like to speak to Mrs. Grice about showing some artwork from the Lakeview Gallery."

"Your name, please?"

"Minnie Hamilton. I'm assistant director at the library."

"One moment."

I hummed my own hold music while I waited. Though in my appeal to Stephen I'd said I'd talk to gallery owners in the plural, I hadn't really meant it. One would be plenty, if only I could convince her.

"Miss Hamilton, this is Caroline Grice. We speak again."

"Yes, ma'am." I put a smile in my voice and started my spiel. I was only halfway through when Caroline jumped in.

"Tell me if I'm understanding correctly. The library will display artwork from the gallery; no art will be sold by the library. We obtain the artists' agreement and select the artwork, which you will need to approve. We deliver the artwork and remove it when the show is over. We will add the library to our liability insurance for the duration of the show."

"That's it exactly." I was about to launch into an apology for all the work this would cause. To apologize for the short notice, but that I hoped we could work out a date to meet within the next week and—

"The selections can be made today," she said. "At some point tomorrow I daresay I'll have contacted all the artists. Correct?"

I blinked. The speed of light had nothing on Caroline Grice. She suggested we meet in two days to formalize the details. I agreed, then hung up and went to get a celebratory soda.

"What's the matter?" Josh was loading his cargo pants with bags of corn chips. "You look funny."

"I am funny," I said. "Did I ever tell you the one about the—"

"You've told me all your jokes." He ripped open a bag of chips. "You know, has anyone ever told you that they're all kind of dumb?"

"Humor is in the ear of the beholder." I ran a dollar bill into the machine.

"Minnie, there you are!" One of the clerks rushed in. "Can you work the front desk for half an hour? My son's car won't start and he needs a ride to work. I'm really sorry, but—"

"Go." I waved her away. "Don't worry about it."

I headed for the doorway, but Josh called me back. "Hey, Min. You forgot your pop." He pointed at the machine.

No food or drinks were allowed at the front counter, so I said, "Consider it a gift."

He grinned. "You're all right. I don't care what the rest of them say—you're not so bad."

I rolled my eyes and headed out.

Time spent at the front desk was always interesting. There were returns to sort, phone calls to take, and patrons to direct. But my favorite thing to do was checking out books. Seeing what people wanted to take home to read, watch, and listen to never got old. There were times, of course, when I wanted to recommend other books.

Because Mrs. Garver didn't really need another book about the value of collectibles. What she

174

needed was a book on organizing. And Jim Kittle didn't really need to read another let's-do-in-all-the-bad-guys thriller. He'd be better off if he'd read through a stack of romances and learned how women see the world.

A tall fiftyish man placed a stack of books on the counter. The stack was so high I couldn't see over the top of it. "Wow," I said, smiling, "I wish I had that much time to read. You know we only have a two-week checkout, right?"

"Yes." His tone was almost curt as he handed me his library card.

The scanner beeped when I aimed it at the card. I glanced at the computer screen. "Looks like you have a number of books out already. Not due until next week, though, so you have some time."

"I put them in the slot," he said.

"Oh." I scanned the titles. *The Name of the Rose. Gone with the Wind.* "*. . . And Ladies of the Club.*" All books that were hundreds of pages long. "Well, I hope you enjoyed them. Those are—" I stopped short as I noticed the man's name. Bill D'Arcy. This was the guy Rafe had mentioned as a possible suspect. The one who went to the diner but kept to himself.

Mr. D'Arcy started tapping the granite counter with his fingernails.

Ooookay. I took the top book—*Moby-Dick*—and opened the front cover to scan the tag. "You know," I said, "this is the only book I ever used

Cliff's Notes for. Just couldn't get through it. I keep thinking about trying it again, but somehow I haven't made time." I laughed.

Bill D'Arcy didn't.

Next book down was *Anna Karenina*. "I always cry when I read this book. Matter of fact, I think I cry when I read anything by Tolstoy. I wonder what he was like in person. Do you ever wonder if he had a sense of humor?"

No comment.

I checked out *11/22/63* and *The Historian*, said a little something about each, and scored exactly zero responses from Bill D'Arcy. Not that I was a brilliant conversationalist, but the guy could have at least grunted a response or two. As an interrogator, I had a lot to learn. "You're all set," I said, pushing the stack over to him. "Good for two weeks."

His mouth was starting to open—he was actually going to say something!—when Mitchell Koyne barged up to the desk, his baseball cap on straight for once.

"Min. Hey, Min! You won't believe what happened the other day. I was out with my buddy in his boat and we almost got this huge fish, a sturgeon. It would have been a record catch, I just know it."

"Just a second, Mitchell, okay? I was talking to—"

But Bill D'Arcy was already gone.

# *Chapter 10*

I looked at Eddie.
     He looked back.

Well, sort of. Even when everything indicated that he was looking at me directly, it still felt as if part of his cat brain was elsewhere.

"You go here." I pointed to the picnic basket I'd bought. The store owner had looked at me oddly when I'd carried in a tape measure, but she'd accepted my story of needing a basket of a particular size so I could carry the oval bowl my great-grandmother had given me to a family reunion. "She always brought potato salad," I'd said, spinning out the tale longer than it needed to go. "And it wouldn't be a real family reunion without it." Such a coincidence that Eddie and the imaginary bowl were the same size.

"Here," I repeated. "It'll only be for a little while. I'll carry you to the car, we'll drive up to the library, I'll carry you into the bookmobile, and then you get to sleep in the cabinet until we get on the road." I showed him the fleece-lined cat bed already nestled into the bottom of the basket. "See? What could be better?"

He twitched his nose.

"There's cat food and bowls in the backpack and a bottle of water in the cooler."

"Mrr," he said.

"Yes, I have thought of everything, how nice of you to say so." I picked him up and put him on the top of the bench seat, then had to wait while he yawned and stretched. There's no hurrying a cat. "Okay, you ready to listen?"

He rubbed the top of his head against the seat.

"Ground rules. No yowling. You have a great big voice and the bookmobile is small. I don't want you scaring the little kids." Or the adults. "And no scratching. If you scratch anybody or anything, it's off to the vet for declawing. No ifs, ands, or buts on that one, pal." He started purring. "No pulling books off the shelves. No hair balls. And if you could cut down on the shedding, I'd appreciate it."

It was a stupid lecture to bother giving. If he understood any of the words, it was "no," a word he knew but had never paid any attention to.

I blew out a small breath and looked at the wall clock. "Ready, Eddie? It's time to go for a ride on the bookmobile."

He leapt to his feet. "Mrr!"

I made the introductions. "Thessie, Eddie. Eddie, Thessie."

My teenage volunteer held out her hand. "Nice to meet you, Eddie."

Eddie put a paw on her palm. "Mrr."

"He said hello!" she exclaimed. "He really did,

did you hear him? What a sweetie of a kitty cat. Can I hold him? Aww, you're just adorable," she said in baby talk as I handed him over. "Just the sweetest little Eddiekins ever, aren't you?"

Appearances could be so very deceiving.

"How could Mr. Rangel not like you?" Thessie held Eddie up in the air, dancing him around. "You should be on the bookmobile every single time."

"Eddie is here to make Brynn happy," I said.

"He's like another volunteer, then, right?" Thessie snuggled Eddie close. "A really cuddly purry one."

"We need to get going." I pointed at Eddie's cabinet. "There's a cat bed in there."

Thessie's eyes flew wide open. "Not in that tiny dark place. That's kind of almost like cruelty, isn't it? What if he's claustrophobic? What if he's scared of the dark? What if—"

"If we don't get going, we're going to be late to the first stop." I took Eddie from her and closed him into the cabinet. "Sleep tight, pal."

My young companion frowned, but sat in the passenger seat and buckled up. "Are you sure he's going to be okay in there?"

I clicked my seat belt and paused before turning on the engine. "Hear that?"

She tipped her head sideways, listening. "The only thing I hear is a funny rumbling sound. Is that some kind of fan? It doesn't sound right."

"It's Eddie. He's snoring."

Thessie blinked, I laughed, and we set out for another day in the bookmobile.

My grin was a mile wide. Thessie's, too. Michelle had tears streaming down her cheeks. Brynn paid no attention to the adults around her as she and Eddie rolled around together on the bookmobile's floor.

"This was so nice of you," Michelle said. "I can't believe you'd go to all this trouble. My husband is really allergic and the pills aren't covered by his insurance, so the kids could never have a cat. I wanted so much to . . . but . . ." She shook her head and let it go in favor of concentrating on her daughter's joy.

"Not that much trouble," I said, ignoring the startled glance Thessie sent my way. "And if it makes Brynn happy, it's worth it."

"Look!" the little girl said. "I have Eddie hair on me!" Beaming, she held out the hem of her dark blue shirt, which was now coated with short black-and-white former bits of Eddie.

"Um, sorry about that," I murmured to her mother.

Brynn rubbed at Eddie's thick fur with both hands to gather up more hair, then smeared it across the front of her shirt. "Now I'll have Eddie with me all the time!"

"Oh!"

The gasp came from behind. I turned and saw last week's surfer girl. "Hi," I said. "Hope you're not allergic. This is Eddie. He's with us for the day."

"Every day," Brynn said firmly. "Every book-mobile day."

"Now, Brynn," her mother said, "Miss Minnie can't bring Eddie with her every time."

"Why not?" The small lower lip trembled. "I love Eddie. He loves me. See?" She grabbed him around his middle and hugged hard.

I made a quick move forward. The one time I'd done that to him, I'd ended up with howls in my ear and a hint of back-claw marks on my stomach. If he did that to Brynn, I'd never forgive myself. I'd never—

Eddie closed his eyes and purred.

I stopped and stared. That rotten, horrible, completely wonderful cat. How had he known to be kind to her? And why wasn't he ever that nice to me?

Thessie was asking surfer girl if she was looking for anything in particular.

"No, not really. Just . . . something to read. It's okay if I look around?" After being assured that, yes, she was free to browse, she started her routine from last week all over again, running a finger over every book with a quiet *thup-thup-thup,* reading each title, but not pulling out a single volume.

181

Thessie looked at me with raised eyebrows. I shrugged. Brynn tugged at the hem of my crop pants. "Miss Minnie? Will Eddie be on the bookmobile again?"

I crouched down. "As soon as he can. He'll miss you."

"I know." She patted his head. He flattened his ears, but let her whack away. "He's my best friend. He told me so."

"That's great." I put on a smile. So much for my hopes of a single dose of Eddie lasting a lifetime. Thanks to his atypical tolerance, we now had an Eddie addiction on our hands. Outstanding.

"When is he coming back?"

I pictured the bookmobile schedule in my head. "I'll call your mom tomorrow and we'll figure it out." Unless Michelle was willing to drive halfway across the county, Brynn wouldn't see Eddie again until we were back in the area in two weeks.

"So I'll see Eddie tomorrow?"

"No, honey." Michelle scooped up her daughter. "Soon, though." She looked at me with happiness on her face, hope in her eyes, and sorrow everywhere else.

"Soon," I agreed.

The pair went down the steps, Brynn waving to Eddie over her mother's shoulder and chattering about the dress she wanted to bring for Eddie to wear next time.

"Pretty cat," Surfer Girl said.

"Pretty much a pain in the butt," I muttered.

"Sorry?" she asked.

"Yes," I said, turning, "he is a good-looking cat. My name's Minnie, by the way." I held out my hand. She shook it briefly, but didn't give her name, and didn't stop looking at the Edster.

"Where did you get him?" she asked.

A sudden and paralyzing fear struck at me. What if Surfette here was Eddie's real owner? What if he'd done the running thing on her, run for miles and miles, and ended up in the cemetery? What if she'd been looking high and low for months? No wonder she was acting so weird.

"I, um." I couldn't lie, not on the bookmobile. "I got him from a friend." Alonzo Tillotson, if I remembered the name from the headstone correctly, born 1847, died 1926.

"Oh," Surfette said, still staring at Eddie, who had settled himself on the carpeted step that ran underneath the shelves.

The fear continued to pick at my stomach. "We only have a few more minutes at this stop," I said. "If you've found a book you'd like to check out, please take it to the front checkout. If you'd like to order a book for us to bring next time, we can do that. All we need is your name and—"

"Oh, no, I'm good. Thanks."

She fled.

Thessie looked from the door to me and back. "What was that all about?"

I put on a puzzled expression. "No idea."

Happily, the rest of the bookmobile run went without a hitch. Eddie and Thessie engaged in a mutual admiration society. He purred, she cooed, and I tried not to make gagging noises. Back at the library, Thessie helped me get Eddie into the picnic basket and spotted for me during the transfer from bookmobile to car.

"Same crew next time?" she asked, winking.

"We'll see," I said.

The next day I got to the library early. With the numbers from the bookmobile continuing to exceed expectations, I wanted some time to think about how to get more runs into the schedule.

I was in the act of carrying my first cup of coffee into my office when I heard the unmistakable sound of Stephen's footsteps.

"Morning," I said, toasting him with my Association of Bookmobile and Outreach Services mug. "Can I get you . . ." But once I got a good look at him, I could see that coffee wasn't going to do him much good. In addition to the previous danger signs of rumpled hair and clothing issues, now Stephen also had the ashen skin that spoke of exhaustion. What the man needed was sleep.

"The library board . . ." He slid his index fingers under his glasses to rub his eyes. When he opened them again, he spied my mug. "Is that coffee?" He held out his hand peremptorily.

I held the mug out to him. "Stephen, are you okay? You look beyond tired."

He knocked back half the contents of the mug, paused, then drank the other half. "I'm fine."

Riiiight. And I was the Queen of the Library. But if he didn't want to discuss whatever it was that was bothering him, I wasn't going to badger him to talk. Not today, anyway. Tomorrow was a different matter.

"The library board," he said, "has been in contact with the executors of Stan Larabee's estate. His relatives have indicated that they'll be contesting the will."

Just as Rafe had said. For once the word on the street had been right. "They won't be able to break it, will they?"

"Extremely doubtful. But the issue could tie up dispensation of the will for as long as his family wishes to pay lawyers."

"I heard he had a lot of sisters."

"Six," Stephen said.

I'd often wondered what it would be like to have a sister or two. I'd never once wondered what it would be like to have six.

"The library board is concerned," he went on. "If the news gets bandied about that the library is losing Larabee's bequest, they fear we'll lose other sources of money, and you know how much this library depends on donations."

"But that's nuts," I blurted out. "No one except you and the board knew the library was getting money from Stan's will until a week ago. And, anyway, why would any potential donor care?"

"The library board is concerned," Stephen repeated. "It's our job to allay their concerns. With that in mind, we need to consider alternative sources for donations. As I recall, you are meeting with Caroline Grice this evening. The gallery will be closed, yes? Good. Sound her out for becoming a library supporter. A onetime 'no' isn't necessarily a permanent no. You have a certain expertise at noting people's reactions and emotions. Notice hers and exploit them."

"I . . . what?"

"The library is depending on you," Stephen said.

"It . . . is?"

"We need to head off any financial troubles before they start. Now is the time, and you're in the right place at the right time. It's up to you, Minnie." He upended the coffee cup, swilling down the last drops. "I'll expect a complete report first thing tomorrow morning."

And off he went, taking my favorite mug with him.

"Minnie? Hey, Minnie!"

I slowed, then stopped in the front lobby, as

Holly hurried to my side. The day had passed quickly, and now late-afternoon sun spilled over both of us, blinding me and putting Holly into dark silhouette.

"Sorry, sorry to bother you," she said, her words running over the top of one another. "I wanted to catch you since I won't be in tomorrow. Do you have a second?"

"Sure. What's up?"

"Remember, a little while ago, I was downstairs and you said . . . you said that you'd try to help prove I didn't kill Stan Larabee . . . and I was wondering, you know, if you really meant it?"

"I promised," I said, stepping close to her and lowering my voice. "So, yes, I meant it."

"Right." She smiled, relief washing over her face. "So, um, have you found out anything?"

What I'd discovered was that many residents of Chilson were getting far too much enjoyment speculating about murder, that rumors did, in fact, travel faster than the speed of light, that the new doctor in Charlevoix was appearing in my dreams, and that it was going to take hours and hours to clean the Eddie hair out of the book-mobile.

I started to say something to that effect. Luckily, I took a good look at Holly before I opened my mouth.

Her brown hair, normally shiny and smooth, had a straggly look. Her face looked almost gaunt and her hands didn't know what to do with them-selves. They were in her pockets, cupped around her elbows, around her upper arms, back to her pockets.

She was worried and scared and she was relying on me. But what could I tell her? Rumors? No way was I going to repeat those stupid stories. Yet what else was there to say?

"There's a chance," I said, "that I'll learn something soon."

"Really?" Hope shone in her eyes.

No, not really, and I was already sorry I'd said so. "Just a chance," I said. Firmly. "It's not as if I have any experience doing this. All I can do is listen and—"

"But you're so *good* at listening!" Smiling, she nodded, apparently reassured by my seeming confidence.

Unfortunately, she was the only one.

"Thank you so much for meeting with me, Mrs. Grice."

"Caroline, please." The older woman smiled. She wasn't showy or even glamorous, but the simple lines of her white shirt spoke of a tailoring that was designed to flatter without being revealing, to complement without drawing attention to itself.

Not to mention the fact that her shirt was whiter than I'd ever been able to get my own shirts.

"Thank you," she said, "for giving our artists a

more public audience." She tipped her head at the gallery around us, a head that didn't have a hair out of place. I had a hunch I was looking at a hundred-dollar hairstylist's creation.

Not that I begrudged Caroline her money. And I liked to work. Work was worthwhile. If I didn't work, what would I do with myself? Of course, I could always volunteer. Maybe at hospitals. In, say, Charlevoix, where there was a new doctor who—

"If we can," Caroline was saying, "I'd like to represent every single one of our artists at the library. All have work that is deserving of purchase, and, to be honest"—she gave a wry smile—"all of them could use the money."

That was another thing that separated the wealthy from the rest of us. They could afford to purchase original art.

"I've talked to the artists, and to a soul, they would be glad to be displayed in the library." She smiled at the walls. "If you see anything in particular you'd like displayed, please let me know."

Since my knowledge of art didn't go much beyond the *Mona Lisa*, I made a positive yet noncommittal noise. "Have you thought about a schedule?" I asked. "We'll want to advertise and the sooner the better."

"Of course."

She opened her leather-bound planner, and I

pulled out my phone. We agreed that a mid-July date would give us enough time to plan yet leave enough time in the season to catch the summer visitors.

We were working so well and so efficiently that I'd lost track of the underlying reason behind the whole thing. It wasn't until Caroline said, "I hear you're the librarian on the bookmobile" that I jerked back to my somewhat sneaky plan.

I suddenly wondered why I'd gone through all this subterfuge. Caroline was a gracious woman; if I'd simply told her I'd like to talk about Stan, surely she would have agreed.

"Yes," I said. "It's great how it's attracting so much attention. The patrons are already calling me the bookmobile lady." And Eddie was the bookmobile cat, but I wasn't going to spread that fun fact around.

"The newspaper."

She didn't say anything else, and I looked at her questioningly. "I'm sorry?"

"Yes." She laid her fingertips across her upper lip and coughed delicately. "Excuse me. A little tickle. I'm told the newspaper reported that the bookmobile librarian found Stan Larabee."

I had no idea what to say, so I went with the simplest possible response. "Yes. That was me." She didn't say anything, so I expanded. "It was a huge shock. See, I knew Stan. He's the one who donated the money for the bookmobile." Still no response. "He was an amazing man," I added quietly. "I'll miss him very much."

"Did he . . . was he . . . ?" She blinked rapidly. "He didn't . . . ?" A great shining tear spilled down her cheek. "Oh, goodness, I'm so sorry. Excuse me." She stood abruptly and hurried to the office.

The door shut softly and I was left alone.

No sound of weeping came through the walls or snuck out from under the door. Maybe all she needed was a minute to compose herself.

A minute went by. No Caroline emerged.

Two minutes.

Three.

When five minutes had ticked past, I got up and went to the door. I knocked softly. No reply. I tried again. I hesitated, then turned the knob and walked in.

The elegant and patrician Caroline Grice was sitting on an office chair, shoes kicked off, heels on the edge of the chair seat, arms wrapped around her knees, shoulders shuddering with silent sobs.

I swallowed the sodden lump in my throat and went to her. Knelt on the floor, wrapped my arms around her shaking body, and put my head against her bowed one. She clutched at my arms. Held me tight.

We were like that for some time.

After the tears slowed, I gave her shoulders a

few rubbing pats, then sat back on my heels and waited. It didn't take long.

"I didn't even know Stan Larabee socially until this last New Year's Eve," she said. "He attended my party with a mutual acquaintance and I'm afraid I neglected a number of my guests for the sheer pleasure of talking to him. I'd known who he was, of course, but we'd rarely spoken until that evening. I had so many preconceived notions about him."

She picked up her head, allowing me to see the ravaged makeup and mussed hair. "Old as I am, I should know better than to trust the impressions of others. My father always told me to make sure I had my own information." She sighed. "I passed on that same piece of advice to my children. I hope it stays with them better than it stayed with me."

I made a comforting, murmuring sort of noise.

"You're a dear," Caroline said. "And you deserve an explanation for letting an old woman cry onto your shoulder."

"Grief strikes in unexpected places."

"Yes, it does." She looked around and managed a small smile. "It certainly does." Her sigh stirred the bangs that now lay flat on her forehead. "You wouldn't think I could get so upset over a man I knew only six months, but he caught me . . . off guard. I wasn't thinking of seeing a man ever again, not in that way." Her smile was sweet and sad. "Did you know Stan sponsored two college scholarships? Every four years, a boy and a girl from a Tonedagana County high school is awarded a full ride."

"The Sunrise Scholarship?" I hadn't been living in Chilson the last time it was awarded. "That was Stan?"

She nodded. "And the new intensive care wing at the Charlevoix Hospital was financed in large part by Stan's money. So was Chilson's community pool. And the waterfront park."

I'd had no idea. All of those projects had been completed, or mostly completed, by the time I'd moved north. Yet if he'd given away all that money, how could his reputation be that of a miser who clutched his cash to his chest? "Were those donations anonymous?"

"No, but he didn't make a spectacle out of giving away money."

I sighed, unhappy that Stan had been so right, unhappy that he hadn't lived long enough to outlive his reputation.

But Caroline was still talking. "In some ways he was very modest. In other ways"—her smile this time was wider—"he was so immodest as to be a caricature of the self-made man."

"Maybe that was part of his charm?"

"Oh, yes. Decidedly. And the man knew how to treat a lady. Oh, not the door opening and the chair pulling, that's mere etiquette. Anyone can do that. Stan had a rare capacity in a man. He knew how to listen to a woman. He had the ability to focus, to make me think I was important. That's why . . ." Her voice caught on itself.

And here was the moment I'd wanted so badly. I needed to press her, to push for answers, and to make my own conclusion on her ability to kill Stan. Only . . . how could I? The woman was grieving.

Of course, she might be sad because she'd committed murder. I had to think about Holly, worrying herself to a frazzle. And I should be thinking about what I'd told Stephen, that I'd ask Caroline for a donation to the library. But that would have to wait. Some things were more important than money.

"Why what?" I asked softly.

A deep breath whistled out from between her teeth. "To my own dying day, I'll regret what I said to him, the last time I saw him."

"The last time . . . ?"

"We had an argument." She looked around the small office. "In this very room." She closed her eyes briefly. "He asked if I wanted to fly to Toronto with him to see *Evita*. He knew how I enjoy that show, but I told him, 'Not if you were the last man on earth. I daresay the next time I see you will be at your funeral.'"

So Lina had heard exactly right.

"Why did I say that?" Caroline bit her lips,

smearing the last of her lipstick onto her teeth. "It was a ridiculous thing to say. I should never have said something like that, no matter how angry I was."

I had to do it. I had to press. For Holly. For Stan. "So why did you?" I asked. "Say it, I mean?"

The air went out of her. "Jealousy. Silly, childish jealousy."

A perfect motive for murder.

But as I watched her fish a handkerchief from her purse and dab at her face, I didn't think she had anything to do with Stan's death. Call it a hunch, call it instinct, call it whatever you want, I simply couldn't picture any reality in which it could happen. Besides, the car parked outside the art gallery would have been hard for someone to miss seeing at the farmhouse. Even I could recognize a Rolls-Royce when I saw a double *R* on the front.

So if Caroline was out as a killer, who was in?

"Jealous?" I asked. "Of whom?"

"Whom. It's so nice to hear that word used properly." Caroline touched the handkerchief to her nose. "Jealousy is an ugly emotion. It's embarrassing to admit to the feeling, especially when you consider the woman who caused it."

"Stan was two-timing you?"

Caroline dipped into her purse for a compact and started patting away the tearstains. "She's the one who killed Stan; I'm quite sure of it. She has hardly a dime to her name. She must have thought Stan would leave her money, worming her way into his affections like that. Wonderful man though he was, he was still a man, and Lord knows men let their heads get turned around by young women."

"Who was it, do you know?"

"I saw them at the diner," Caroline said. "I was downtown on errands and saw them sitting together. Stan said it wasn't what it looked like, but I saw them. I saw *her*—I saw the way she looked at him. She wanted something from him, there's no misinterpreting that. A woman knows."

"Do you know her name?"

"Stan said I could trust him, but how could I trust a man who'd lie to me? I had enough of that with my first—"

"Her name?"

"The woman who runs that boardinghouse. Frances," Caroline spat. "Frances Pixley."

# Chapter 11

Aunt Frances?" I asked. "How could Aunt Frances have been involved with Stan?"

Eddie's eyes were closed. He was listening, though, I was sure of it. So while I tugged socks over my feet and tied my shoes, I kept talking.

"Caroline must be wrong, that's all. The whole last winter I did nothing but go on and on about the bookmobile and Stan donating money, and Aunt Frances said she didn't know him at all."

I flexed my foot and realized I'd tied the laces on my right shoe too tight. Start the day like that and you never get them the way you want them. Growling to myself, I undid the laces, pushed the shoe off with the toes of the other foot, and started over again.

"And even if she did know him, it's outside of the realm of any reality that she . . . that she . . ." I couldn't make myself say the words. Then a thought started to ping around inside my head. If Caroline suspected Aunt Frances of killing Stan, would she tell the police? Had she already? Should I warn Aunt Frances?

"What do you think, Mr. Ed?"

My feline flopped over on his side and batted at my elbow.

I pulled my arm away. "Quit that. I'm not a cat toy, you know."

He gave me the humans-are-soooo-stupid look and closed his eyes again.

"Thanks so much for your help." I lightly thumped the top of his head, making it bounce up and down like a bobblehead. "See you later, Eddie-gator."

His mouth opened and closed without making a sound, but I knew what he meant.

Mrr.

The boardinghouse was full of the beginnings of love. Unfortunately, it resembled the second mixed-up act of *A Midsummer Night's Dream* more than *My Big Fat Greek Wedding*.

"It turned out okay in the end, though," I whispered to Aunt Frances. The starry-eyed, middle-aged Quincy was handing twenty-something Dena a bowl of strawberries. Paulette, who'd been picked for Quincy, was giggling with sixty-five-year-old Leo, and Zofia was chatting with Harris, who was a perfect age to be her grandson. "Hermia ended up with Lysander," I said quietly, "and Helena with Demetrius, just like they were supposed to."

"That was a play," Aunt Frances whispered back fiercely. "More than four hundred years old."

My lips twitched as I watched Quincy pass Dena

the powdered sugar. Shakespeare might have written it in the late fifteen hundreds, but it was still relevant.

The eight of us ate waffles and strawberries and whipped cream and sausages until we couldn't eat any more. "More coffee, anyone?" Zofia, the cook for the day, held up the carafe. "Minnie? Or do you need to get to the library?"

I held out my mug. "Working tomorrow afternoon, off today."

Zofia *tsk*ed at me. "They work you too hard down there. One of these days you're going to work yourself into illness."

"She does it to herself," Aunt Frances said. "She makes up the schedule."

I glanced at her as I poured cream into my coffee. Aunt Frances knew perfectly well that the library had a tight budget. Payroll was the library's largest expense and since I was salaried, working more hours myself was money in my budget's pocket.

"Say," Leo said. "Did they ever figure out who killed that guy you found? What was his name? Stan something."

Since my gaze was on Aunt Frances when Leo asked his questions, I saw her flinch as clear as the horizon on a cloudless day. "Larabee," I said quietly, still watching her.

Leo snapped his fingers. "That's it. So, did they? Find who killed him?"

"Not as far as I know," I said. My aunt put her silverware and napkin on her plate and stood to take the dishes to the kitchen. "Aunt Frances," I asked, "have you heard anything?"

She stopped. "No, I haven't. But then, why would I?"

Zofia chuckled. "You know everyone in this town. How could you not know the richest man in Chilson?"

"Well, I didn't," Aunt Frances said, a little too quickly. "There are lots of people I don't know. And there are some I know far too well." Abandoning her plate, she took quick steps to the back door and left the house, letting the screen door slam behind her.

After a short silence, Harris was the first to speak. "Wow, I've never seen her like that. She sure seems mad about something."

"Oh, dear." Zofia fiddled with her spoon. "I hope I didn't offend her."

Paulette poured Leo another cup of coffee. "What do you think, Leo?"

He smiled at her. "I think this is a beautiful day. How do you feel about a drive up to Cross Village and lunch at Legs?"

Dena glanced around the table, ending with me. "Shouldn't somebody go after her? She sounded pretty upset."

"Not to worry." Quincy patted her shoulder, his touch lingering a beat too long. "Give her some time to work it out herself. If she's still upset this afternoon, I'll talk to her."

Through it all, I said nothing.

But the worries in my brain were starting to run in tiny little circles, around and around and around.


Chris Ballou sat cross-legged on my boat's front deck, a bilge pump in each hand. "You want the good news or the bad news?"

I was sitting on the deck, too, looking at him across the open engine hatch. "I hate questions like that."

He grinned. "The good news is that your problem isn't the bilge pump. I can put the old one back in and sell this to some other poor slob."

Since I wasn't completely ignorant of boat maintenance issues, I could see where this was going. "It's electrical, isn't it?"

"Got to be," Chris said cheerfully.

"How much is it going to cost?"

"Well, that's the bad news."

I squinched my eyes shut and slapped my hands over my ears. "Don't want to hear it, don't want to hear it—"

Chris spoke loudly. "I got another set of good and bad newses." I uncovered my ears and waited. "Bad first. Job like this on a boat like this, we're looking at five hours if it's easy, double that, or more, if it's not."

My chest went tight. Five hours of a boat mechanic's time was equivalent to slightly less than a week of the Chilson District Library assistant director's take-home pay. Ten hours was an amount that would require payments on my credit card for longer than I wanted to think about. My student loans were far from being paid off, my car wouldn't be paid off for almost two years, and the houseboat loan was—

"Hey, don't look like that," Chris said. "You haven't heard my good news." He lowered his top half deeper into the engine compartment and his voice came out echoey, in a disembodied sort of way. "Rafe Niswander could do the work for you a lot cheaper." His right hand extended up into the air. "Hand me those wire cutters, will you, Min Pin? Thanks. Yeah, Rafe used to work here, summers. He's got those long skinny fingers that fit into tight corners no one else could reach without pulling the freaking engine."

I'd never noticed that Rafe had long skinny fingers. I would now, though.

"But you know Rafe," Chris said. "You'd have to work with his schedule. And he's got that thing going with his arm right now. He says it's good, but if it's that good, why is he still wearing that ratty old bandage?"

Rafe. I grumped a grumpy noise to myself. Anyone with half an ounce of sense would have changed the bandage daily. Not Rafe. Oh, no, not oh-it'll-be-fine-quit-worrying Rafe. The man needed a wife something fierce, but I couldn't think of any woman I disliked enough.

Another couple minutes, and Chris pushed himself out into the sunlight. "There you go. All shipshape and seaworthy."

Seaworthy I didn't care about. "Is it lake-worthy?"

"Well." Chris scratched his bristly chin with the end of a Phillips screwdriver. "I wouldn't take her out on the big lake, but she's probably okay for a one-cocktail cruise out there." He pointed the screwdriver out at Janay Lake.

"How about tied up to the dock?"

He started putting his tools back into the red toolbox he'd brought with him. "If nothing changes, you might be fine for the season. But you know boats."

Wind gusted my hair into my face and I reached into my shorts pockets for a hair elastic. My too-curly hair never wanted to stay in a ponytail, but better that than have my hair blowing into my mouth every time I tried to talk.

As he tidied his tools, he said, "Hey, did I tell you we're full up?" He went on to list, slip number by slip number, the people who were up north already, the people who would be up for the Fourth of July, and the people who paid to have their boats put in the water but who rarely made it up at all.

I sat there, half listening, half not, enjoying the wind and sun on my face. Then something he said caught at me. I asked, "Did you say the Olsons wouldn't be up until the Fourth?"

"Well, yeah. They never are."

"But I saw some lights on board a couple of weeks ago."

Chris was shaking his head. "Couldn't be. There hasn't been a car in their parking space all summer. Besides, he always calls and has me run a shakedown the week before they get here."

He had to be right. Chris knew the marina and its inhabitants better than I knew the contents of my own closet. But still . . . "I saw lights."

"Okay, you saw lights." He clipped the toolbox shut and stood. "And Skeeter still says he saw a cougar up in the hills above town last year. See you later, Minster." He reached out to pat me on the head with his greasy hand.

I ducked away. "Yeah, yeah. Thanks for coming over, Chris. I'll talk to Rafe about the wiring, if you don't mind."

"Hey, why should I care? I like taking care of your boat, but your paycheck ain't exactly like that one's." He tipped his head in the direction of Olson's boat. "Or their pension." He nodded at Ted and Louisa's boat. "You're okay, even if you're not from here." He grinned again, got one pat on my head before I could dodge it, and headed off.

I sat there, elbows on my knees and chin in my hands. I *had* seen lights on Gunnar Olson's boat. I'd been studying the angles and there was no way I could have confused the beams from his looming boat with anything else.

But, really, who cared? It wasn't any of my business if Gunnar or his wife had snuck up north for a quiet weekend. I yawned and pushed myself to my feet, then stopped cold.

The lights. I'd seen the lights on Gunnar's boat the night Stan was killed.

Sunday was a quiet day at the library. We had afternoon hours only, from one until five. During the school year, most of the patrons were middle and high school students ostensibly working on homework. During the summer, the patrons were either parents looking to entertain their children, summer folks stocking up on a week's reading, or tourists who wanted a tour of the library. Sundays in the library felt like a Sunday, somehow, and working hardly felt like working at all.

There was one consistency, however, winter, spring, summer, or fall, Sunday, Monday, Tuesday, or any other day of the week.

Mitchell Koyne.

He'd started an inane conversation on Sunday, put it on hold when I shooed him out at closing, and continued it Monday afternoon when he walked into the lobby, dripping rain off his baseball hat, shirtsleeves, pant legs, and finger-tips.

I spotted him as I was walking from the reference desk to my office, a stack of books and papers under each arm.

"Hey, Minnie," he said. "I think I figured out what we should do if we get a hurricane. It all depends on the direction of the wind, of course, and since the only way we'd get a hurricane is if it came up the St. Lawrence Seaway—hurricanes die out over land, you know, so it'd have to—"

"Paper towels," I told him.

"For a hurricane?"

"Go into the men's room and dry yourself off with paper towels."

"Nah, I'm good." He shook himself like a dog and sprayed water all over the floor, a free-standing sign announcing the summer reading club, and me. "See?" He grinned, not seeing or not caring about the water droplets on my face, arms, hair, and, far, far worse, the books I was holding. "Now," he said, "if you look at a map, you'll see that . . . Hey, Minnie, where are you going? I got this all figured out. Minnie?"

I retreated in the direction of my office, ignoring Mitchell's calls. There were days when Mitchell was interesting and a treat to talk to. Other days, it was front desk scramble to see who got stuck with him.

As I passed the open doorway to the break

room, there was a reverberating crash of splintering china and splashing liquid. I peeked in the room and saw Holly standing with her hands to her mouth. Her wide gaze flashed to me, darted behind me, then dipped back to the monstrous mess on the floor.

"What did she do this time?" Josh shouldered past me. "Oh, great. Coffee. Nice. All sugared up, I bet. That'll be nice to clean up. Who's going to do it for you this time?"

"Josh," I said sharply. "It's just a cup of coffee."

He snorted. "Cup of coffee today. The other day it was a whole pot. Bam! Coffee over the counters, over the floor, it even got in the refrigerator. Princess over there was too upset to clean it up, so guess who got volunteered?" He thumped his chest.

Holly started to say something, but stopped and crouched down to pick up the biggest shards of her former mug. "I'm sorry," she whispered. "I don't know what's wrong with me."

"It was an accident," I said, trying to smile at them both. Not an easy task since they were on opposite sides of the room and neither one was looking at me, but I did my best. "These things happen."

"Oh, yeah?" Josh smirked. "Last week Reva Shomin brought in a plate of cookies for everybody. Guess who let the full plate slip out of her hands? We didn't get a single cookie, thanks to butterfingers over there. If we had a three-strike rule for breaking things, she'd be on her way out of here."

I saw a tear trickle down Holly's cheek. Enough.

"Josh!" My voice whipped his head around. "It was an accident. There's no need to make her feel worse than she already does."

"I don't think—"

"What you think doesn't matter right now. If you're not going to help clean, why don't you go do something more productive than mocking your coworkers?"

He narrowed his eyes at me. Though my assigned tasks in the library included personnel issues, I'd only once before had to cross over into being the disciplinarian. The experience had left me shaking, yet oddly elated. From that experience, I'd learned that it made no sense to put off tasks that you knew were going to make you uncomfortable. The delay only gave you time to worry, and what was the point of that?

"The printer in the bookmobile room is creasing the paper," I said. "It would be great if you have time to take a look at it."

He gave me a curt nod and stomped off.

I dropped my armloads of books onto a table. "Holly, sit down. If you don't, you're going to fall over into that sticky mess, then you'll have to go home to shower and change, I won't be able to send Mitchell over to you, and I don't have time today to answer his questions about hurricanes."

Her hands shook as she pulled out a coffee-free chair. "We don't get hurricanes here, so why does he care?"

I grinned as I took the chair next to Holly. "Ask him. I dare you."

Her smile was shaky. "No, thanks. I'll leave him to you today, if you don't mind. And I will clean this up, no matter what Josh says." She cast a mournful eye at the mess. "And I would have cleaned up the other messes. I just need a minute, that's all."

"Nothing wrong with that," I said, hesitated, then asked, "Is something wrong with Josh? He seems a little on edge."

Holly nodded. "We all are, I think. The police are still asking questions, and now that thing with the will. Stephen's hardly come out of his office in days. The rest of the clerks keep asking me what's going on with him and I have to keep telling them I don't know. Do you?"

"Going on?" Stephen himself came into the room. "Why should there be anything going on?"

I put on a smile. "Hello, Stephen. How are you today?"

He put his hands on his hips. "You never reported back to me about your talk with Caroline Grice. I'm now forced to come fetch information from you. Is she or is she not going to donate money to the library?"

My face froze. During Caroline's revelations the other night, I'd decided that soliciting for a donation wasn't that important. I still felt my decision was the right one, but coming up with a cover story would have been an excellent idea. "Our meeting was interrupted," I said. "We didn't have time to discuss anything except the—"

"Do you have another appointment with her?" he said, enunciating each consonant very, very clearly.

"Not yet, but—"

"See that you call her today," he snapped. "More donations are imperative if we're going to keep this library functioning at its present level." He spun around and marched out.

"Well," I said, turning to Holly. "That was—"

But she was gone, having slipped out the side door. I looked at the shards of former coffee mug. At the spatters of coffee.

Shards and splatters and splinters and sarcasm, and it was only Monday.

I sighed and got up to hunt down the mop and vacuum cleaner. My happy library world was falling apart and I had no idea what to do about it.

When I left work at six, light rain was still coming down. I stood in the front doorway, backpack in hand, staring out at the sodden world.

"Want a ride?" Mitchell appeared at my side, jingling a set of keys. "I'm parked right over there." He pointed to a maroon pickup that had a beige driver's door and a yellow hood.

"No, thanks." I smiled. "I have a couple of errands to do on the way home." In my youth, I'd owned cars that had looked worse than Mitchell's, but mine had never had stacks of empty pizza boxes piled so high on the passenger's seat that you could read "Fat Boys Pizza" from fifty feet away.

"You sure?" Mitchell squinted out into the rain. "It's coming down pretty good."

"Thanks, anyway." I pushed the door open and went out into the wet.

To make good on my statement of having errands to run, I stopped at the grocery store for cheese and fresh lettuce and at the fudge store for a slab of chocolate with walnuts. Both got shoved unceremoniously into my backpack at the point of purchase, and both were slightly dented when I got home and put them on the kitchen counter. Sugar and salad. The ideal dinner to soften the edges of a cranky day.

I cut open the cheese and nicked off a small corner. "Hey, Eddie, I have a treat for you."

No padding of cat feet, no sleepy *mrr*s.

"Hey. Ed."

Silence.

I picked up the cheese and started the Eddie hunt. "Here kitty, kitty, kitty."

No Eddie under the kitchen table, no Eddie

behind the bench seat's two small throw pillows. No Eddie under the kitchen sink, no Eddie under the bathroom sink.

I trod down the three steps to the bedroom . . . and found pieces of paper strewn everywhere. White bits on the floor, white bits on the bunks, white bits magically stuck to the walls.

"Eddie!" I shrieked. "What have you done?"

I crouched down to pick up two crumpled sheets of paper that looked largely intact. Underneath was Eddie, sleeping in a meat loaf shape. When the light hit his face, he blinked, yawned, and rolled over onto his side, purring.

"You are a horrible cat," I said, scratching him behind the ears. "And as soon as I think up a suitable punishment, you'll be the first to know."

"Mrr," he said, opening his eyes and looking at me intently.

"Oh. Right." I placed the piece of cheese directly under his chin. "This is for you."

He didn't even sniff at it. Instead, he continued to look at me with an unpleasantly direct gaze.

"Cut that out." I put my hand over his eyes. "You know I can't think when you do that."

"Mrr." He jerked his head away.

"Yeah, to you, too." I knelt and started gathering up his mess. "What did you destroy, anyway?" Since the boat didn't have a second cabin, I used the second bunk as office space. Laptop in the middle, printer on a bed tray behind the laptop, papers for filing on the right, bills to pay on the left. But what Eddie had shredded was neither.

"Huh. I thought I'd thrown these away." It was the papers I'd printed when I was trying to find a genealogical link between me and Caroline Grice. "Wasted effort," I told a recumbent Eddie. "I found a better way to talk to her."

Of course, that way had ended up with her accusing Aunt Frances of Stan's murder.

He flopped down onto the two intact sheets of paper. "Mrrrrowww!"

"Chill a little, will you? No need to scare the neighbors." I reached to gather in the biggest bits of Eddified paper. Mr. Ed scrambled to his feet, stalked to a small pile of clawed-up paper, turned to face me, and sat in the middle of it.

"Fine," I said. "Your work, your toy. But just until bedtime."

"Mrroww."

"Back at you." I snatched the unwanted cheese offering from the floor and went to make dinner.

Cats.

# Chapter 12

After I left the library the next day, I strolled down the sidewalks outside the gallery and loitered long enough to see Caroline walk out the door. I'd called the gallery earlier and Lina had told me she was there and when she'd likely be leaving.

"Caroline," I called, hurrying up to her while trying to look as if I weren't hurrying. Short people have this down to a science. It's all in the arms.

"Minnie." She smiled politely. "How are you this evening?"

"I feel as if we have a little unfinished business," I said. "So I was wondering if you'd be my guest to dinner tonight."

"How kind of you." Caroline glanced at her watch and I knew the battle was half lost. Charge!

Before she could open her mouth to ever-so-kindly reject my invitation, I plunged forward into the cannon's maw. "My friend Kristen owns the Three Seasons, have you been there? Tonight she wants to try out a new recipe on me and anyone I bring. Since we have a few things to discuss, I thought this would be a great opportunity. Please say you'll come."

I smiled at her as winsomely as I could. When

I'd talked to Lina, I'd also asked if she knew anything about Caroline's eating habits. One call to Kristen and the plan was laid. "Do you think you'd like fresh linguine and asparagus with a light butter cream sauce?"

Caroline blinked. "Fresh asparagus? This time of year?"

I nodded. "Kristen found a woman in the Upper Peninsula who drives it down twice a week as long as it lasts." I inched closer and lowered my voice. "And I happen to know the truck came in today."

Caroline looked at her watch once again. "We do have things to discuss. Let me call my house-keeper. I'll meet you at the restaurant in ten minutes."

Score!

As per my request relayed via Kristen, the hostess settled us at a small table in a quiet corner. She laid down menus and a wine list—"The wine steward will be with you in a moment"—and disappeared into the labyrinth that was the main eating area of the Three Seasons.

Many restaurateurs would have made major changes to this former residence and bed-and-breakfast. Eliminated the walls between the front parlor, rear parlor, morning room, and breakfast room. Combined the formal dining room, sun-room, and library. The only major renovations

Kristen had contracted were in the kitchen. Otherwise, she'd let it revert to the posh summer residence from days of old, white wainscoting here, pine paneling there, coffered ceiling over there.

Caroline and I were seated in the library, its shelves still heavy with a century of family books from Robert Louis Stevenson to Dickens to Ayn Rand. Kristen had vowed she'd let people borrow books if they asked, but so far no one had.

Caroline looked around. "I've never been seated in this room. What a delight to see so many old friends."

I beamed. A woman after my own heart. But though I deeply wanted to talk books, I stuck with the topic of her first sentence. "You've been here before?"

"A handful of times, yes. Stan and . . ."

She paused as the wine guy approached. Since Kristen had already told me what would go best with dinner, I ordered a bottle as if I actually knew what I was doing. I passed the tasting honors on to my companion and was satisfied with her smiling nod.

Wining and dining. This trolling-for-donations thing wasn't so bad. I decided to let the comment about Stan go for now. Give the wine and Kristen's magic a little time to take effect.

Over the bread we discussed the wide variety of artists, mediums, and subjects we wanted to bring to the library show. During salad, we firmed up the mundane details of dates and hours. Then, with the pouring of our second glasses of wine and the arrival of our entrées, I broached the big subject.

"I suppose you know that Stan was one of the library's major donors."

"He was a generous man." Caroline cut a small piece of asparagus even smaller.

"Very," I agreed. "His will mentions a large bequest to the library, but the family is challenging. It may be a long time before the library sees any of that money."

I twirled a piece of pasta onto my fork, wondering about the six sisters, wondering if any of them had thought they'd inherit. Though I had no idea what it took to successfully challenge a will, I was sure Stan would have made sure his will was locked up watertight.

"But," I said, "the library board hadn't made any firm plans for the money, so there's no direct loss."

Though Caroline's face showed only courteous interest, I felt the click-click-click of conclusions being reached. "An indirect loss remains a loss," she said.

"My boss is afraid that our regular donors are going to get cold feet because of the situation." I smiled at her crookedly. "When I told Stephen I was going to try to have dinner with you tonight, he wanted me to ask you for a check."

"But you haven't." Caroline tilted her head. "Or . . . have you?"

"I'm no good at this kind of stuff. Never have been. When I was a kid, I hated selling Girl Scout cookies."

Caroline laughed. "Tell Stephen I'll consider a donation."

My eyes bugged out. "You . . . will?"

"But there is no way on this green earth that I'm going to join the Friends of the Library."

Since I was very familiar with the give-me-an-inch-and-I'll-take-ten-miles personality of the current Friends president, I understood her feelings exactly. I couldn't say that out loud, but I nodded. "Understood. Thank you, Caroline. Very, very much."

She held a forkful of pasta over her plate. "No promises, mind you. I'll need to talk to my accountant first."

"You're considering a donation," I said. "If I can pass on that quote to Stephen, he'll be a happy camper. But he'll spread it all over town," I said in a warning tone. "Are you okay with that?"

"Stan would have liked it," she said quietly, concentrating on her plate. "He was always trying to get me to donate more money."

"And how is your dinner, ladies?" a male voice boomed.

I flinched. Caroline did not. Clearly, she was the better woman.

"Very nice, thank you." She smiled at Larry, the new chef, whose arm was now brace-free. "Every bit as good as the party you catered for me at New Year's. How is your lovely wife?"

He nodded. "Now, is there anything else I can get you? Mrs. Grice, if I recall correctly, you have a small weakness"—he held his thumb and index finger a fraction of an inch apart—"for strawberry shortcake. As it happens, we got a fresh delivery of strawberries this morning, and I can't think of anything I'd rather do than bring you a special creation."

"Thank you, Larry." Caroline kept smiling. "That's a wonderfully kind offer, but I'm afraid I've eaten too much of your cream sauce. And strawberry shortcake?" She shook her head sadly. "I'll lose my figure in a week if I continue down that path."

"Too bad about Mr. Larabee," Larry said. "I remember him from your party. He seemed like a real nice guy. He said with talent and skills like mine that I had a bright future. I told him all I needed was a little money and he said money is easy enough to come by if you know the right people." Larry colored slightly. "I'm talking too much again. Sorry, Mrs. Grice. Let me know if you need anything else." Smiling, he left.

"You miss him, don't you?" I asked softly. "Stan, I mean. I miss him very much, but I'm guessing you miss him even more."

She gazed at, then through me. "There are so few people who are true friends. It's heartbreaking to lose even one."

The deep truth of her words kicked me back. Then I pushed it away. I'd think about it later. "Do you know his sisters?"

"Only through Stan's tales." A brief smile flickered, then faded. "He dearly loved to tell stories. I was certain many of them were sheer fabrication, but he swore they were all true. When he claimed to have bought and sold a piece of property three times and doubled the profit each time, I demanded proof."

"And he had it?"

"If anything, he'd played down the money he'd made."

Stan. "What a character."

"It's unfortunate he wasn't more successful at family relations," Caroline said. "He thought it would be enough to purchase them each a house of their choosing and establish a trust that would pay for their health insurance."

It sounded generous, and I said so.

"I'm sure they don't agree." Caroline dabbed at the corners of her mouth with her linen napkin. "Their attorneys will make their case. Meanwhile, our county sheriff's office continues to flounder about, looking for a killer in all the wrong places."

"Oh. Right." I shifted in my comfortable chair. Maybe she meant Stan's sisters. Because it sure seemed as if they should be suspects. Who could be better suspects than people who thought they might inherit even part of Stan's fortune? Unfortunately, she was probably talking about someone else. "There's something you should know."

But Caroline wasn't listening to me. "I've never let anyone say a word against law enforcement, against the men and women who put their lives on the line every time they go on duty. I've supported the city and the county officers, gone to their fund-raisers, voted for their millages, and now they barely tolerate my phone calls."

I knew the feeling.

"It's that Frances Pixley," Caroline said. "One of her former boarders works for the Chilson Police Department, did you know? She's using her influence over the officers to make them look the other way."

"I'm sure that's not true."

"You think not?" Caroline's voice was rising. "Then why haven't they investigated her actions? Why haven't they had her in for questioning? Why haven't they arrested her?"

"Um, they probably need some proof."

"Proof?" She *tsk*ed the problem away. "They'd find proof if they only looked. Frances Pixley is—"

I'd had enough. "Is my aunt."

"Your . . . ?" Caroline Grice was speechless.

"Aunt." I nodded. "She's my dad's sister."

"But you . . ."

"I know, we don't look anything alike. But we're blood relatives, I love her very much, and I don't think she killed Stan any more than I think you killed him."

"Than I?" She drew back.

"Sure." I shrugged. "From what you've said, you have the same kind of jealousy-induced motive. Why shouldn't you be a suspect, too?"

"Why . . . why . . ." She picked up her purse. "Excuse me," she said, and left.

"Don't say it," I said.

"Wouldn't dream of doing such a thing." Kristen grinned from behind her desk. "But may I point out that this makes three—yes, three—career-killing moves inside of two weeks?"

"No." I slid down in the chair.

"How about mentioning the fact that I warned you about trying to figure out who killed Stan?" Kristen put her feet up on an open drawer and her hands behind her head.

"You didn't."

She frowned. "I must have."

"You said helping Holly was going to take up too much of my time. You never once said I shouldn't investigate."

"And if I had?"

"I'd have ignored you."

"Exactly. Which is why I saved my breath."

I gusted out a sigh. "Caroline will never donate any money to the library now. Stephen's going to be way mad."

"Probably going to fire you," Kristen said comfortably.

"You think so?"

"Oh, sure. He could replace you in a snap. Bet people are already lining up for your job."

Another sigh. "Yeah, you're right. They probably are."

"Just so you know, don't come to me looking for a waitress job. You'd be terrible."

She was right, I'd be the worst waitress ever. I'd get talking to people and forget I had orders to take, and I'd be a disaster at giving people the right change. "How about dishwashing?"

"Nah." Her feet came down. "You're too short to put away dishes on the top shelves."

"Isn't that discrimination?"

"Most likely." She stood and whipped a cloth from a small table that, in my misery, I hadn't even noticed was there. She lifted covers off two desserts. "Crème brûlée topped with shavings of dark chocolate," she said, handing me a plate and spoon and putting a second set on her desk. "Eat up."

I looked at the custard-filled ramekin. "This is supposed to make me feel better?"

"It is and it will. Eat."

I didn't see how, but I picked up the spoon and cracked open the sugar. At the sound, I felt a small smile whisper onto my face. I loved crème brûlée. I loved dark chocolate. Most of all, I loved them together, and Kristen knew it.

Three bites in, the world looked brighter. "Stephen isn't going to fire me, is he?"

"Nope."

Another bite. "And there aren't a bunch of people who want my job, are there?"

"Are you kidding? With the hours you work?"

I crunched into a big piece of caramelized sugar. "You're a true friend."

"Yeah, well, it takes one to know one."

One more bite of custardy goodness and I asked, "Would you really turn me down for a waitress job?"

"Do you really want to know the answer?"

"Not really."

"Good choice."

Even true friends deserve an occasional tongue-sticking-out. So Kristen got one.

I decided to walk home not along the waterfront but through downtown. Now that school was done, the summer tourists were out in force even on a weeknight, and a walk by the water would be punctuated by baby-stroller dodging and small-child evasion.

The crowds were part of summer, just like the

smell of suntan lotion and cut grass, but I didn't want to mingle tonight. I wanted to get home quickly and quietly and have Eddie purr at me until I fell asleep.

So I walked east through the downtown blocks, head down, hands in my pockets, not seeing much, not thinking much, trying not to feel sorry for myself because I was such an idiot, trying not to see the look on Stephen's face when I told him that it'd be a cold day in you-know-what before Caroline Grice gave the library any money.

My efforts weren't working very well, so I was easily distracted by the sight of a man sitting on the bench outside the Round Table. A familiar-looking man. I'd seen him at the library . . . yes. It was Bill D'Arcy. He'd checked out a monstrous pile of books. He was on Rafe's list of suspects. And he was sitting there, typing away on his laptop, catching the Round Table's free Wi-Fi.

Was using free Wi-Fi provided by a restaurant when you weren't inside the restaurant itself weenie-like behavior? I wasn't sure, and made a mental note to ask my mother next time we talked. Mom was always good for making sure my moral compass pointed straight north.

I crossed the street and sat down on the bench. "Bill D'Arcy, right?"

The look he gave me was guarded, but not overtly hostile. "I am."

"Hi." I smiled wide and held out my hand.

"Minnie Hamilton. I'm assistant director at the library. We met the other day when you were checking out a bunch of books."

He glanced at my hand. Hesitated. Shook it briefly. "Nice to meet you," he muttered, going back to his computer.

"You're not from around here, are you?" I asked. He grunted, but I couldn't tell if it was one of agreement or disagreement. Still, it was a reply of sorts, so I kept going. "Not that it matters, of course. I'm not from here, either. Turns out that spending your childhood summers up here doesn't count at all. If you didn't graduate high school here, you're not from here. Actually"—I made a *hmm* sort of noise—"you have to be born here. A friend of mine, his parents moved up here when he was starting middle school, and he's not considered a local." Which annoyed Josh to no end, but there was nothing he could do about it.

"Where are you from?" I asked.

He hunched away from me and typed rapidly.

"I don't care, really," I said. "Just curious. It's a standard question. I bet a lot of people have asked you already, right?"

"Too many," he muttered, whacking at the keyboard keys.

"Sounds familiar," I said, laughing. "I tell people I'm from Dearborn, and next thing they want to know is, what high school did I go to? Then it's what year did I graduate? After that, we're talking restaurants and what street I lived on. Conversations like that can go on forever."

He gave me a pointed look. I smiled. "But lately all anyone wants to talk about is Stan Larabee. You know, the man who was killed? Well, not so much talking about him, but who killed him. I've heard all sorts of theories, from my boss to his sisters to some guy named Chris. Some people even think I did it." I laughed heartily. "Since you're not from here, I bet your theory has less baggage than anyone else's."

Either he'd managed to turn off his ears, or he was intentionally ignoring me. I talked louder.

"Outside points of view can be very helpful. If you know anything about Stan, anything at all, you should tell the police. You look like an observant man; I bet there's something you know. I bet—"

He slapped his laptop shut, stood, and walked away without even the courtesy of a backward glare.

There were two ways to interpret that little scene, I thought, watching him stalk off, his legs stiff and his shoulders set. One, that he was trying to become a hermit and was well on his way to success. Two, that he knew something about Stan's death that he didn't want to share.

I stood and walked the rest of the way home, thinking that I wasn't ready to cross Bill D'Arcy off the suspect list. Not by a long shot.

Five seconds after I walked in the door, I walked back out again. Rafe. I needed to ask Rafe about working on my electrical stuff.

The lights were on in his house, which, when he was done restoring it to its original status as an early-nineteen-hundreds Shingle-style cottage, would be a showpiece. Now, however, it was a cobbled-together mess of tiny apartments on the inside and was covered on the outside with the widest variety of siding seen anywhere but a lumberyard. The former owners hadn't exactly been concerned with aesthetics.

I knocked on the front door. "Rafe? It's Minnie. I know you're in there—I can hear that horrible music you play."

"No one's here."

Uh-oh. Rafe always defended his music. "What's wrong?" I asked.

"Nothing. Go away."

I banged on the door with my fist. "Let me in or I'm coming in anyway."

The door swung open slowly, making a creepy screeching noise. Rafe stood in the doorway. "Has anyone ever told you what a pain in the heinie you can be?"

"Daily. What's the matter with your arm?"

He was holding it away from his side at an awkward angle. "Nothing."

I stepped inside. "Let me see."

"Aw, Minnie, don't—"

"Let. Me. See."

Once again, the Librarian Voice did the trick. His shoulders slumped and he let me pull him into the brightness cast by the halogen work lights scattered around the entryway. "It'll be fine," he said. "It just needs a little more time."

I pulled at a corner of the first aid tape and started tugging. "This might hurt a little."

"Jeez, Min, that stings like a you-know-what. Do you have to?"

With one quick rip, I yanked off the tape.

"Ow!"

"Quit being such a baby," I said. "Now let me see your stitches. Come on. Show me."

"Don't want to," he muttered, but held out his arm.

I took hold of his wrist, pulled off the gauze, and turned the wound to the light. I sucked in a quick breath. "We're going to the hospital. Now."

"Aw, Min—"

"Rafe Niswander, your arm is red and puffy with infection. Next thing is you'll get those red streaks and then you'll get a staph infection and then they'll cut off your arm, but by then the infection will have gone too far and you'll spend two weeks in the hospital sliding toward an early death, all because you wouldn't listen to me."

"Can't die, I got too many things to do."

"Rafe." I swallowed. "Come to the hospital with me. Please."

He looked at my face. I don't know what he saw there, but for once he didn't argue.

Forty-five minutes later, we were back in Charlevoix's emergency room. The attractive Dr. Tucker Kleinow came in as I was helping Rafe up onto the hospital bed.

"Back again?" he asked. "Another problem with your saw?"

"Nah," Rafe said. "Minnie here is all worried about that cut you sewed up a while back. Tell her it's okay, will you? She's getting on my case something fierce."

I crossed my arms. "Only because you're not taking care of yourself. If you had, this wouldn't have happened."

Dr. Kleinow snapped on gloves and examined Rafe's arm carefully. "You definitely have some infection going on. Did you fill the prescription for antibiotics that I gave you?"

"Sure did," Rafe said.

I glared at him. "But did you take them?"

"Well, yeah."

"*All* of them?"

"Not all in a row, like," he said. "I forgot a couple of days and it looked good, so what was the point, right?"

I drew in a long breath, the better to yell at him

with, but the doctor stepped in between us. "I'll clean this up again, if you two don't mind putting a pause on your argument. You can yell at your husband on the way home."

"My . . . what?" Surely he hadn't said what I thought he'd said.

Rafe chuckled. "Don't know what's funnier, thinking that she'd marry me, or that I'd be dumb enough to ask her."

I frowned. "Was I just insulted? Because it sure sounded like it."

Dr. Kleinow looked from one of us to the other. "Siblings?" He looked a little closer, undoubtedly noting the complete lack of family resemblance. "Adopted, maybe?"

Rafe and I shook our heads. "We're just friends," I said. "Neighbors."

"Only relatives are allowed with the patient in the examination room," the doctor said.

Rafe and I looked at each other. We shrugged simultaneously. "Everybody must have thought we were married," Rafe said. "I can see it. Did you hear how she was ragging me for not taking those pills?"

"She was right," Dr. Kleinow said.

"Oh, sure, take her side," Rafe said. "The cute girl's always right, is that it?"

"There are worse reasons to take sides." The doctor grinned. "Now, let's get a closer look at that arm."

• • •

After another forty-five minutes, Rafe was cleansed, rebandaged, and more or less beaten into submission about taking the newer and much stronger prescription. His post-emergency-room care, however, was being more problematic.

Rafe looked at the doctor mournfully. "Don't tell me Minster here was right, that I could lose my arm. Taking these new freaking horse pills will be enough, right? You're not going to cut my arm off, are you?"

"It's been known to happen." The doctor handed Rafe a handful of papers, all of it with teeny tiny print. "Here's what you need to do."

"Man." Rafe hefted the paperwork. "This is a lot of reading. I really need to look at all of it?"

Dr. Kleinow started to say something. Stopped. Eyed Rafe. Eyed me. "Well . . ."

I grinned. He couldn't have transmitted what he was thinking more clearly if he'd written it on a chalkboard. "Though Mr. Niswander here is a born and bred northern redneck wannabe, he not only graduated from high school, but he earned a bachelor's degree from Northern Michigan University and a master's degree from Michigan State."

"A Spartan?" The doctor frowned. "Yet you're certain he can read?"

"Hey!" Rafe sat up.

I pushed him back down. "He'll read it. And he'll follow the directions this time." I thumped a gentle fist on his leg. "Won't you?"

"Yeah, but jeez . . ." Rafe was scanning the instructions.

"Just think of the story you'll have for the kids in September."

Dr. Kleinow gathered up the empty gauze packets and dropped them into a wastebasket. "You're a teacher?"

"Nah. Worse."

I snorted. "He's principal of the middle school, if you can believe it."

Rafe flipped a sheet. "Lucky for me they didn't have any other applicants."

An outright lie. There had been dozens, and Rafe had been the school board's unanimous choice for the job.

"We done here?" Rafe kicked his feet over the side of the bed and slid to the floor. "There's a little boys' room that's calling my name."

Dr. Kleinow watched him go. "I'd guess he's an excellent principal."

"He is, actually." I picked up the papers Rafe had left behind. "And will be for a long time, assuming I don't kill him first."

"What are friends for?"

I smiled at him. He smiled back and the moment became something that made my heart beat a little faster.

"So you two are just friends?" Dr. Tucker Kleinow asked.

I nodded. "All we'll ever be." Or want to be. Rafe was a wonderful friend, but it was a brother-sister kind of friendship. The thought of a life spent with him made the inside of my mouth pucker.

"And is there anyone who would be angry if I asked you out to dinner?"

"Not a soul."

He moved a half step closer. "I find that hard to believe."

My smile went wider and I moved half a step toward him.

"Hey, Min!" Rafe stuck his head inside the doorway. "Are you ready to go, or what? Back home I got slow glue setting up something fierce."

"See why we're just friends?" I asked Tucker.

He nodded. "Of course, it's good to have friends."

"And even better to make new—"

Rafe slung his arm around my shoulders and marched me away, yelling my phone number to Tucker.

Later that evening I thumbed off my cell phone. "Looks like I have a date," I told Eddie. "What do you think about that?"

He yawned and gave the impression of settling even deeper into the scraps of paper he'd decided were his new home. I wasn't sure he'd moved at all in the last twenty-four hours. Well, there was litter-box evidence that he'd engaged in some physical activity, but that could have been a trick.

My intention had been to clean up the mess he'd made, but every time I touched the papers, he'd started such a horrendous howling that I was afraid the neighbors would call the police. Not Louisa, since she and Eddie were good friends and she understood how odd he could be, but some of the newer arrivals were blithely ignorant of Eddie's presence and could easily interpret certain events erroneously.

In the end I'd shoved the shredded papers into an Eddie-sized pile and let him nest on it. He was a truly strange creature.

Now I sat on the floor and ran my hand over him from head to tail-tip. "The last time I went out with anyone was with Kristen and her old boyfriend and a friend of his." The friend had driven north to ski and the four of us had gone out for dinner at Red Mesa in Boyne City. It had been a fun evening, but we'd parted with a hand-shake and a quick hug. Though we were good Facebook friends now, even via the Internet it was obvious that no love was going to bloom.

Tucker, though. There'd been a little flame right at the start.

"And a doctor," I told Eddie. "Go figure." My one and only serious romance had been with a medical student. We'd met when I was a grad student at University of Illinois at Urbana-Champaign and he was halfway through med school. We'd dated, then lived together while we finished school. Stayed together while he did his residency and I found my first job at a nearby library. Then, when he was done, we discovered we had nothing to talk about. We'd fallen out of love years earlier, but had been too busy to realize it.

"Should I tell Mom?" I asked.

"Mrr." Eddie rolled on his back, scrunching more papers and offering up his stomach for rubbing.

"You're right," I said. "Wait a while and see how it goes. No sense in getting her all excited about grandchildren at this point. I could tell Kristen, though. And Aunt . . ."

I sighed. And Aunt Frances. I wanted to talk to her. Needed to talk to her.

But would she talk to me?

# Chapter 13

The next day was a Bookmobile Day. Thessie, Eddie, and I headed to the southern part of Tonedagana County and today was our first run to an adult foster care facility, a small facility where residents need some care, but not the high-level care of a traditional nursing home. If the visit went even marginally well, I had a long list of similar facilities that were excited about the possibility of having the bookmobile make a regular stop.

Actually, the term "excited" wasn't even close to the reactions I'd received when making the invitational phone calls. After two, I'd learned to hold the receiver away from my ear to prevent permanent damage to my eardrum.

I parked the bookmobile in the shade cast by the tall maple tree outside Maple View Adult Foster Care. As soon as I'd set the brakes, Thessie jumped out of her seat and headed to the back to start wrestling with the heavily laden book carts.

Thessie started down the steps, then paused. "What about Eddie?"

The cat in question was sitting in the middle of the floor, licking his paw and swiping the backs of his ears with it. Lick. Swipe. Lick. Swipe.

"Why can't he come with us?" she asked. "He follows you like there's a leash on him."

There'd been no reason to tell Thessie about Eddie and Stan's farmhouse, so I hadn't. "I don't want to take any chances," I said. "If he saw a . . . a chipmunk or a bird, he could take off. We'd spend an hour hunting him down and we'd be late for the next stop."

While we were opening the back door and pushing the buttons to lower the wheelchair lift that could also carry the book carts, Gayle came out to the parking lot. Gayle, the manager of Maple View, had volunteered to be the guinea pig for the first AFC bookmobile stop.

"Hi, Minnie," she said, smiling. "Hope you brought lots of books. The residents are more excited than I would have guessed."

I was introducing her to Thessie when a large voice trumpeted forth. "I spy a cat," she said. "Right there in the window of the bookmobile." The size of the voice matched the size of the woman who filled the wheelchair from one side to the other. Her white hair was short and curly and she wore a matching knit shirt and pants of lavender. "Gayle? Gayle, do you see?" she called, pointing to my little buddy. "It's a cat come to see us."

"Yes, Polly, I see." Gayle glanced at Eddie, then at me. "Unfortunately, I'm not sure the cat is here to visit Maple View."

Polly wheeled herself down the short concrete walk and across the parking lot. "We haven't had a cat here in ages and I miss hearing a nice purr. He's got that nice white chest, just like a tuxedo. What's his name?"

I made a note to myself to go back in time ten minutes, shut Eddie up in his cabinet, and avoid this entire scene. "Eddie. He's friendly, but . . ."

Gayle smiled. "The residents are used to cats. I have one of my own that I bring in once in a while."

"Please?" Polly looked up at me beseechingly. "I miss my own cats so very much."

My heart panged with sympathy. Now that I had a cat, I couldn't imagine life without one. At least one particular one. I looked at Gayle. "He's friendly, but he isn't declawed."

She smiled. "Mine isn't, either. The residents know what to do."

"And we can't stay long. We have to be at the next stop in a little over an hour."

"I'll kick you out in plenty of time."

"Well, then . . ." I got an image of a head-shaking Stephen, then banished it from my brain. "If you're sure, let's give it a try."

"Great!" Gayle clapped her hands. "Polly, let's get you back into your room so you can greet Eddie properly. Minnie, I'll send Audry out to show you things, okay?"

"Who's Audry?" Thessie asked. She'd rolled the book carts off the ramp and was ready to take them inside.

"No idea. But I'd guess that's her."

Walking toward us purposefully was a woman who looked to be about ten years older than Gayle's sixtyish, though while Gayle was short and round, this woman was short and slender, moving with a comfortable ease that put me in mind of a cat trotting on its way to do cat things.

An odd noise came from inside the bookmobile, but I ignored it in favor of holding out my hand in greeting. "Hi, I'm Minnie and this is Thessie. You're Audry?"

"Audry Brant. I help Gayle a couple days a week." She smiled. "Helping out until I have to move in here myself. Thessie, could you be a big help and take those into the dining room? In through the double doors, then straight on until morning. The readers are ready and waiting. Well, those who aren't waiting for your cat."

The odd noise grew odder. I started to turn to look, but Audry laid a hand on my arm.

"Minnie, can I ask you a question?"

"Sure." I prepared myself for the standard bookmobile inquiries. What kind of gas mileage does it get? (Awful.) Did you have to get a commercial driver's license to drive it? (No, but I did take a truck driver's course.) How do you plan the route? (With difficulty.)

"I hear," she said, "that you're—"

She stopped because this time the odd noise was too loud to ignore. Eddie was making

240

enough noise scratching at the window and yowling that people in the next county could have heard.

"Excuse me," I said to Audry, and hurried into the bookmobile. By the time I'd climbed up the steps, Eddie was perched on the headrest of the passenger's seat, moving his head around to peer out the side window at who knew what.

"What is the matter with you?"

All cats are masters of the evil eye, but the frozen glare Eddie sent me was in a class by itself. I shook off the foot-thick ice with which he'd tried to cover me. "Will you cut it out? There are a bunch of nice elderly people inside. For some bizarre reason they want to see you, but I can't take you in if you don't stop acting like you have ants in your pants."

He jumped down to the seat and banged his head against the console.

*Bonk! Bonk!*

"Eddie!" I picked him up. "What is with you?"

He pulled back to look me in the eye. "Mrr!"

"Well, yeah, but I don't know what that means. I don't talk cat."

*"MRR!!"*

I sighed and stroked his fur. "You know, sometimes I really think you're trying to tell me something and I'm just too stupid to . . . Oh, sure, *now* you start purring, you silly cat." I kissed the top of his head. "Are you ready to make some new friends?"

He snuggled into my arms. "Mrr," he said.

"Is that a yes or a no?"

"Mrr."


The rest of the day went smoothly enough. Polly and a number of the other residents got to pet the kitty, Thessie picked cat hair off her clothes and wondered out loud if it could be spun and knitted, and Brynn—who'd bounded aboard the book-mobile at the next stop wearing a headband with fuzzy cat ears attached—got her Eddie fix while her mother watched with moist eyes. The little girl's blood count numbers were all where they should be, I was told, and having a regular visit from Eddie was doing wonders for keeping her cheerful.

I drove us back to Chilson. "Eddie's getting to be more of a draw than the books."

"Oh, I don't think so." Thessie put another collection of Eddie hair into the plastic bag that had formerly housed her peanut butter and jelly sandwich. "Did you see the stacks of books those kids checked out?"

I was thinking about that when I took an evening walk. Could we manage to secretly market Eddie as an attraction for the bookmobile? Eddie as an inducement to reading. The mind boggled. My brain was whirring away as I walked through downtown, which was probably why I didn't see that I was on track for a collision until I ran smack into someone.

"Oh! Sorry about—" I shook myself out of boggle mode and looked up at the woman I'd almost run over. "Aunt Frances! I didn't see you." I started to laugh at myself, but then remembered her abrupt departure on Saturday morning. The phone messages I'd left that she hadn't returned.

The pause hanging between us grew bigger and fatter and wider. "How are you?" I finally asked.

"Fine," she said.

The pause, which had shrunk slightly, started ballooning again. I felt it grow larger and larger, wondered if it would pop or just keep expanding forever.

A cane tap-tapped along the sidewalk. "Miz Pixley," Lloyd Goodwin said, nodding. "Miz Minnie. How are you two lovely ladies this lovely summer evening?"

"Fine," we chorused. And for some reason, that made us both start laughing. The balloon shrank to nothing and suddenly everything was okay.

"Come on," Aunt Frances said, taking my arm. "I need to visit someone."

I resisted her light tug. "You sure you want me with you? Do I know her? Him?"

"It'll be fine," she said. Which, of course, made us both laugh again.

• • •

She was right—it was fine. The bag she carried held hand clippers, a dandelion puller, a hand cultivator, and a pair of gloves. She took us straight to the oldest part of the cemetery and held out the clippers.

"Do you mind?"

We stood facing the headstone of Mary Alvord, born 1815 in London, England, died 1877 in Chilson, Michigan.

"It's the oldest headstone in the cemetery," Aunt Frances said. "There's no one around any longer to tend her grave, so I take care of things for her."

Tears sparked in my eyes. "I had no idea you did this. It's . . . really nice of you."

"I just hope that maybe somebody will do the same for me someday. Ready?"

Fifteen minutes later the grass was trimmed, the weeds were gone, and the marigolds Aunt Frances said she'd planted on Memorial weekend were looking tidy again.

"Now." She took the clippers from me. "As a reward for your labor, I will treat you to a complete explanation of my odd reactions to comments about Stan Larabee. To be honest, I was being an idiot. I just didn't . . . couldn't . . ." She sighed. "I don't even know where to start."

"At the beginning." I led her to Alonzo Tillotson's bench, looking around with mild trepidation. One Eddie was wonderful, but if there were two, and if they met, the universe would surely explode. Or I would.

We settled down and sat in comfortable silence watching the waters of Janay Lake. Boats went this way and that. The wind blew a light breeze. The sun was on our faces.

My eyes were starting to close for a little nap when Aunt Frances started her story.

"It was a family feud," she said, sighing. "A very private, very old feud inside Stan's family, and Stan had made me promise not to say anything to anyone about it."

"That's not a beginning," I said. "That's more like an explanation."

"I suppose." She watched a seagull soaring past, her eyes slits against the sharp sun. "Stan stayed with me the winter before you moved up north."

I made a squeak of surprise, but managed to keep my mouth shut.

Aunt Frances was still focused on the seagull. "He hated hotels. Hated them with a serious kind of hate. He stayed with me while that house of his up on the hill was being renovated. He moved out of my place and into his just a few weeks before you moved up." She shifted her gaze from sky to me. "He had the corner room near the stairway," she said. "Just to be clear about things."

"Crystal," I said.

"Good." She looked at me a moment longer, then returned to the lake view. "As far as I know, no one realized that Stan stayed with me that winter. He didn't want his relatives knowing he was in town and I was willing to keep his confidence."

At that time of year it would have been easy enough to keep his presence a secret. The houses surrounding the boardinghouse were all summer cottages. The closest year-round residence was almost a quarter mile away, and that was occupied by a couple who worked in Traverse City and were willing to drive the hour-long commute, one way. As long as Stan had a vehicle no one recognized, he could have driven out to the old highway, headed up to U.S. 31, and blended with the traffic before anyone paid any attention.

"The only thing," Aunt Frances said, "is I'm good friends with one of Stan's nieces. Gwen's the daughter of his oldest sister and isn't much younger than Stan." She went quiet. Stayed quiet.

"That's not the end of the story, right?" I asked.

She watched another seagull wing past. "No. It wasn't until a few months ago that I connected Stan and Gwen. He never talked about his family and she didn't mention that Stan was her uncle until he donated the money to the bookmobile. That's when . . ."

"When . . . ?"

"I decided to play master of other people's lives." Her voice was harsh. "I talked to Stan, over and over, on the phone, at the Round Table, at his house, trying to convince him to call his sisters. Tried to convince Gwen to see Stan. All in the name of trying to make people happy."

She shoved at her hair, trying to push it into a place out of the wind. "It's not enough that I think I can help people find their true loves. Oh, no. I have to try to end a family feud that has been going on for decades. And look what happened. So stupid." Creases appeared around her lips.

My mind made a small, frightened leap. "You think you're responsible for Stan's death?"

"I don't know what to think." The creases went deeper. "The feud . . . I don't even know what it was about." She made an impatient gesture. "Something stupid. Feuds always are. But what if old hurts were opened up because I tried? What if my attempts at reconciliation brought it all back? What if . . . ?"

Her strong voice wavered. Quavered. Fell apart into a choking sob. "What if it's my fault?"

I wanted to say, *That's nuts, of course it's not your fault. You didn't have anything to do with Stan's death and it's ridiculous to think so.*

But I didn't know what was true anymore. So I took her hand. Held it tight between mine.

And didn't let go.

● ● ●

Eddie and I sat on the houseboat's front deck that night, watching the sun go down and the stars come out. At least I was watching the sun and the stars. Eddie was alternating between being a motionless cat statue and chasing the tip of his tail as if his life depended on it.

I'd turned off all the lights in the cabin to let my eyes adjust to the darkness, and a sense of invisibility had enveloped me. No one could see me, and since I was lying quietly on the chaise lounge, no one could hear me. But I could hear them.

A few boats down, a new couple was welcoming friends to their boat. Wine corks and beer cans were popping open, toasts were being toasted, and a wild happiness was emanating from all.

Closer, a woman with small children was trying to convince her youngsters that, yes, it was bedtime, that just because they were still awake didn't mean it wasn't time for sleepy eyes and if they wanted to go to the beach tomorrow, they'd better get into bed right now, and don't make me count to three. One, two . . .

Next door, Louisa and Ted were putting away the dinner dishes they'd just washed. Silverware rattled and plates tinked as they chatted in voices too low for me to hear. Not that I was trying to hear, of course. Eavesdropping was a nasty habit and those who indulged in it often heard things they didn't want to hear. Take the time when I was five and had listened in on my older brother and his girlfriend when they—

"He got what he deserved," Gunnar Olson said.

Eddie, whom I saw in silhouette against the lights of the dock, perked up his ears and turned his head to look at our other immediate neighbor, the one whose mere presence allowed me a discount rate on my boat slip. When I'd seen his lights on earlier that night, I'd wondered what he was doing up here a full two weeks before the Fourth of July, but had hoped I wouldn't have to find out.

With Gunnar going full force, my quiet evening was done. I should go in, anyway. There were bills to pay and Eddie hair to vacuum. I swung my feet to the deck and started to stand when Gunnar's voice boomed out through his open cabin windows. "Larabee lived about twenty years too long, if you ask me."

Then again, listening in to someone else's conversation could hardly be considered eavesdropping if you were sitting on your own boat enjoying the evening. I sat back down.

"Yeah, tell me about it," Gunnar said to the person on the other end of the phone. "You know, I was up here when he died."

I bolted to my feet. I *knew* it! I *knew* I'd seen lights on his boat that night.

Eddie padded across the deck and wound around my ankles. "Mrr," he said.

I put my finger to my lips and waved at him to keep quiet.

"Mrr."

Why, *why* is it that cats only seem to understand English when it's to their own benefit? I knelt on the deck and pulled Eddie to me. He allowed the snuggle for a second and a half, then slithered out of my grasp.

"Flew the Cessna up," Gunnar said. "I got the itch to play a little blackjack. Good thing the cops don't know I was in town. They'd slap me on the suspect list in a flash, with my history." He chuckled. "The wife? Nah, she doesn't know I came up that weekend. She thought I was in Chicago on business. . . . Sure, I told her I'd quit gambling, but this was the first time since Christmas and I won a couple hundred bucks, so it doesn't count. Besides, she'll never know. I didn't get the car out of storage until today. When I was up before, I hired some local to drive me around for next to nothing."

Which explained why there'd been no vehicle in their reserved parking spot.

"Not until tomorrow," Gunnar said. "She's flying up from Grosse Pointe with some friends. Corporate jet . . . yeah. We have some wedding we have to go to in Charlevoix. . . . That's the one. At Castle Farms. Waste of a Saturday, if you ask me."

I thought about what he'd said about Stan. The

comment about being twenty years too long—was that important? And if so, how was it important?

"Yeah, I'll be picking her up at the airport. Pain in the butt, it'll break up my whole day. Makes me think I should hire that local yokel to drive her around. Get her to show some cleavage and bet it'll be even cheaper."

He laughed. My fists clenched. This guy was really getting on my nerves. Maybe next year I'd chin up to the expense and pay full price for a slip in another spot. It would mess up my student loan repayment schedule, but it might be worth it to move away from this yahoo.

"Some guy I met at the bar," Gunnar said. His voice faded and was replaced by the clinking of ice cubes and the pouring of liquid. "Yeah, he's . . ."

But I couldn't hear what he said. Chilson wasn't exactly a huge metropolis, so odds were good that I knew whom he'd hired to drive him around. That, or I knew someone who knew him.

And when I did track down the driver, a few pointed questions would be in order. Question number one—did you drop Gunnar off at the farmhouse where Stan died? Two. Did you pick him up later? Three. Had he been carrying anything? Say, a rifle?

In the name of trying to keep my head literally down, I got down onto the deck in case Gunnar looked out a window, and crawled on my hands and knees to the very front of my boat's bow. I always docked nose out to take best advantage of the lake view, and the tip of my boat matched the midship region of Olson's vessel. Luckily, that was its galley area and was where Gunnar was pouring himself a drink.

Closer, closer . . . I poked my head outside the railing. Heard snippets of words, but nothing clear. Close, but not close enough. I rose to a crouch and slid outside my boat's railing, put my toes on the deck's edge, grabbed the top railing with one hand, and leaned out as far as I could.

"Nah," Gunnar was saying. "That's the last thing I'm worried about. This guy isn't any mental giant. Says he reads a lot. Comic books, maybe." He laughed.

"Say his name," I murmured. "Say his name."

"Mrr."

There I was, ninety-eight percent of me precariously over the water, and my cat was walking along the top railing as if he'd been doing it all his life.

"Eddie!" I whispered. "Get down! You're going to—"

One of his back paws slipped off the railing. His tail went down, a front paw slipped, and without thinking, without breathing, I released my single-handed hold on the rail and pushed him boatward. He gave a howling yowl and, twisting, fell to the deck feetfirst.

I windmilled for a grip on the rail, on the boat, on anything. Failed completely, and hit the water with a monstrous *splash!*

My feet hit the lake's sandy bottom. I let my legs collapse and pushed myself back up. When I surfaced, spluttering out icky marina water, Gunnar Olson was stomping out onto his deck.

"Who's that? Who's there?"

I flung my hair around to get it out of my eyes. "Just me, Mr. Olson."

"Who?"

"Minnie," I said, treading water. "Your next-door neighbor." I swam toward the end of the floating wooden dock that ran between my boat and Louisa's.

"What were you doing out there?" he demanded. "Hey, don't leave when I'm talking to you! You get back here right now!"

I climbed up the ladder fastened to the dock's end, clambered over my boat's railing, and, dripping, went to look for my cat while Gunnar Olson continued to shout at me. I found Eddie under the chaise lounge where he'd compressed himself into the smallest Eddie-ball I'd ever seen.

"Hey, bud," I said softly. "Come on out. I'm sorry I scared you, but I didn't want you falling in the water, see? You would have gotten all wet like I did and you'd hate that."

"Who are you talking to?" Gunnar shouted. "You were listening to me, weren't you? What did you hear? Invasion of privacy, that's what you were doing. That's against the law, you know. I could call the cops and have you arrested."

Oh, please. I stood tall and faced the man. A difficult task, since his six feet of height combined with the height of his boat's deck made his face roughly fourteen feet above mine, but when there's a will, there's a way.

"Privacy?" I asked. "Expectation of privacy is quite low in a marina, Mr. Olson. And are those open windows I see on your boat? That lowers the expectation even further. Almost like being in a public campground, I'd say."

He paid no attention to me. "The only reason you'd fall off that little tug of yours is if you were outside the railing. And there's no reason for you to do that unless you were trying to listen to my conversation!"

"For your information," I said with exquisite politeness, "I was trying to keep my cat from falling in the water."

Gunnar scoffed. "You don't have a cat. You were intentionally eavesdropping. Admit it."

A low *rrrrrrr* noise came from underneath the chaise.

"What was that?" Gunnar slapped his big, meaty hands on his railing and loomed over me. "No more of your little-girl games. Tell me the truth and there's an outside chance I'll let this episode—"

Eddie hissed, a long indrawn breath that raised the hair on the back of my neck. I'd never heard him make a noise like that. Not ever.

Gunnar drew back. "But you don't have a cat."

"I didn't." I smiled up at him. "But I do now."

"You can't," Gunnar said. "Not a cat, not right next door to me."

Eddie spat. Hissed again. Gave a long, low growl.

I hunched down. "You okay, pal?" Even in the dim light I could see that he was puffed up to half again his normal size. "Shhh, it'll be all right. No one's going to hurt you, okay? Shhh."

Eddie subsided and let me scratch the back of his ears. He came out from under the chair and I scooped him up for a snuggle. With a sigh, I decided the right thing to do was introduce cat to human and human to cat. "Eddie," I said, turning to face my irate neighbor, "this is . . ."

But Gunnar was gone.

When I got out of the shower, my skin was a splotchy pink from the heat. Swimming in Janay Lake was one of my favorite summer things to do, but swimming in yucky marina water had never been on any of my mental lists.

"List of things to avoid, maybe," I told Eddie.

He was lying on the narrow shelf that ran above

the bed. In former summers, I'd decorated the shelf with vases of dried flowers, Petoskey stones, and bits of driftwood. Early on in my life with Eddie I'd discovered that these things are all cat toys. Of course, when you got down to it, everything was a cat toy if a cat chose to make it one.

Eddie stretched out a front paw and rearranged himself on the shelf. He was a teensy bit too wide to fit comfortably, but that didn't seem to bother him. Apparently he didn't care if his back leg hung over the edge. At times it seemed he even liked it.

"Wonder how you're going to like it at the boardinghouse?" I asked him.

He didn't say anything.

"Well, we won't move until October, so—" The floor under my bare feet crinkled. I peeked out from underneath the towel I'd been rubbing my hair with and saw that I was standing on Eddie's papers. Or what had become Eddie's papers after he'd decided to shred my Grice-Hamilton genealogy research. "Done with these, I take it?"

Since he didn't say no, I herded the bits into a pile and dumped them into the wastebasket. "I suppose I should be grateful you didn't mistake those for your litter box."

Eddie gave me a look that was obviously meant to say I should be grateful for a lot more than that.

I slid on undergarments, shorts, and a T-shirt and

chucked him under the chin. "I'm always grateful for your presence, pal, but especially tonight. Did you see Gunnar's face?" I giggled. "Mr. Big Shot Consultant Don't Mess with Me or I'll Sic My Lawyers on You is scared of cats."

Eddie yawned, showing his sharp teeth. I grinned. If Gunnar had seen those, he would have run for his life.

"And that's his style," I said, pulling my fingers through my wet and unruly hair. "Lawyers. If someone gets in his way, he'd hire a battalion of attorneys to fight for him. He wouldn't do any fighting himself." My fingers caught on a snarl and I yelped as I tugged through. "Still, did you hear what he said about Stan?"

Another yawn came from the Eddie quarter. He jumped down, made a beeline to the wastebasket, and started rubbing the side of his face against it.

"Cut that out," I said. "I just filled that. With your mess."

He rubbed harder and the wastebasket tipped over, sending small bits of paper halfway across the carpet.

"Oh, good job." I knelt down to clean it up a second time. Eddie sat tall as an Egyptian cat statue and watched me work. "I'm spending twice as much time cleaning up this research as I did doing it."

"Mrr."

"Yeah, well, thanks for your comments, but the suggestion box is closed. Try again next . . ." My voice tailed off as I looked at the piece of paper in my hand. It was the only piece still intact and it was kind of a flowchart I'd made of names. I'd added circles and arrows and scrawled questions that had led to no answers whatsoever.

I remembered how I'd stared at it, thinking of previous generations and families and long-ago loves and hates and deaths and motivations.

"You know," I said slowly. "Gunnar looks guilty as all get-out, but maybe . . . maybe the reason behind Stan's death isn't a recent reason. Maybe it came from a long time ago. Maybe . . . I wonder . . ." All those sisters. What were the chances that one of them had murder lurking in her heart? Were the police looking into their alibis? Then again, Stan had been seventy. How likely was it that his sisters were still hale and hearty?

"You know what?" I mused out loud. "I need to know more about Stan's past."

My cat catapulted himself onto my shoulder and clonked his forehead against the side of my skull. "Ow! Eddie, jeez, what's with you?" He started purring loud enough to rattle my teeth. I reached up to pet him. "You are such an Eddie."

"Mrr," he said, and purred some more.

# Chapter 14

I rolled out of bed early the next morning and trotted up to the library as the sun was creaking over the hilltops. No one else would be in for at least two hours, so I had a nice slice of time to start my research into Stan's past.

Though many of the old local newspapers had been microfilmed, microfiched, or scanned, many had not. The grant I'd obtained had paid for archiving about half of the library's newspapers. After long debate, we'd decided to start with the most recent issues and work our way backward. It was a decision I now regretted. Deeply.

We'd shoehorned the unarchived papers into the local history room. I turned on the overhead lights, shocking the sleeping books, and went straight to the narrow drawers that held seventy-year-old copies of the *Chilson Gazette*.

There were a lot of newspapers.

A *lot*.

"Well," I said out loud. This project could possibly take longer than I'd hoped it would. But was there any other way to get the information I needed? Any easier way?

I couldn't think of one. So I scraped out a chair, sat down, and got to work.

• • •

In the end, it didn't take as long as I thought it might. I knew the year Stan was born, so all I had to do was find the page of the newspaper where the births were typically printed and hunt through the papers until I found the right announcement.

"Stanley Warren Larabee," it read, "born at home to Silas and Belinda Larabee. Seven pounds, ten ounces. Mother, infant, and his six older sisters are doing well."

"Onward and upward," I said, and put that newspaper away. Next was high school. Back in Stan's day, Chilson was the location of the only high school in the county. The library didn't have a complete set of old yearbooks, so the paper was the next best source. I had no idea if Stan had played any sports, been a member of any clubs, or excelled at anything that might have been considered newsworthy fifty-odd years ago, but I had to look. Who knew what I'd find?

What I found, after an hour and a half, was nothing. Maybe Stan had been too busy on the family farm. Maybe he didn't care about sports, maybe he hadn't wanted to join the debate club. Maybe—

"Oh, my," I breathed. "My, my, my." I'd found the edition of the newspaper with pictures of the graduating seniors from Chilson High School. There, in black and white and gray, was a photo of a young Stanley W. Larabee. I could see no resemblance between the Stan I'd known and this young man, but there was his name, and there was the picture right above it. And since there were only thirty-seven kids graduating, it wasn't likely that the paper had gotten the names mixed up.

"Wow," I said. "Stan was *gorgeous*." Saying the words out loud made me cringe. Somehow, admiring the youthful looks of a murdered elderly man felt downright weird. And a little creepy, to boot.

For a moment, I wondered if I was being disrespectful. I couldn't see it, but maybe it was another moral question for my mother. One of these days I should write them all down and actually ask her.

Idly, I paged through a few more editions. What I'd hoped for hadn't materialized. I'd hoped to find evidence of sport- or activity-oriented friendships, hoped that I could find some of the friends, hoped to ask a few questions that would lead me to something that would lead me to—

And there it was. Black and white and no gray, this time, because it was a short text-only announcement. Extremely short. Like one sentence short.

"Marriage license to Stanley W. Larabee, 18, and Audry M. Noss, 17."

Audry. That was the name of the woman in the bookmobile, the one who'd been helping out at

Maple View. Her name had been Audry. And how many Audrys roughly seventy years old could there be in Tonedagana County? What were the odds that my Audry and Stan's were the same?

I didn't know, but I was going to find out.

"Here's a nice table for you two," the hostess said, grinning from ear to ear. "Here are your menus and this is the wine list." She aimed the latter in Tucker's direction. "The wine steward will be with you in just a moment." She winked at me broadly and left.

I sighed. "This may not have been a good idea."

"No?" Tucker picked up the wine list but didn't open it. "I've wanted to eat here ever since I moved up north. Everyone says it's great." He studied me. "Have you had a bad experience here? Because we don't have to stay. We can—" He stopped and looked up. "Hello," he said politely.

"Good evening," Kristen said, grinning wide. "My name is Kristen and I'll be your server tonight."

I stared at her. "You will not."

She opened my menu and slid it in front of me. "I can think of nothing I'd like to do more than help you plan your dinner."

"You are an evil woman," I muttered.

"And you, sir?" she asked, turning to Tucker. "Do you have any questions about the menu?"

"Not the menu, no." He looked from Kristen to me, then back again. "But I'm getting the impression there's something going on here that I don't know about."

Kristen's smile went even wider. "Our menu has a considerable depth—it's one of our trade-marks."

"Something in here is deep," I said. "Not sure it's the menu."

Kristen batted her eyes at me. "Let me treat you to an amuse-bouche. On the house. The smallest of quiches with pesto, cheese, and sun-dried tomatoes. Yes?" She beamed. "Of course, yes. I'll be back directly with your wine."

Tucker frowned after her. "But we didn't order any wine."

I rarely did, not at Kristen's restaurant. The day she'd caught me drinking a glass of white zinfandel had been a memorable one. She hadn't let me near her wine list since.

"Um," I said. "I should probably tell you that—"

"Hey, Minnie!" Josh appeared, escorting a young woman over to our table. "This is Megan."

Well, well, well. So after months of soulful sighs, Josh had finally taken Holly's and my advice and found the courage to ask Megan out. Wonders never did cease. "Nice to meet you," I said to the girl, and introduced Tucker. Megan's

263

freckles and open countenance made her look cheerful and warmhearted. I hoped looks didn't deceive and that she wouldn't break Josh's heart.

"Josh says you drive the bookmobile," Megan said, her tone rising at the end, making it sound like a question. "That must be like the coolest job ever!"

I spared Tucker a glance. While I'd told him I was a librarian, I hadn't gone into detail. He looked almost as interested as Megan. "Two or three days a week," I said. "We don't have the staffing to do more than that."

She was starting to ask more bookmobile questions when Kristen came back with our wine. With a professional expertise, Kristen shooed Josh and Megan off to their table and presented us with the wine she'd chosen.

"Malbec from the Chateau Chantal label. You'll enjoy it." She popped the cork and poured a swallow for Tucker. He sniffed, tasted, and got a happy look on his face.

"As I said"—Kristen filled our glasses to the appropriate height—"you'll enjoy it. As to your dinner selection, Miss Hamilton here is going to have a simple yet elegant meal of filet mignon, medium rare, with roasted red-skin potatoes and fresh young carrots steamed long enough to be tender yet cooked lightly enough to retain a slight bit of crispness. For you, sir, I'd like to suggest the same. Yes? Yes. Your amuse-bouche is being prepared this very moment by Chef Larry. Enjoy your wine." She wafted off.

Tucker took another sip of wine and his slightly furrowed brow smoothed. "Is this kind of service typical?" he asked. "I know things are different up here, but even so . . ." He looked at me expectantly.

"Well," I said, "this restaurant in particular is—"

"Minnie, is that you?" boomed a male voice.

I closed my eyes.

*Quincy,* I thought. *Please let him be with Paulette.* If he wasn't, if he was still infatuated with the much-too-young Dena, Aunt Frances's summer plans were not in a good place. Aunt Frances was already upset enough over Stan. She didn't need matchmaking guilt piled on top of that.

"It is you!" Quincy said. "Didn't you hear me calling? Hey, you all right?"

I opened my eyes. "Hey, Quincy. How are you?" My gaze drifted to his companion. Not Paulette. I smiled. "Hi, Zofia." I made the introductions.

"Lovely, lovely." Zofia's flowing dress billowed as she turned. "Our table's over there, Quince. Nice meeting you, Tucker. Come *on,* Quincy." She tugged on his arm so hard that he almost lost his balance.

Tucker looked at me. "Do you know everybody in this town?"

"I've only been here three years," I said. "That's not nearly long enough to—"

"Good evening, Minnie," Mr. Goodwin said, his cane tapping as he drew near. "Are you having a nice dinner?"

The entire meal went like that. Every time Tucker and I would start a typical first-date conversation—where did you grow up, where did you go to school, sisters, brothers, do you ski/bicycle/hunt/kayak/run?—someone would pause at our table to talk to me or Kristen or Chef Larry would barge in to serve more courses.

The only things I learned about Tucker were that he didn't have any allergies and that he'd never been to the Grand Canyon. And I'd only learned that because Kristen asked about allergies and because a passing Louisa and Ted Axford happened to mention their spring trip to Arizona.

"I knew this was a bad idea," I muttered as the restaurant's door shut behind us and we started walking to the marina.

"What's that?" Tucker asked.

"Sorry. Nothing. It's just—"

"Yo! Minster!" Mitchell Koyne called through the open passenger window of his pickup. "Your car break down? You guys want a ride or something?"

"Thanks," I said, waving, "but we're good. Nice night for a walk."

"Sure?" He revved the truck's engine. "I can get you home in a flash."

"Thanks, anyway."

Mitchell roared away and I thought I heard Tucker make an odd noise.

"What's that?" I asked. "Did you say something?"

"No, it's just—"

"On your left," a male voice called. "Oh, hey, Minnie." Cookie Tom, riding past on his bicycle, braked to a squeaking stop. "I've been thinking, if you want cookies for the bookmobile, give me a call and we'll set something up. Discount rate, and you can come to the back door and not have to stand in line."

"Tom," I said, "you are the love of my life."

"Ah, that's what they all say." He waved and was off.

"So," Tucker said. "Your bookmobile. It's a new addition to the library?"

"Practically brand-new. It's only—"

One of the hardworking Friends of the Library waved at me from the other side of the street. "Minnie, hey, glad I caught you. Got a second? Did I hear that you've convinced Caroline Grice to do an art show? However did you do that?"

Almost an hour later, we'd finished walking the route that usually took me fifteen minutes. Between various Friends, library patrons, coworkers, business owners, and marina rats, I was pretty sure we'd been stopped by everyone I knew. As a first date, the evening was a complete bust. Any element of romance that managed to bloom had been squashed within seconds. I would never find someone to date in this town. There were mail-order brides; maybe I could find a mailorder husband.

We came to a slow stop at the dock that ran out to my boat. "Would you like to come in?" I asked without much hope.

"That would be nice," he said, "but I have to be in the ER early tomorrow morning."

"Oh. Sure. I understand."

We stood there, not talking. Boats moved gently in the water, straining against the lines that held them in place. Waves lapped, distant voices murmured, and a boat far out on Janay Lake puttered past. All peaceful, calming nighttime noises, all summer sounds that I loved, but tonight I hardly heard them at all.

A handshake. I'd be lucky to get a handshake, let alone a peck on the cheek. I was doomed to die alone.

I took a deep breath. "Look—"

"Minnie." Tucker moved close. Took both of my hands. Rubbed the backs of them with his thumbs. "There's just one thing I want to do right now."

Go back in time and change his mind about asking me out, probably.

Instead, he leaned down. "Minnie," he whispered. "Look at me."

The kiss was gentle and tender and soft and warm, everything you could want in a first kiss. Except for one thing.

"Hey, Minnie-Ha-Ha!"

We broke apart as Chris Ballou shouted out a second time. He was on his little Boston Whaler, coming in after an evening's fishing. "Hey, you two aren't doing anything I wouldn't do, are you? Hah! Say, Min, I got an idea on how to fix your electricals. You know, that problem you been having with your bilge? Tell Rafe to stop by."

There it was again, the odd noise Tucker had made when we were walking back to the marina. I looked more carefully this time. "You're laughing," I said in surprise.

"Of course I am." He got the words out between what were now obviously bursts of uncontrollable laughter. "Your bilge? Of all the ways to ruin a kiss, that's got to be in the top ten."

The funny side of the evening finally hit me. I grinned. "Maybe even the top five."

"Next time," Tucker said, "let's go somewhere out of town."

His good-bye kiss was the classic peck on the cheek, but inside my heart was singing. There was going to be a next time!

The next morning I made a quick phone call to Gayle Joliffe of Maple View AFC. Out of thin air I conjured up a story about a book title that her assistant Audry and I had been trying to remember. I told Gayle I'd found the book, and if I had Audry's last name, which I'd been told but couldn't remember, I could look her up and give her a call.

"Oh, honey, you don't need to go to all that trouble." Gayle rattled off her phone number.

I hung up, thinking that the impossible had happened. Someone had been too helpful. What I really wanted was Audry's last name. With that, I could do some library research magic and find out if this Audry and Stan's Audry were the same person. But all I had was a first name and a phone number.

Of course, I had a phone number. And a computer with multiple search engines.

Minutes later, I had Audry's last name (Brant), her address (17981 Valley Road), a map to her house, and enough information about her to confirm that, yes, she'd been married to Stan. Privacy? What was that?

I thought about what to do next as I finalized the July employee schedule, thought about it at lunch when I went out for a walk with Holly, thought about it all afternoon while I staffed the research desk, and thought about it while we ate dinner. "We" being Eddie, who was eating cat food, and me, who was eating take-out sesame chicken.

"What do you think?" I asked Eddie.

Since his face was in his food bowl, he paid no attention to the question.

I waited until he sat down and was licking his paw and swiping it across his face. "So, what do you think? Go talk to her? Or do I just ask around?"

Eddie picked up his head, gave me a look, then went back to concentrating on his cleaning efforts.

"Yeah," I agreed. "Asking around could take forever. The fastest way is just talk to her, I suppose. A few questions is all I have, see if she knows anything about the family feud that Aunt Frances talked about. Do you think I should call, or should I drive out there?"

Eddie put his right front paw down and picked up his left one so he could wash the other side of his face. Eddie the Clean.

"You're no help," I muttered.

"Mrrr."

Since the evening had three hours of daylight left to it, I decided to take a drive out to Audry's house. And her husband's, I supposed, since she wasn't using Larabee or her maiden name.

The thought of a husband slowed me down in my walk to the car. Maybe he was a huge hulking man who won arm-wrestling contests all over the country. Or maybe he was one of those militia guys and had high gates circling the property, owned lots of guns, and was prepared to shoot trespassers on sight.

"Don't be stupid," I told myself. If I saw any signs of that, I'd drive by, that's all. Same if there were big growling dogs or chickens. Large groups of chickens scared the snot out of me, and by large groups I meant any number more than zero. They'd peck me to death, given half a chance, I just knew it.

By the time I turned onto Valley Road, I'd imagined Audry's house as a ramshackle 1960s ranch with aluminum siding that had needed replacing for twenty years and a roof that was rough with age and stained with pine needles. There'd be no porch, just concrete steps, and the garage would be so crowded with junk that the cars—a rusted pickup with bullet holes in the side and an ancient Oldsmobile that didn't run most of the time—would be parked outside.

Which was why I drove right past Audry's house. I was so intent on finding the horrible picture I'd imagined out of absolutely nothing that it wasn't until I saw the mailbox numbers were in the 15000s that I stopped and turned around.

House number 17981 was far from a broken-down ranch. It was an old farmhouse with a Centennial Farm sign out front. The roof was new and white trim set off the warm clapboard siding's yellow paint. The wide porch that ran across the front of the house held a set of wicker furniture, swing included, with flowered cushions. The window boxes were filled with happy red geraniums that bobbed in the light breeze. And there, in the front yard, was Audry on her knees, weeding an exuberant flower bed.

Since there was no sign of a hulking husband, firearms, or any other sort of weapon, I pulled into the driveway and got out of the car.

Audry stood, putting her hands to the small of her back and wincing. "It's the bookmobile girl," she said, smiling. "What brings you out my way?"

"Stan Larabee," I said simply, and watched her smile change to wariness. "Once upon a time," I went on, "you were married to him. If you don't mind, I'd like to ask you a few questions."

"Why?" she asked.

I saw a shadow of stubbornness starting to form on her face, but I also saw what looked like a question. And something that might have been sorrow.

"He was my friend," I finally said.

She looked at me the same way I'd looked at her. Then, "Come on up."

We sat on the front porch, glasses of lemonade in our hands, drinking in the view. This part of Michigan had been carved out by glaciers ten thousand years ago. Ice a mile thick had scoured the land underneath, then retreated, leaving high hills running north and south with valleys and lakes between. Audry's house was nestled in the flat of one of those valleys, looking north across the valley's expanse and up the length of the hills.

I sat there, enjoying the view, while Audry assembled lemonade and cookies. She set a tray on the small table between the two cushioned porch chairs. "Here we go. Yes, please go ahead and pour." She settled into the empty chair and took the filled glass I offered. "So, you know about my first marriage. Odd that a stranger should know when everyone else has forgotten. Bill and I have been married for so long I'd bet even my brothers don't remember I was married before. How did you find out?"

In a few short sentences I'd told her about my hunch that Stan's death had to do with his past, and my searching into the newspaper archive. She nodded, then asked, "You say you were Stan's friend? How did that come about?"

I explained about the budget situation at the library, the closings of the small outlying libraries, the idea of the bookmobile as a solution, then Stan's donation and his wish to be involved with the planning and purchase of the bookmobile.

She settled back, the white wicker creaking about her. "Sounds like Stan. He always had to be in the thick of things."

That, I knew. What I didn't know was anything about his past. "I hear there was some sort of feud between Stan and his sisters. Do you know anything about that?"

Audry gave me a measuring look.

"It's not idle curiosity," I said quickly. "It's just . . . Stan never mentioned his sisters. I met with him almost every day for nearly a year and I didn't know anything about his six sisters and the nieces and nephews he must have. The great-nieces and great-nephews, there must be lots more of those. He didn't have any pictures of them on his desk; he never talked about them at all."

Audry gave a deep sigh and looked out at the hills. "Ancient history," she said heavily. "What can it matter now?"

I let the silence sit a little, then said, "Maybe it's the reason he was killed."

"After more than fifty years?" She shook her head. "I can see one of his sisters taking a frying pan to him back then, but now? They're too old for that kind of thing, the ones who are left. We're all too old."

"Are you sure?" I asked quietly. "The police haven't arrested anyone for Stan's murder. Do you want to take even the smallest chance of letting his killer go free?"

"Of course not."

"Then . . . tell me."

She sighed and kept her gaze on the hills.

I waited. Waited some more.

The ice cubes in the lemonade had melted to tiny bits before she started to talk. "Back then," she said, "no one understood how ambitious Stan was. He'd talk on and on about making pots of money, but everybody laughed at him. He was a farm kid, how was he ever going to make the money to buy all those things he wanted? No, he was going to be a farmer, just like his dad and grandpa before. That was the future everybody saw for him."

"But it wasn't the future he wanted," I said.

"He wanted money," she said flatly. "He wanted to be lord and master of the manor. He wanted every single person who'd laughed at him in high school for smelling like manure to come crawling to him for money and then he'd turn them down and laugh in their faces."

I blinked. That didn't sound like the Stan I'd known. And yet . . . and yet . . . he turned down almost everyone who'd come to him for a loan. He'd bought and renovated that huge house up in the hills, its windows showing little but lake and property that he owned. Lord and master.

"Do you know how he got started as a developer?" I asked.

Audry gave a smile, but it wasn't a pretty one. "Unfortunately, yes."

I swallowed. I'd liked Stan. I didn't want to learn things about him that weren't nice; I wanted to remember him as my exuberant friend who tried hard to get good things done. "What do you mean?"

"Stan's mother died when he was in grade school, complications from another pregnancy if you can believe it. His dad died the year he graduated high school." She looked pensive. "In April, during maple syrup season. He had a heart attack out in the sugar bush. Stan was the one to find him."

"That must have been hard."

She gave me a sardonic look. "You'd think, wouldn't you? By the next spring, Stan had sweet-talked his sisters out of their share of the farm, got it put in his name only, and sold it to a man he'd found from downstate who had big dreams about turning the property into some kind of ski resort. Stan took off for Florida with the money and his sisters never talked to him again."

My jaw went slack. "Stan stole the family farm from his sisters?"

"That's not the way he looked at it. He said he'd pay them back. With interest."

"Did he?"

"Eventually." She made a gesture that suggested frustration, sadness, and tolerance. "He always needed more money, Stan did. Another property he needed to buy, another building with great potential, another whatever. By the time he got around to repaying his sisters, he had buckets of money to spare, but the damage was permanent. They took the money, of course," she said with a twisted smile, "but they wouldn't talk to him. Not even after he bought them houses and who knows what else."

Just as Caroline had said. "Did you go with Stan to Florida?"

Her merry peal of laughter filled the porch. "No, I didn't go to Florida. Stan was a good-looking son of a gun, but I got over that two weeks into the marriage. And once he sold the farm? I was done. Smartest thing I ever did was divorce that man and find my Bill."

"How did Stan take your divorcing him?"

She snorted. "The way I heard it, he found a second wife before he'd unpacked his suitcase down there in Florida. If a man gets money, he can get a wife, easy enough."

"You weren't interested in his money?"

She gestured to the stupendous view. "I've woken up to this every day for almost fifty years. How could I get any richer? And Stan came back to this, in the end. Who's to say which one of us was more successful?"

I looked at the green hills and the arching blue sky above, felt the peace and the calm, breathed in the clean air, heard nothing except birds and the rustle of leaves on the trees. Who indeed?

"So," I said, "the feud started when Stan sold the family farm?"

"I wouldn't call it a feud, really." Audry considered her lemonade. "More of an 'us against Stan' attitude. His sisters all hated him and taught their children to hate him."

"And unto the next generation?"

"I imagine." She sighed.

Up until that point, I hadn't considered her as old, but she suddenly looked every inch of her seventy years. I knew I should leave, but there were questions I needed to ask. "Are his sisters still alive?"

"Goodness." Audry squinted at the horizon. "Four of them moved either downstate or out of state years ago. The other two . . . ? I really have no idea. One moved to Petoskey, the other down to Traverse City."

I studied her, wondering if she truly didn't know or if she was protecting a friend. "Do you know anything about Stan's nieces and nephews? The great-nieces and nephews? Do any of them live in Chilson?"

She gave a small shrug. "I know almost nothing about that group. About all I know is that whole family tended toward having lots of children, and they liked naming the children all with the same first letter. Don't ask me why, it's just what they did."

I blinked. "You mean all the sisters had names starting with *S*?"

"Sarah, Shirley, Stella, Sadie, Sylvia, and Sophie," Audry recited, smiling faintly.

"There's a niece named Gwen," I said, remembering the friend of Aunt Frances.

"One of Sarah's, as I recall. She had boys named Gordon and Gerard. And one of them used names that started with *K*. Kevin, Kyle, Karla, and Kendra." She frowned. "Or was that the next generation down?"

As she'd said, lots of children, all of whom turned a year older every twelve months. Was this the definition of multiplicity? I found it hard enough to keep track of the ages of my brother's children, and there were only three of them.

"But there is one thing that's been bothering me," Audry said slowly.

The weight she was giving to the words made the insides of my wrists tingle. "What's that?"

"The farmhouse where you found him? That was where he and his sisters grew up."

# Chapter 15

I left Audry's house with one thought and one thought only: Find the closest Tonedagana County sheriff's detective.

I drove straight to Chilson and parked in the empty sheriff's office lot. It took a little bit of doing, but I eventually convinced the deputy on duty that tracking down either Detective Devereaux or Inwood would be in everyone's best interest.

He hung up the phone and looked at me with a schooled expression of blankness. "Detective Inwood was at the grocery store. He said he'll stop by in about five minutes."

"Inwood. He's the short round one, right?"

The deputy actually laughed. "Nope. Devereaux is the short, round one. He looks like the letter *D*, see? And Hal Inwood is the tall, skinny one. He looks like the letter *I*."

Clouds parted and the light shone down. "That's brilliant," I said sincerely.

He waved me off to a plastic chair, but he was smiling as he did so, and a few minutes later, Detective Inwood walked in. "Ms. Hamilton. What can I do for you?"

I stood, but didn't move much closer. He was too tall (like the letter *I*) to make a face-to-face talk much of a reality. "Sorry to bother you on a Friday night," I said, "but I just found out something."

"Yeah, what's that?" He put an angular elbow on the front counter.

"Well, it's a couple of somethings, actually." I gave him a quick summary of the origin of Stan's fortune. "His sisters were furious when he sold the farm, I was told."

"Who told you about this?" While Inwood's pose remained casual, the expression on his face was sharp.

"Oh. Well." I mentally fast-forwarded through the next part of the conversation and decided it was best to tell the truth now rather than have it dragged out of me later. "Audry Brant. She was Stan's first wife."

Inwood reached into his pants pocket and pulled out a small pad of paper. "His first wife, you say."

I winced. Audry was going to get a police visit and it was all my fault. *Sorry about that,* I told her silently. "She had no reason to kill him, though. They were divorced about fifty years ago. And anyway, that's not an important something."

Inwood used the pencil he'd pulled out of the memo pad's spiral binding to dot a period. "What is?"

"The farmhouse where Stan was killed? That was where Stan grew up. That was the farm he sold out from under his sisters."

"Now that is a something." Detective Inwood nodded, a faint smile lurking around the corners of his mouth. "Ms. Brant give you that bit of information?"

"Yes, so I was wondering. Have you looked at Stan's sisters? I mean, with him being killed at their old farm, it makes you think there's a connection, right? They were all older than Stan, but it doesn't take much strength to pull a trigger."

But the detective was shaking his head. "All six sisters are accounted for, either passed away or moved out of state decades ago."

"Oh." I deflated. "The ones still alive, they have alibis? I mean, I'm sure you checked, but . . ."

"Of the three," he said, "two are in nursing homes. The other is living in Arizona, and according to the golf course manager, she hasn't missed her daily game of golf since she moved there fifteen years ago."

"What about their children? I've heard the sisters all had a lot of kids. And the kids probably all had kids. Have all of them been checked out?"

The detective stuffed his memo pad back into his pocket. "The six sisters had twenty-three children. The twenty-three of them have had a total of seventy-two offspring. So, we're working on it, Ms. Hamilton. Plus, there are other—" He stopped. Gave me a short, assessing look. "We're investigating all avenues," he said. "In addition to the family members, Stan Larabee had many friends and business associates across the country. A thorough investigation takes time."

I nodded my understanding. And I did understand, but I was also pretty sure I knew what that look of assessment had meant—that he'd remembered whom I worked with.

They were still considering Holly a suspect.

Saturday's breakfast of omelets made to order was delicious, but since I was scheduled to work that morning, I didn't have time to get Aunt Frances off into a cozy corner for a chat. I wanted to tell her about Audry and Stan's sisters and the reason behind the feud, but it would have to wait until the next day.

Sunday morning I decided to stop at the farmers' market and see if I could find some raspberries to take up to Aunt Frances. While I wasn't bearing bad news, not exactly, hearing the slightly sordid tale might be easier if the first raspberries of the season were involved.

Even at eight in the morning, the waterfront market was crowded. White tents over the bright colors of produce against the blue of Janay Lake was a feast for the eyes long before the food itself would be a feast for the tummy. I dawdled at the wide selection of lettuces—most of which I couldn't put a name to, other than lettuce—and so heard Gunnar Olson before I saw him.

"Dear," he said in a strained tone, "I'm getting hungry."

I looked up and saw his wife ignoring him completely. A bunch of radishes were dangling from her hand. "Now," she said to the woman behind the table, "these are organic, right? How organic are they?"

The two women started what was clearly going to be a long conversation about fertilizer and manure and irrigation. Gunnar heaved a huge sigh.

Mrs. Olson, who must have a first name, though she had never made it known to me, glanced my way. "Hello, Minnie, how was your winter? Gunnar, catch up with Minnie a moment, I need to learn more about these radishes." She turned back to her conversation, leaving me and Gunnar standing face-to-face. My face to his collarbone.

What I needed was a stroke of brilliance in how to deal with a social situation in which one of the parties was a potential murderer. None came. Then again . . .

I put on a polite smile. "When did your wife get into town?"

"Couple of days ago. My dear wife and I had a wedding to attend yesterday," Gunnar said, booming his voice across the two feet that separated us. The dear wife shot him a look. He put on a smile and waved his fingers at her.

"You know," Gunnar said, turning back to me,

"I've been thinking about the importance of libraries in small towns. What would you think about a donation to the Chilson District Library?"

My eyes thinned to the merest of slits. Was this a bribe? My jaw went forward and my chin went up. "What I want is the truth," I said quietly. A donation would be nice, naturally, but I wasn't going to tell him that.

He sucked in a breath through his teeth. My gaze locked on his. There was no way I was going to be the first one to blink, not if my eyeballs dried up and fell out of my head.

Gunnar looked away. "Half an hour," he muttered. "The Round Table."

"Fifteen minutes," I said.

"Half an hour." His ruddy skin colored. "Have to help the wife carry the groceries to the boat."

Minnie: one point. Mrs. Olson: one point. Mr. Olson: a big fat zero. In victory, grace. I nodded. "Half an hour."

To hang on to my advantage over Gunnar, I headed for the Round Table straightaway. Let him see me with the remains of my breakfast scattered all over the table; let him think he was late. I could feel my mother shaking her head and saying, "Minerva, aren't you being a little petty? Take the high road, you'll feel better about yourself."

At the front door, I hesitated. Maybe she was

right. Maybe I shouldn't be messing around like this. Maybe I should just—

"Nah," I said out loud, and went inside.

The Round Table was a diner, Up North style. Walls of wide pine paneling, ceiling of faded acoustic tile. The only thing new in the last twenty years was the flooring, and that was because the regular customers had signed a petition to replace the worn linoleum that had been laid down in 1952.

Vinyl-covered booths lined the walls and tables filled the middle. Small square tables, with the exception of the one round table in the back. This was the table where the elder men of the town congregated on weekday mornings. Opinions were aired, politicians dissected, and decisions were made, whether or not any facts were taken into account.

The whole scenario irritated me, but since it was Sunday, the table was empty. I sat in a booth, triangulating myself into a position equidistant from a couple with small children and a man in the back booth hunched over a laptop.

The waitress, Sabrina, brought me a mug of coffee and a glass of ice water without me saying a word. "Here you go, hon. Cinnamon apple pancakes with sausage links."

I grinned. "You're amazing. I haven't had time to come here since early April. How do you remember this stuff?"

"Here's your cream." She took three tiny plastic cups from her apron pocket and set them on the tabletop. The pencil behind her ear got pulled out, was used to scribble down my order, then pushed back into her bun of long graying hair. "How do I remember? Easy." She winked. "I'm a professional." She headed off to the kitchen and I was left with my own company.

The direness of the situation suddenly struck me. All by myself for half an hour, and I had no book. I did have my cell phone and a book app, but since I couldn't remember the last time I'd charged the battery, I'd probably get all of five minutes of reading before the thing died on me.

So, no book. Also no newspaper, and no magazine. I started to get up to grab a booklet of real estate listings from the stack next to the cash register when I recognized the man with the laptop.

Bill D'Arcy.

Mr. I-Don't-Have-a-Word-to-Say D'Arcy. Mr. Suspect-Through-Sulkiness D'Arcy.

I sat back down, sipped my coffee, and studied him. He didn't seem to be using the keyboard or touch pad often, but I could tell by his arm movements that he was using one of them regularly. I counted, and every thirty seconds he made another click.

Hmm. Could he be reading? Who did that much reading on a computer? I rubbed at my eyes.

"Here you go, Minnie." Sabrina put my breakfast in front of me. "Can I get you anything else?"

"Actually, do you have a minute? There's something I want to ask you."

"Important, huh? Hang on a sec." She checked on the other tables, got a "No, thanks," from both, and came back to slide into the opposite side of my booth. "Okay, lay it on me. Ask me anything except the recipe for those pancakes, because I'm not telling. And eat up. No sense in good food going cold."

Obediently, I forked into a pancake. With the bite hanging off the tines, I leaned forward and quietly asked, "What do you know about Bill D'Arcy?" I nodded in his general direction.

She glanced over her shoulder. "Not a blessed thing. That man hasn't the foggiest notion of how to make small talk."

"No idea where he's from, why he came up here, anything?"

"Only thing I know about him is he orders whatever the special is every morning, drinks three pots of coffee, most always stays through lunch, orders the lunch special, and stays until we close at three. He stares at his computer the whole time. Tips real good, though," she said reflectively. "Of course, he'd better, hogging a table like that."

"He comes here every day?"

"The most regular customer we have."

We gawked at the rut-bound Mr. D'Arcy.

"But I take it back," Sabrina said, the booth's vinyl squeaking at she turned back to face me. "There was one day he wasn't here at all. About three weeks ago, I'd guess." She hummed a tune. "Must have been a Friday, because the breakfast special was the Western omelet, that's his favorite, and he wasn't here. Cookie in there"—she tipped her head to the kitchen—"figured he must have died, but the next day he was back again, just like normal."

"Did he say where he'd been?" I asked.

"Eat," she commanded. It wasn't until I was chewing that she answered my question. "He didn't say word one about where he'd been. Just plopped himself down in that booth like he'd never been gone and didn't unglue his eyes from that stupid computer for hours. Look at him. He'll reach for his coffee without even looking. Does the same thing with food."

But I wasn't thinking about Mr. D'Arcy's eating habits. "The Friday he was gone," I said slowly. "Was that the day Stan Larabee was killed?"

She drummed her short fingernails on the table. "You know, I think it was."

I suddenly felt a large, solid presence next to the table. We looked up and saw a glowering Gunnar Olson looming above. "You must need to talk to Minnie," Sabrina said, sliding out of the booth. "What can I get you, Gunnie?"

"Coffee," he growled, dropping into the seat she'd vacated. "And make it quick."

"Keep your pants on." She leaned over and whispered to me, "Give me the high sign if you need help with this guy."

Gunnie? "Thanks, but I'm good."

We sat there, listening to the occasional click of Bill D'Arcy's keyboard, listening to the parents struggle to keep their toddlers in line. I listened to myself chew and swallow. Gunnar sat with his arms folded and stared out the front window.

When Sabrina returned with a carafe of coffee and a mug, she asked, "Anything else?" Gunnar sipped his coffee and glared at me. I said, "No, thanks, Sabrina."

Gunnar waited until she was out of earshot before he pushed his coffee aside and leaned forward, his arms spread wide on the table, the better to intimidate me with. But that kind of domination attempt didn't work on me. I wasn't even five feet tall. Everyone was bigger than I was. It was something I was accustomed to and knew how to ignore.

"What did you hear?" he asked. "The other night, when you were eavesdropping. How much did you hear?"

I wanted to say, "Pretty much all of it," but there was a reasonable chance that the man sitting across from me was a killer. What I needed was to be smart, and to be smart in such a clever way that he didn't realize I was outsmarting him.

"I told you the truth. I fell in the water because I was trying to keep my cat from falling in."

"Cats don't fall," he said flatly.

"And cats don't like bread, either, but Eddie loves the stuff."

"You named your cat Eddie?"

I shrugged.

For some reason, the idea of a cat called Eddie amused him. He snorted out a laugh. "Eddie. What a stupid name for a cat." He snorted again, then leaned low across the table. "I didn't kill Stan Larabee," he said quietly.

I cut my cold sausage into bite-sized pieces. Speared one piece. "Okay." I popped the bite into my mouth.

"Nothing wrong with a nice grudge between former business partners, is there? But I didn't kill him."

Since I was chewing, I held out a hand, palm up, and made a tell-me-more gesture with my fingers.

His nostrils flared as he breathed in and out, in and out. "Twenty years ago, when I was down in Florida for a business conference, a mutual friend introduced me to Larabee. He thought it was funny that I summered where Larabee had grown up. Real funny," he said, making fists with his hands. "I'm laughing hard enough to hurt myself."

I swallowed. "So, twenty years ago . . ."

"Yeah. Back then life was good for buying

property in Florida, putting in some roads, slapping up modulars, and making a killing. Larabee said he'd come across this sweet property—the owner needed cash and was selling it for a song. Larabee said he was thinking about getting out of the development business, but if I wanted in, we could make a limited liability corporation, each put in half, each get half the profits." His face was turning a deep shade of red.

"I take it things didn't go like that?"

"Stan Larabee was a thief," Gunnar said stonily. "We bought the property, laid out thousands for the engineering, laid out tens of thousands for the infrastructure—then when time came to sell lots, we got nothing but rumors of hidden limestone sinkholes about to cave in, toxic waste dumps, and contaminated water. Didn't matter what we said, the word was out. Couldn't sell a single lot."

"Were there any sinkholes?"

"No!" he shouted, his face now almost purple. "We had geological reports up the wazoo. We had hazardous-materials guys declare the site clean. We had the health department sign off that the water was well within tolerances. It was fine!"

I hoped he wasn't prone to heart attacks. "Then why the rumors?"

"Stan Larabee was behind it all." Gunnar spoke through gritted teeth. "He said he was sorry it was turning out this way, said he'd buy back my share."

"That doesn't sound so bad."

"Buy back my share for pennies on the dollar. Pennies!" His fist hit the table so hard even Bill D'Arcy looked up. "And you know what happened? The minute Larabee bought the property off me, the rumors disappeared. Vanished." He flicked his fingers out in a magician-style move. "In the end he makes a bundle with barely more than half the investment he should have put into it. And what do I get? Nothing. Nothing!"

"Did you talk to an attorney?"

"What, you think I'm stupid? Of course I did. He said he'd be glad to take my money, but it'd be a waste. If Larabee did start all those rumors, it'd be a job and a half to prove it and even if I won, I'd probably end up spending more in lawyer fees than I'd recover." He grabbed his coffee mug and took a hefty slug. "Still, I thought about it. Thought about it hard."

I eyed him. "All that sounds like an excellent motive for murder."

He stared back. "I have more money than I know what to do with. I hate to lose, is all. Sure, I was madder than a wet snake over the deal, but not mad enough to kill him. And two things. One, this was over and done with years ago. Two, I didn't have a car that weekend. What was I going to do, hire Koyne to drive me on a murder gig?"

I blinked. "Mitchell Koyne?"

"Yeah, that's him."

Mitchell kept turning up in the oddest of places. Mr. Koyne and I were going to have to have a chat. Soon.

I laid my knife and fork on the side of my plate. Added my wadded-up napkin to the pile and pushed it toward the edge of the table. Gunnar Olson had a nasty temper and he was a misogynist and a bully, but I wasn't sure he was a murderer. Of course, I wasn't sure I'd recognize a killer if I met one. They didn't tend to wear labels.

"Say," he said, "you didn't hear what I said about my little spin at the casino, did you? No reason to tell the wife." He tried a chuckle. "I mean, what she doesn't know won't hurt her. Besides, she's the worrying kind, and I don't want her worried about nothing."

If his grip on the handle of the coffee mug hadn't been white-knuckled and if his other hand hadn't been trembling, I might have believed him. But that, on top of his rapidly blinking eyes and his fast, short breaths . . . no. I didn't believe a word of it.

"You know," I said, "your wife looks like a cat person. How much are you two going to be up this summer? Do you think she'd like to take care of Eddie when I go on vacation? He'd probably like to stay on that big boat of yours."

The red on Gunnar's face paled to gray. "Is that a threat?" he asked hoarsely.

"Just thinking out loud." I slid out of the booth. "Just thinking out loud."

"Hey, when's your vacation?"

The completely correct answer would be that I didn't have one planned. "Later," I said, giving him a wide smile. "I'll let you know." I handed a ten-dollar bill to Sabrina, and left.

I spent Sunday afternoon with Aunt Frances, sorting through emotions and working through fears, trying to do a clean sweep of it all and not doing a very good job. I told her about the Larabee feud. We cried a little, hugged a little, and talked a lot, but when I left, I wasn't sure either one of us felt much better than when I'd arrived. Stan was still dead, and Aunt Frances still felt guilty about it.

Monday wasn't much better. It was one of those days that everyone on the entire library staff was in a bad mood.

Holly was frazzled, stressed about household chores that weren't getting done, and concerned about her son's scratchy throat. I asked if she'd told her husband about Stan and the police. Her teary expression answered my question, and I patted her shoulder while she gulped down sobs, choking out that he was too far away, it would just make him worry.

It didn't go much better with Josh. When I asked

him how the date with Megan went, he shrugged and said it went okay. "But she said she was busy this weekend, so I guess that's it."

"What do you mean?" I asked.

He popped the top of his soda can. "She said she was busy, don't you get it? That's the same as saying she doesn't want anything to do with me."

"Or maybe she's busy. People are."

He made a rude noise and stomped off.

And Stephen had holed himself up in his office and did nothing but make grunts of displeasure every time I talked to him. I'd tried to get him to open up about whatever weight was pressing him down, but he'd repeatedly rebuffed my attempts. Even when I told him both Caroline Grice and Gunnar Olson were considering donations, the response wasn't any different. "Consideration," he'd said, "isn't a check in hand."

In spite of my vows to stay upbeat, perky, and positive, by lunchtime my own mood had been pulled down. At the end of the day, for the very first time, I was glad to escape the library.

Happily, Tuesday was Bookmobile Day. Thessie was spending the week with her grandparents in the southeast corner of the county and since the day's route covered that area, I'd told her I'd pick her up and drop her off.

We met in the parking lot of a nearby township hall and the three of us, Thessie, Eddie, and me, headed off into the wild blue yonder to spread knowledge all across the land.

The day was a good one. Maybe it only felt like a good day compared to the horrible yesterday, but everything in bookmobile-land seemed to go smoothly. Eddie stayed on his self-appointed perch on the passenger seat headrest, we found books to suit all the children, and the adults who'd ordered books remembered ordering them. We even paired up a slightly sullen adolescent with a copy of *The Hitchhiker's Guide to the Galaxy* I'd accidentally put on a shelf next to the DVDs.

"Maybe there are no accidents," Thessie said. "My mom says there's a meaning to everything."

Thessie's mom also believed that the earth was under the control of aliens who had to consume people's blood to maintain their human appearance, but in this case she might actually be right.

I dropped Thessie off at her sagging sedan and headed home. Sort of.

Though I'd logged hundreds of miles in my car while planning bookmobile routes, driving the same route in the vehicle itself was a far different experience. I'd taken into account hills and curves and narrow roads, but what I hadn't considered enough were the potholes. Thanks to the freeze-and-thaw cycle of late winter and early spring, the roads are full of the little buggers, and some of them aren't so little. And it quickly became clear that hitting a pothole in a small sedan was a far different experience from hitting the same pot-hole in a thirty-one-foot bookmobile.

The poor bookmobile didn't like it. Thessie didn't like it. The books didn't like it. And Eddie really didn't like it.

"Mrrrooowwww!" he'd yell, then give me a dirty look.

After dropping Thessie off, I taped the county map to the dashboard and looked at Eddie. "This isn't about you, you know. You're not supposed to be here in the first place. As far as this rerouting is concerned, you don't exist. This is about the bookmobile and minimizing its maintenance."

Eddie settled into the passenger seat and closed his eyes. He didn't believe a word of it.

I patted his head and dropped the gearshift into drive.

The sunlight was starting to slant low when it happened. I'd wanted to find a new east–west bookmobile route in the middle part of the east side of the county and wasn't completely happy with any of the three possibilities. I drove over each of the roads three or four times, trying to imagine their surfaces in ice-slick winter, eyeing the cracking asphalt, anticipating future potholes.

"Which do you like best, Eddie?"

Mr. Edward opened his eyes just wide enough for me to see the yellow in his irises, then went back to sleep.

In spite of his lack of interest, I continued to articulate my thoughts. "The county road is probably in the best shape, but that stretch near the potato farm is going to drift over like crazy in winter. If I take the most direct way, that hill—"

*BAM!*

The bookmobile gave a bucking lurch and started pulling hard to the right. "Hang on!" I yelled to Eddie. The steering wheel tried to spin itself out of my hands.

"MMrrrrrRRR!!!"

But I didn't have time to calm Eddie—it was taking everything I had to calm the bookmobile. My foot was off the gas, I was pumping the brake lightly, staying out of a skid, I could do this, I could do this, I was doing this, I would—

*BAM!*

The bookmobile lurched again.

Eddie hissed and howled and spat. "MMrrrrrRRRRRR!!!"

The little control I had over the bookmobile vanished. My mouth tasted of metal as the adrenaline flowed through my body, into my heart, into my tingling skin.

To the right, the road's shoulder dropped away fast into a hill that rolled down steep to a narrow creek. If I couldn't keep out of that, if we pulled that way . . . into my head came an image of the bookmobile falling and rolling and tumbling, all the books, Eddie, and me, jumbling together in a broken heap.

"No!" I shouted, and gripped the steering wheel with all my strength and all my might. I kept on pumping the brakes. Was it doing anything? I didn't know, but I had to think it was helping. I had to try.

My arms quivered with the strain of keeping the vehicle headed straight. We were slowing, but not fast enough, not nearly fast enough. My jaw muscles bunched. My lips went dry. "Steady, Eddie," I whispered. "It'll be okay."

The steering wheel was doing nothing. I was doing nothing. My pumps on the brakes were doing nothing. There was nothing I could do except try to steer and try to brake and hope hope hope that something I was doing would do something.

It had to work.

We had to stop.

We *had* to.

Bare inches from a steep slope that would have carried us off without a second thought, the bookmobile came to a slow screeching stop.

We'd made it.

I sat there, panting, my hands still gripping the steering wheel.

"Mrr," Eddie said.

I blew out a breath and reached out for a cat snuggle. "You and me both, pal, you and me both." My laugh was a little too loud.

Then my brain started working again. "What on earth happened?" I asked Eddie.

He butted his head against my shoulder. Comforting, but not much of an answer.

"You stay here," I said, putting him on the seat of my chair. "I'll be right back." I opened the rear door and jumped to the ground, stumbling a little at its steepness.

I looked at the back end of the bookmobile. The right rear tire was flat. I looked at the front end. "Oh, jeez . . ." The right front tire was flat, too. How on earth could both tires have gone flat at the same time?

A motor-ish sort of noise came from behind me and I saw the hunched figure of a guy on a four-wheeled ATV, a quad, roar across the road and up a narrow trail. The driver wore dark pants and a dark hooded sweatshirt. Sticking out behind the driver was a rifle strapped to the vehicle's carrier rack.

A rifle.

I shrank back behind the bookmobile, but poked my head out to see the quad wind up the hill and disappear into a thick tree line. The engine's roar faded to a dull buzz; then that, too, disappeared.

# Chapter 16

I climbed back aboard the lamed bookmobile and pulled my cell phone from my backpack. I studied the screen, sighed, and put the useless thing away. There was a certain inevitability to the fact that there was no signal.

The last house we'd passed had been at least a mile back and it had had that abandoned look houses get when they're unoccupied. I didn't remember the road ahead well enough to know how close the nearest house might be, but there wasn't one in sight.

In the cabinet behind me was the emergency road manual, but since I could recite the entire contents from memory, I knew without looking what it said about a situation like this. "Call for assistance." So helpful. It also said, "Use your best judgment when dealing with emergency situations."

Well, that would have to do.

I turned on the four-way flashers and kissed the top of Eddie's head. "I'll be outside, okay?" He started a light and steady purr. Which wasn't truly helpful, but it did make me feel a little better.

I headed out and rummaged around for the battery-operated emergency lights I'd bought myself and stored in an outside compartment. Set one on its small tripod stand a little ways in front of the vehicle, set another one a little way behind.

Then I used my hand to brush dust off the front bumper. Sat down, crossed my legs at the ankles, and started waiting.

Waited some more.

Tried to enjoy the sounds of early evening.

Recrossed my legs and realized that summer evening sounds were really the sounds of bugs.

Waited. Thought about going inside and getting a book. Didn't.

Waited.

At long last, I heard the hum of a vehicle.

I jumped to my feet and stood, a happy and expectant smile on my face, formulating the words of thanks with which I'd shower my rescuer.

The vehicle came closer, closer, and suddenly there it was, small and silver and moving fast. I waved my arms high in the air, flagging the car down, calling for help. The convertible zoomed past. BMW Z4, I was pretty sure, since I'd admired one in the marina's parking lot all last summer.

I gave its taillights the meanest, nastiest glare I could glare. "Jerk!" I yelled to the driver. "You're nothing but a big jerk!" The driver hadn't even looked at me. He'd just ignored me and the poor bookmobile and zipped on his merry way.

People.

I plomped myself down on the bumper.

Waited.

Roughly a year and a half later, a rattletrap of an SUV appeared. I'd heard the sputtering muffler long before it came around the long curve, so I was already standing in the middle of the road, feet spread across the centerline, hands out in a *Stop!* gesture by the time it came into view.

This time, everything was different. The driver's window rolled down and a blond head poked out. "Miss Minnie? What's wrong with the book-mobile?"

I walked up to the ancient Jeep Cherokee. It was Surfette, the young woman who'd been on the bookmobile twice, hunting for a book she wouldn't let us help her find. "Hi," I said. "Two flat tires and I'm not getting any cell coverage."

"Oh, wow. What can I do?"

And they say the youth of today is self-centered. I wanted to hug her. "I don't want to leave the bookmobile, so if you could find a phone and call our mechanic, that would be a lifesaver." I gave her the name of the garage that did the bookmobile maintenance.

"You bet. I know the people who live a couple miles up the road. I'll be right back."

She took her foot off the brake, but I waved at her to stop. "There's another phone call to make." While I didn't want to scare her, this had to be done. "I need you to call the police."

"What?" Her mouth dropped open, showing perfectly white teeth. "Why? What happened?"

I gave her as brief a description of the event as possible, and her reaction wasn't anything close to fear. "Some rotten kid, I bet," said the girl who couldn't be much more than twenty. "Stupid jerks. Some of them have nothing better to do than take potshots at anything that moves."

She eased her vehicle forward a few feet, then braked. "Um, this may sound like a weird question, but is your cat with you?"

My heart did an odd thump-thump. This was Eddie's real owner. She'd cried buckets over losing him and I was going to have to give him back. I deeply, desperately wanted to lie, but was stopped by an image of my mother shaking her head at me and saying, "Minerva, I am so disappointed in you."

"Thanks a lot, Mom," I murmured.

"What's that?" Surfette asked.

"Eddie's in the bookmobile."

She nodded. "Okay, good. Is there anything I can get you?" I shook my head and she pulled away, speckles of rust falling off the wheel wells as she accelerated.

I stood, slump-shouldered, and watched her Jeep vanish into the distance. She was going to take Eddie away from me and I was going to have to be grateful to her for rescuing the bookmobile. And to think I'd started this day happy.

Hands in my pockets, I scuffed my way back to the bookmobile. If I only had a little time left with Eddie, I was going to make the most of it.

I climbed up the steps and found him in the back corner, sitting on a small pile of children's books he'd pulled off a shelf. Any other day this would have earned him a scolding and a threat of no treats for a week. This time I lay on the floor next to him, stomach down, and laid my head on one arm while I petted him with the other, not thinking, just being.

In what felt like three minutes, I heard the Cherokee's muffler return. I got to my feet, scooping up Eddie on the way, and sat on the carpeted step to wait.

Surfette knocked on the back door and came on in, all bright smiles and energy. "Your garage guy said he'll be out as soon as he can. He didn't see how you'd blown two tires, though. He must have asked me six times if I was sure it was two tires."

I laid my hand on Eddie's flank. My friend, my companion. "Did he say how long he thought it would take to get here?"

"Less than an hour, he figured." She introduced herself as Hannah, thereby blasting the surfer girl image to bits. Surfettes would be named Didi or maybe Jenny. Never Hannah. "He said he'll bring an extra guy and the big tow truck."

I nodded. "That's great. Thanks so much for

your help, Hannah. I could have been here all night if you hadn't come along."

"Oh, anybody would have stopped," she said, shrugging. "I must have been the first person by. Just luck it was me."

Luck. You could call it that. There was a pause that neither one of us seemed in a hurry to fill. "So," I asked, "do you mind if I ask you a question?" My inquiry came at the same time Hannah asked, "Is it okay if I ask you something?"

We both laughed and I gestured for her to go ahead. "Rescuers get to go first. It's a rule."

Hannah giggled and pushed her sun-bleached hair back behind her ears. "You know how I've been in here a couple of times looking for a book? Well." Her voice went low, almost into a whisper. "My fiancé and me, we're getting married in the fall."

For the first time, I noticed the diamond ring on her left hand. A very small diamond. Hannah spun it around on her finger, smiling a little.

"Anyway, both our families want this great big wedding. Our parents really can't afford it, and anyway, Bobby and me don't *want* a big wedding. Too much money for one day, and you're still just as married if you go to a justice of the peace, right?"

My mouth might have dropped open. "Yes," I managed to say.

She gave a sharp nod. "That's what I keep

telling my mom. I tell her we don't want them to run up their credit cards for a wedding, but she kind of tells me to go away, that she has to pick out napkins since I haven't done it yet." She rolled her eyes. "I mean, it's *our* wedding. Shouldn't we be able to say that we don't *want* napkins?"

"Absolutely."

"So what I was looking for was a book on having a small, cheap wedding. There's got to be a way."

I smiled. "I know just the book."

Her eyes lit up with hope. "You do?"

"Not here, but I'll put it on the bookmobile as a reserved book and you can pick it up anytime."

"Really?" She grinned wide. "This is so cool. I thought for sure if I checked out a wedding book, you'd tell my mom—she knows everybody, it seems like. Bobby and me, we'll figure out a plan first, and then we'll just, you know, go ahead and do it."

I looked at her happy smile. It wouldn't be that easy, but given the firm look in her eye, she probably knew that already. We fell to talking about weddings, easy happy talk that stretched out long.

Finally Eddie gave a wide yawn and said, "Mrrr."

"Oh, hey." Hannah snapped her fingers. "That's another thing I wanted to ask. . . . Um, are you okay?"

I patted myself on the chest, playing at pretending the sharp gasp I'd let out had been something else entirely. "Fine, thanks. What's the question?"

"Him." She pointed at Eddie and I thought my heart was going to freeze. "Is he a silver tabby?"

It took me two tries, three, to say, "That's what the vet said."

"Cool." She squatted down in front of Eddie. "He's a good-looking cat. Bobby and me, we're breeding boxers, but we're thinking about doing cats, too." She squinted up at me. "Are you sure you're okay?"

My muffled laughter smoothed out into a wide smile. "Eddie was a stray, and he's been neutered."

"Oh." She made a face. "That's too bad."

The honking of a truck startled all three of us. We looked through the bookmobile's windshield to see my second set of rescuers pile out of the biggest tow truck I'd ever seen.

"Well, guess I'll get out of your way," Hannah said.

I gave her a quick hug. "Thanks again. I'm glad it was you who stopped."

She hugged back. "Me, too." Halfway down the steps she turned. "Hey, you wanted to ask a question, too. What was it?"

"You know, I really don't remember." I smiled and hugged Eddie to my chest, holding him tight.

• • •

I was averting my eyes from the sight of the front end of the bookmobile being hoisted onto the tow truck when a sheriff's cruiser pulled up.

The deputy who climbed out looked familiar and I realized it was Deputy Wolverson, the officer who had dripped rainwater all over the bookmobile the day I'd found Stan.

"Ms. Hamilton," he said, nodding. "Sorry it took so long for me to get here, but I was on another call. What's the problem?"

"Thirty aught six, I'd guess," the head mechanic said. He kicked at the shredded tire they'd removed. When I'd ordered the bookmobile, I'd also ordered a spare rim and tire and had it stored in their garage. Ordering two in case someone attacked the bookmobile had never occurred to me.

Wolverson lowered himself into an easy crouch and studied the remains. "Got it a good one, didn't he?" He glanced up at me. "You okay?"

"Mad, mostly."

He smiled. "Healthy reaction. Good for you." Standing, he walked to the front end and looked at the ruined tire that was still attached. "No damage other than the tires, looks like. Some fine driving on your part, Ms. Hamilton." He took a small notebook out of his shirt pocket. "How far apart were the shots, timewise?"

We did the question and answer routine for a

few minutes. I pointed to where I'd seen the rifle-toting quad rider drive off, and the deputy made extensive notes. When he was done, he lifted his gaze to the distant line of hills. "You know that Larabee's farmhouse is that way, just two or three miles, right?"

I nodded. Steep and rough miles, but nothing for a quad.

"Maybe there's no connection between your book-mobile's tires being shot out and his murder," he said, "but maybe there is. I'll take some pictures and do what I can out here, but I'm going to pass this on to the detectives in charge of the Larabee case."

I'd guessed as much and had actually hoped for it, because at this exact moment Holly was working at the library. Had been, all afternoon. If there was any silver lining to this episode, it was that now Holly would be dropped to the bottom of their suspect list.

After Eddie and I got home, courtesy of the tow truck's narrow backseat, I made the dreaded phone call. "Stephen? Sorry to bother you at home. It's Minnie. I'm afraid I have some bad news."

At the end of my recitation of the afternoon's events, Stephen grunted and asked, "The book-mobile will be out of commission for how long?"

"Just a few days, they told us."

"Us?" Stephen's voice was sharp. "You had a volunteer on the bookmobile when some maniac with a rifle was shooting at you?"

"No, no," I assured him. "I dropped Thessie off long before that. By us I meant me and the bookmobile and three thousand books." I laughed as if I hadn't a care in the world. Stephen didn't laugh with me. I tried not to take that as a bad omen, since Stephen had never been prone to breaking into uncontrollable laughter, or any kind of laughter for that matter, but a sick sensation started gnawing at the back of my brain. Stephen hated the bookmobile. He would use any excuse to take it away.

"We'll be off the road one week maximum," I said, projecting assurance into my voice. "And the guys said the tires may even get up here in time for Saturday's run."

Stephen grunted. "Keep me informed," he said.

He sounded grumpy, but not the world-class grumpy that he'd been. "Say, Stephen, you're starting to sound more like your old self. Have you had one of those summer colds?"

"No, it's my . . ." He stopped. "I'm fine." A pause. "But thank you for asking."

Thank you? Stephen had unbent enough to say thank you? It was a day to remember. "One more question," I said. "Do you know if Holly scheduled the summer book sale with the Friends?" I'd meant to do it myself the day before, but had forgotten and asked Holly to take care of the small chore.

"Holly went home early," he said. "One of her children was sick, I was told."

Sighing, I hung up the phone. "So much for Holly being dropped to the bottom of the list," I told Eddie. While I'd been on the phone with Stephen, Mr. Ed had placed himself exactly in the center of the dining table. By rights, I should be enforcing the No Cats on the Table rule. Somehow, though, I didn't have the heart. Not tonight.

"Mrr," he said, then shut his eyes and purred.

Smiling, I scratched him behind his fuzzy ear. He wasn't so bad for an Eddie.

The next morning I was hard at work sorting through applications for a new part-time library clerk when the detectives stopped by.

"Can we have a moment of your time?" Detective Inwood asked.

"Sure." The one guest chair for which my office had room was piled high with books. "Do you want to go into the conference room?"

"No, thanks," said the short stout detective who was shaped like the letter *D*. Devereaux. "We just want to get your story about yesterday." He pulled a small notebook from his jacket pocket. Its cardboard covers were curved slightly, molded to the shape of his body.

As clearly as possible, I related the events of the day before. The lurching of the bookmobile. The second lurch. My sighting of the quad and the rifle. And how the distance from where the book-mobile's tires had been blown out to the farm-house wasn't that far, not cross-country with a quad.

Detective Devereaux flipped his notebook shut. "Bet it was some kid messing around," he said, chuckling. "Probably he was shooting at a stop sign and missed." They both laughed.

If I'd been a cartoon, steam would have poured out of my ears. "He came close to destroying a vehicle worth a quarter of a million dollars," I said.

The laughter stopped. "Yes, ma'am," said Detective Inwood. "We realize that. We'll find him. People talk, and kids talk even more. It won't take long to track him down."

I nodded, slightly mollified.

"What garage is working on the vehicle?" he asked. I told him and he nodded. "We'll take a look at the blown tires. Where were you when this happened?" When I gave him directions, he said, "We'll check it out."

He was saying the right things, but I sensed that I was losing them. "Do you think there's any link between Stan's murder and the bookmobile?" Yesterday I'd spent hours driving up and down the same few roads, trying out routes. The bookmobile was a big thing and didn't move very fast. Easy enough to follow it, if you wanted.

I didn't want to come out and ask if they thought my life was in danger, but how could it not be a possibility? I was very attached to my life and I wasn't keen on it ending any time soon.

The detective smiled. "Ma'am, like I said, we're investigating every possibility. If there's a link, we'll find it."

And with that, they were gone.

I stared after them, my face red with the effort of restraining my temper. They'd find it? Sure they would. Right after they figured out what really happened to the lost colony on Roanoke Island and right before they tracked down D. B. Cooper.

"Hiya, Minnie. What's that you're doing?"

I jumped. I was doing a stint at the research desk and Mitchell Koyne had done his usual trick of walking up from behind and scaring the living crap out of me. I pushed back from the desk and looked up at him. "Hey, Mitchell. I've been meaning to ask you something. You know Gunnar Olson, right?"

"Olson . . . oh, yeah. Big guy, too much money, not enough nice?"

I smiled. Mitchell had pegged it. "He said you did some driving for him a few weeks ago."

"Yeah. Buddy of mine said a bud of this guy he

knows was going to be in town for the weekend without a car and needed somebody to drive him around." He shrugged. "Paid me decent. Cash, too."

"Where did you take him?"

"Did more waiting than taking. Don't know why he didn't rent a car. I told him so, but he said I was stupid to talk myself out of a job." Mitchell shrugged. "Hey, I was trying to save him money, but whatever."

"You drove him around town?"

"What?" He tipped his head the other way to look at my computer from another angle. "In Chilson, you mean? Hardly any."

My breath stopped, but my heart beat on and on, whooshing air through my veins and arteries so loudly that I could hardly hear anything else. I sucked in air and my ears started working again. "Then where did you take him?" To the farmhouse? The answer to Stan's murder couldn't really be so simple, could it? If anyone could have missed a murder happening under his nose, it would be Mitchell.

"Casino." He pointed at the computer. "You looking to buy some property? I could find you some cheap acreage, if you want. There's a sweet quarter section I know about, lots of maples you could harvest, probably pay for itself and then some. And the guy who owns an eighty next to me wants to sell."

I swallowed down a laugh. Me, buy eighty acres of land? Mitchell obviously didn't know the size of my salary. "Which casino?"

"More like which one didn't we go to." Mitchell shook his head. "I don't get gambling. I mean, sure, maybe you'll win sometimes, but those places aren't dumps. You got to figure they're making money hand over hand."

Little spin, Gunnar had said.

"You don't gamble, Minnie, do you?" Mitchell asked.

Not unless you counted waking up every morning. "So you drove Gunnar around to casinos? You didn't drive him around the rest of the county?"

"Here, you mean?" Mitchell pointed at the map on my computer screen.

I'd been using the county's geographic information system. This view showed property lines and I'd zoomed into the eastern part of the county. One click on a parcel and up came details like legal description and taxable value. And property owner. I was poking around at the properties near where the bookmobile had been damaged, but I wasn't reaching any conclusions. I needed more information and I had no clue how to get it.

Mitchell tapped the screen. "Can you move the picture over this way? A little more . . . yeah. This long skinny property here? I was out there

318

cutting trees for some guy a few weeks ago. Ash. Dead from that emerald borer bug. Ever see one? They're kind of cool looking, for bugs."

"A few weeks ago?" I echoed. "Around when Stan Larabee was killed?"

"Uh, yeah. I guess. A little before, maybe." He put his index finger on the screen, guaranteeing a streaky fingerprint I'd have to clean up later. "Is that where that farmhouse is? Can you turn on the picture?"

I clicked a few clicks, changing the base map from property lines to aerial photography. Though the resolution wasn't anywhere near *CSI* standards, it was easy enough to make out the straight lines and regular planes of a roof. "There it is," I said, trying not to see into my memory.

"That's the place? Huh." Mitchell rubbed his jaw, which, since it looked like he hadn't bothered to shave in three days, made a sandpapery sort of noise.

"What?" I asked.

"Sometimes your brain just clicks things together, you know?"

I wasn't sure I wanted to know what things were rattling around in Mitchell's head, but I asked anyway.

"Well," he said. "Two things. That Olson guy. I asked him why he came to Chilson instead of Petoskey or Traverse, and he said his dad used to bring him up here hunting. From what he said, this is the place." He left another fingerprint on the screen, one that was centered on a property maybe half a mile south of the old Larabee farm. "He said there was this old junky cabin they stayed at. Wonder if it's still there?"

The back of my neck tightened. "What was the other thing?" I whispered.

"What's that? Oh, the other thing. When I was out there, cutting that wood, I saw some guy on a quad going up the hill behind that farmhouse where you found Larabee. Pretty sure, anyway."

"Pretty sure that was the house or pretty sure you saw a guy on a quad?"

"Huh?" He stared at me. "Oh. Both, I guess."

"You have to tell the police," I said.

"Why the . . . I mean, why should I?"

I gave him the Librarian Look and started the lecture. "Because Stan Larabee was killed there. Because, not too far from there, someone on a quad shot out the bookmobile's tires. Because it could be important. Because—"

"Okay, okay." He reached up and reset his baseball cap. "I'll stop by the cop shop, uh, later on."

"Today," I told him, but to Mitchell, the term was a fluid one. Later, he'd said. That meant he'd stop by the sheriff's office when he got around to it. Or when he happened to remember. Mitchell-time, Holly called it. There was a reason Mitchell spent so much time at the library reading books

320

and magazines he could have checked out; his overdue fines were nearing the three-figure mark. Right after Christmas, Stephen had laid down the law—no more lending books to Mitchell Koyne no matter how much he begged and pleaded, not until he paid up his fines. And maybe not even then, Stephen had thundered.

But this was too important to leave to Mitchell-time. The police needed to go back to the farmhouse and search for quad tracks. And I needed to tell them about Gunnar. Sure, Detective Inwood had said they were looking at Stan's business associates, but how many of those associates had hunted near the old Larabee farm? If the cabin was still there, Gunnar could have hidden the quad and walked down to the farmhouse. How that worked with Gunnar's lack of transportation, I wasn't sure. Maybe he had a car stashed somewhere at the airport and only hired Mitchell to drive him as a cover and—

"Which reminds me," Mitchell was saying. "It's what, Wednesday? Do you want to, maybe, go out to a movie or something with me on Friday?"

Thanks to a good fortune I didn't deserve, my mouth did not drop open and I didn't blurt out the first thing that popped into my head. I took a breath, smiled kindly, and said, "Thanks, Mitchell, that's very nice of you, but I'm seeing someone else right now."

"Oh, yeah? Anybody I know?"

"I don't think so. He's the new emergency room doctor in Charlevoix."

"Oh." Mitchell's shoulders drooped.

My heart ached for him. It was a brave thing to do, to ask someone on a date, and here I'd crushed his ego with one short sentence. He'd be despondent for weeks and—

He raised his head. "Say, do you think your friend Kristen would go out with me?"

I blinked, then smiled, remembering the night she'd barged into my date with Tucker. Paybacks can be glorious. "Why don't you ask her?"

Late on Friday morning I decided I couldn't wait for Mitchell any longer and decided to take matters into my own hands. Besides, I hadn't taken a break yet and what better way to spend a morning break than at the sheriff's office?

I passed the front desk, but stopped when I saw Holly, biting her lower lip and staring at nothing. "What's the matter?" I asked. She shook her head and didn't meet my eyes. "Hey, are you okay?"

Her head went up and down in a slow-motion nod. "It'll be fine," she said. "Right? The police . . ." She stopped, either not knowing where to go or not liking where she was going.

"It will be fine," I said firmly. "Very fine. Matter of fact . . ." But then I stopped, too. I had no right to give her hope, no right to promise anything.

She turned to look at me. "What?"

Think, Minnie, think! "Matter of fact, I have the perfect thing to make you feel better. What do you think about a cinnamon roll from the Round Table?"

A wan smile came and went. "That sounds nice."

"If anyone asks, I took a late break. I'll be back in a few, okay?"

Out in the warming sun, I walked down the backstreets as far as I could, staying out of the heavy pedestrian traffic that was bound to be in the downtown's core. At the last possible street, I dove into the downtown flow, stepping around a stroller, avoiding a woman talking on her cell phone, slowing down to avoid bumping into a tall, thin man walking with a short, round one who looked as if they'd just come out of the cookie shop.

Tall and thin, short and round. The letters *I* and *D*.

Serendipity was my friend. I fell into step behind the two men, then surged forward to split them apart. "Hello, Detectives, how are you this fine morning?"

They came to an immediate halt, one on either side of me. Since even the short detective was taller than I was by a good seven inches, this wasn't a position of power for Ms. Hamilton. I took a quick step away from them. "I'm fine, thanks," I said in response to their nonresponse. "Has Mitchell Koyne talked to either of you recently?"

Detective Inwood shook his head. So did Detective Devereaux.

Mitchell-time had struck again. "He said something you should know." They exchanged a glance that was over my head. Literally over my head, not figuratively. I could guess what that glance was all about. It meant, *I bet this is nothing, but we have to listen to her, don't we?* Why, yes, you do. "A few days before Stan was killed," I told them, "Mitchell was cutting down some trees near that farmhouse. He saw a guy on a quad."

Their faces, which had been politely blank, stayed that way.

"A quad," I said. "It was a guy on a quad who shot out the tires on the bookmobile, remember?"

Detective Devereaux said, "Ms. Hamilton, do you know how many quads are in this county?"

I didn't know and I didn't particularly care. What I did care about was that the detectives apparently hadn't followed up on the tire-shooting incident. They'd chalked it up to a kid messing around and hadn't bothered their pretty little heads about it any further. A sharp anger started to heat up inside me. Somewhere, I heard my mother saying, "Now, Minerva, don't lose your temper. You know it never helps anything," but she wasn't talking loud enough for it to have any real effect.

"It seems to me," I said, "that you should look for quad tracks near the farmhouse. Maybe the guy cleaned up the tracks close by the house, but maybe there are still tracks nearby."

Detective Inwood started to say something, but I wasn't done.

"And you said you were investigating Stan's business associates. Have you come across Gunnar Olson by any chance?" My sarcasm was starting to show and I knew I needed to dial it down. I released the fists that my hands had become and went on.

"He has a summer slip at Uncle Chip's Marina and was partners with Stan in a development deal. Gunnar lost out big-time. He still carries a huge grudge. And what I just found out is he used to hunt up in the hills behind the farmhouse. There was a cabin up there."

This part seemed to matter to them. Devereaux took some notes, and even made sure he had the correct spelling of "Olson."

"Thank you for the information," Detective Inwood said. "We'll follow up on this."

He made a move as if to go, but I wasn't done yet. My anger was still too hot. This was when Mom really should have spoken up. "Will you? Will you really?" I asked. "You're detectives for the Tonedagana County Sheriff's Office—at least that's what your badges say—but what detecting have you been doing?"

"Ms. Hamilton," Detective Devereaux said. "Give us time to do our job. Can we investigate as fast as you'd like? No. But—"

He was patronizing me. I hated that. "But meanwhile," I cut in, "Stan's killer is running around free, and innocent folks are suffering because you're questioning the wrong people."

"Ma'am, we're doing the best we can."

"I'm sure you are," I said with exquisite politeness. "But the killer isn't in jail, is he? Maybe it's time to contact the state police. I'm sure the post in Petoskey would be happy to talk to me."

"Gaylord," said Detective Inwood. "The regional post is in Gaylord. There's not much going on in the Petoskey post these days."

I stared up at him. He stared down at me. Neither one of us was going to budge a fraction of an inch. We were both going to die in this spot, frozen to death come January.

An electronic ringing sallied forth from Detective Devereaux's chest. He thumbed on his cell. "Yeah . . . yeah . . . okay. We'll be there." He slipped the phone back in his pocket. "Let's go, Hal. Ms. Hamilton, you have a nice day, now."

They swung around and headed off.

I stood there, watching them go, my hands on my hips, then started walking in the opposite direction. The detectives were blowing me off. They were ignoring everything I said. Had they done a single thing I'd suggested? No. If they had, I'd surely have known.

Holly was a mess, Aunt Frances wasn't much better, and the detectives were ignoring the person (yours truly) who was handing them clues on a freaking platter.

*Oh, Stan . . .*

"Working on it, Stan," I said out loud, startling a middle-aged couple who were walking toward me, hand in hand.

Not only was I working on it, I was moving it to the top of the list.

# Chapter 17

In spite of the odd hour of eleven a.m., the Round Table was packed with people. Half of them were having a late breakfast; half were eating an early lunch.

I waited my turn at the cash register, listening to the conversations about boat rides and weekend plans and where the next meal was going to be eaten. When I got to the front of the line, I asked if there were any cinnamon rolls left.

"Not sure," said the young woman. "Hang on, okay?" She scurried off through the narrow double doors that led to the kitchen. On the wall behind the register hung a calendar displaying a picture of the Petoskey breakwater and lighthouse. I simultaneously admired the photo and wondered where the month of June had gone. It was the last Friday of the month, a month to the day that Stan was killed.

*Oh, Stan . . .*

I turned away, looking for a distraction. And there, in the back corner, I found it. Bill D'Arcy's booth was occupied by someone else. Four someone elses, to be exact, and they looked as if they'd been there for some time, judging by the breakfast detritus scattered about.

I spotted Sabrina, weaving through the crowded

tables with plates of burgers and fries. When she'd distributed the meals, I called to her. "Morning, Sabrina. Where's your best customer?"

She made a face. "Mr. Won't-Talk D'Arcy? Don't know and don't care."

That sounded a little harsh. "Has he been in today at all?"

"Nope."

Just like the day Stan had been killed. One month ago, exactly. I frowned. Something was tickling the back of my thoughts. What would take someone away from a favorite haunt? What would be four weeks apart? Did men get their hair cut that often? But how could that take all day or even half a day?

*WHUMP!*

The entire building shook. There was a short second of silence; then children screamed, women shrieked, and men yelled. Dust filtered down. "Earthquake!" someone yelled. But I was already running through the front door with Sabrina and half the restaurant patrons on my heels.

It wasn't an earthquake. Not only were earthquakes exceedingly rare in this part of the country, but through the window I'd seen the cause of the whump.

Half a dozen running steps and I'd reached the passenger door of the car that had struck the building. I grabbed the handle and flung the door open. "Are you all right?" I hunched down and saw large hairy arms flailing around, shoving aside the released air bag. I half sat on the passenger seat. "Sir? Are you all right? Do you need an ambulance?"

"No!" he yelled.

"Bill?" Sabrina ran around to his side of the car. "Bill! Are you okay?"

It was Bill D'Arcy. How Sabrina had recognized his voice, I didn't know. I wasn't sure he'd ever spoken more than one word in a row.

"Yes, yes, yes." He shoved aside more air bag and opened the car door. "I'm fine." He stood, swayed, put his hands out.

Sabrina was right there, supporting him, guiding him. "You get back down. You've had a nasty little scare and you need to sit." She got him settled back into the driver's seat, ignoring his bleats of disapproval. "You need to get your breath, hon. Just sit for a minute." She looked around at all the people. "Anybody here a doctor?"

"Don't need a doctor," Bill said.

Sabrina gave him a considered look. "Oh, you don't, do you?"

"Just came from one."

"Oh, really?"

He should have recognized the tone in her voice. And if he'd taken one look at her just then, he would have seen more danger signs. Hands on her hips, eyes thinned, chin jutting forward. No good was in store for Mr. D'Arcy.

"And what, pray tell, did this doctor say?" Sabrina asked.

"None of your business," he muttered, staring straight ahead.

"Really." She folded her arms on her chest. "I've waited on you every day for weeks. I know how you like your coffee, I know how you like your hash browns. I know you don't read the sports section, I know what stocks you watch. I know you're less grumpy when the sun is shining and that you don't like to go out in the rain. I know you have high blood pressure and are trying to do something about it. I know—"

"You don't know anything!" he roared.

She bent down, pushing her face closer to his. "Because you don't tell me anything! How can I know what you won't tell?"

"I didn't want to worry you!"

Over on the sidelines, I blinked. He didn't want to make her *worry?* What on earth . . . ?

"Do I look like someone who would worry?" Sabrina shot back. "How about you, sitting with that laptop, never looking up, never seeing what's going on around you? You're hiding from something, and that means you're worried. Tell me what it is." She poked him in the shoulder. "Tell me!"

He kept staring straight ahead, seeing nothing but car dashboard, windshield, and the brick wall he'd whacked. "I have a bad case of macular degeneration," he said. "I do nothing but read because I won't be able to for much longer. The doctors say my sight will be gone within two years. I've been seeing a specialist in Traverse City for treatments once a month, but that's just slowing the inevitable."

Sabrina stood up straight. Looked up at the bright blue sky. Swallowed. Then bent back down again. "You drove to see an eye specialist? Let me guess, you got those shots, and then you drove all the way back here."

He nodded.

"Are you in*sane?*" Sabrina yelled. "You must be certifiable. Too bad the hospital in Traverse isn't a psychiatric hospital anymore—you could have checked yourself in for a nice long stay."

"I thought—"

"That's the trouble, you *weren't* thinking! Driving after an eye treatment? And here I thought you were smart. Do you realize what could have happened?"

"I'm only fifty-two years old." He pulled himself out of the car and faced her, eye to eye, glare to glare. "And I'm not blind yet."

"You going to keep driving until you are? How many buildings do you have to run into?"

"This was the only one!" He waved his arms around. "It was an accident! Everyone has accidents."

"Up here most people hit deer, not buildings

that haven't moved in a hundred years," she said drily.

"Look, I'm sorry I hit your precious restaurant, but—"

"I don't care about the stupid building."

"You . . . don't?"

"No, I care about you."

"You . . . do?"

She crossed her arms. "Don't be more of an idiot than you can help, okay? Of course I care about you. Why else would I be yelling at you like this in front of fifty strangers?"

Bill D'Arcy didn't look at the fifty strangers. He didn't look anywhere but at Sabrina. "You care about me?"

She heaved a huge sigh. "For now. Keep up the stupid questions and the stupid driving habits and I might change my mind."

"Sabrina . . . my darling Sabrina . . ." He lifted a hand and held her face gently, caressing her cheek with his thumb. "I had no idea. I . . ." He leaned in for a kiss and I could almost see the fireworks going off.

The crowd clapped, whistled, and cheered. "You go, girl!" "Got a good one there, pal!"

Sabrina and Bill paid no attention. They wrapped their arms around each other and held on as if they'd never let go.

The fifty strangers dispersed, laughing and smiling. After I retrieved Holly's cinnamon roll, I went along with them, unsure whether to cry for happiness or stomp my foot at human idiocy. Those two had come close to not connecting the dots. That it had taken what could have been a serious accident was silly in the extreme.

And due to the month-ago doctor's visit, Bill D'Arcy wasn't a suspect for Stan's murder. One down and far too many to go.

I sighed and headed back to the library.

Via multiple text messages, Tucker and I decided on Short's Brewing Company as the location for our second date.

"Not Chilson," Tucker had typed.

"Not this county," I'd returned.

Short's fit both those requirements. A happy addition to the small town of Bellaire, which was about thirty miles south of Chilson, the brewpub was famous for its wide variety of beer selections. We arrived after the Friday night dinner rush and scored a small table as soon as we walked in the door.

Fifteen minutes later, we were eating thick sandwiches, drinking adult beverages, talking about nothing in particular, and enjoying ourselves immensely. Sooner or later we'd get around to discussing the potentially problematic issues that could doom a relationship, but right now it was time to have fun.

I looked around the room. "You know, I don't

see a single person that I know. How about you?"

Tucker scanned left and right. "Not even anyone I've seen in the ER. Which is good, because that can get awkward. Especially if he's cooking your dinner."

I frowned, then figured it out. "Oh, you mean Larry? You stitched him up after he sliced and diced himself?" I made vague sword-fighting motions. "If you did as tidy a job with him as you did with Rafe, I'm sure he's healing fine and . . ." But Tucker was shaking his head. "What?" I asked.

"It was a broken hand, not a sewing job. He'd fractured his—" His words screeched to a halt. "What I just said. Can you forget it?"

I flicked a stray piece of lettuce off my finger and tried to figure out why he'd ask. "Larry told me he'd cut his hand. But . . . he broke it?"

Tucker looked at me over his sandwich. "I was way out of line to say anything. Please forget it."

An odd itch climbed up the back of my neck, but I nodded because I now understood what he was talking about. "Librarians know all about respecting privacy laws."

Tucker's nicely broad shoulders lost a little bit of tension. "Thanks," he said. "I'd give you a hug, but . . ." He held up his hands, still filled with gooey sandwich.

I smiled. "Can I ask a question, instead? How hard is it to break a bone in your hand?" I laid down my sandwich, made a fist with one hand, and pressed it into the opposite open palm, pushing hard. "And how long does it take to heal?"

If you were hitting something, say the back door of a farmhouse, how much force would it take to break your hand? How hard would you have to hit, how much damage would you inflict on yourself, how much would you inflict on what you were hitting?

But a better question was, why had Larry lied? He'd told Kristen the injury was from softball and he'd told me he'd cut himself, yet it was really a break. Why the multiple lies? Maybe he was just one of those guys who was trying to tell the best story. Sure, that could be it.

"It's easier than you think," Tucker said. "Saw a lot of it, downstate. From street fights, but also people who'd get mad and haul off and hit a wall. Metacarpals with spiral fractures? Those guys are in a world of hurt for a long time. Surgery, nerve damage, sometimes they never get their strength back a hundred percent."

He talked about the importance of physical therapy for full recovery and how the length of recovery varied tremendously, but all I kept hearing was the loop of my question and his initial response.

How hard is it to break a bone in your hand?
Easier than you think.

• • •

Eddie and I sat out on the houseboat's front deck, me on the chaise lounge in shorts and sweatshirt, Eddie warming my lap as the sunset glow faded. I'd set the chaise in the exact center of the deck. No chance of any accidental fallings-in tonight.

"Mrr," Eddie said, snuggling in closer to me.

"Yeah," I told him, petting him long from head to tail. "It's nice, isn't it?"

I'd asked Tucker if he wanted to come aboard. "Love to," he'd said, and I'd started smiling. "But I have to work tomorrow, so I'd better get home." So, once again, it was me and my pal Eddie hanging out.

In a minute, I'd go figure out who was hosting the Friday night party. One dock down, maybe two. It wasn't far. Over the quiet water I could hear music and laughter and the popping of beer cans. Eddie and I would sit here for a while and then I'd put him inside and head for the lights and the noise.

Soon.

The stars came out, bright in the moonless sky. The scattered white of the Milky Way eased into view. It must be at least eleven o'clock. I should find the party before the diehards were the only ones left.

Soon.

Eddie purred gently. "Trying to get me to stay?" I asked, resting my hand on his back, feeling the vibrations up through my arm, shoulder, and deep into my heart. "I should really go and be social."

He shifted and his purrs became lower and even more soothing.

I thought about Stan, about how he'd died, how he'd lived, and about how much I owed him. I thought about my responsibilities to the library, to the ever-increasing number of bookmobile patrons, to Holly, to Aunt Frances. I thought about my obligations. Which overlapped quite a bit with the responsibilities, but wasn't an exact match, somehow.

What is a friend obligated to do? Did I want to be the kind of person who ran the risk of being taken advantage of, or be the kind of person who walked away? And what is a niece obligated to do? More than a friend? Less?

I thought about the times I'd talked to the detectives. Had I been too impatient? Unrealistic in my expectations? Maybe I'd assumed too much; maybe I hadn't listened to them just as much as they hadn't listened to me.

The party noises faded. Up above, a yellowy green curtain waved into view, a slow dance moving to a beat I could almost feel in my bones. The northern lights, gorgeous and unworldly, beautiful and primeval.

I watched the show all the way to the end, hours past the time I should have gone to bed, watching and wondering.

And thinking.

# Chapter 18

The next day, Saturday, had been scheduled to be a Bookmobile Day. Unfortunately, the bookmobile was still in the mechanic's garage. I'd called all the stop contacts and volunteered to bring a selection of books in my car. "Tell me what you're interested in, and I'll make sure I bring something that suits."

They'd all asked the same question: "Is Eddie going to be with you?"

When I'd said no, there wouldn't be enough room in my small car for books and cat, I'd gotten a universal response. "Thanks for the offer, but we'll make do until you come around next time."

So instead of driving around southwestern Tonedagana County, I headed to the library itself to cover for a part-time clerk who was in the Upper Peninsula attending a family funeral.

"You believed that story?" Josh laughed. He was in the break room, up to his elbows in printer parts. Why he hadn't taken it to his office I didn't know, but some questions were best left unasked, since if you asked, you ran the risk of getting an answer that included things you didn't want to know.

"Yes, I believed her," I said, "and so would you if you'd seen how upset she looked."

He snorted. "What I see is the U.P.'s weather forecast of eighty degrees and sunny all weekend when it's supposed to be maybe seventy and rainy down here. They're saying really heavy rain, too."

"So young, yet so cynical." I mock-sighed heavily and left him to his tinkering.

I was deep into the task of processing the Friday night returns when Stephen strolled past. "Good morning, Minerva," he said. "How are you this fine day?"

"Uh . . ." I stared at the apparition. Though the presence in front of me resembled my boss, it couldn't be him. Stephen had made it a Thing that he was never at the library on a Saturday. He'd said repeatedly that if he was doing his job properly, overtime hours weren't necessary. Plus as far as I knew, Stephen had never once wasted time on the casual conversational exchanges made by everyone else in the universe. "Uh, hi. You seem . . . chipper this morning."

"Why, yes. Yes, I am." He smiled broadly. "Last night we got the news that my sister and the new baby are going to be fine. Out of the woods and out of the ICU today."

I blinked. Stephen had a sister? "That's great. Your family must be thrilled."

"Thrilled and relieved both." He laughed, an unexpectedly rich sound.

"This is a younger sister?" I asked. "Have you been to see her?"

Up until that point, his face had been open and easily read. Now it closed down. "Younger," he said shortly. "She and her husband live in Oregon."

I grinned on the inside. Crankmeister that he was, it was good to have the old Stephen back. "Well, I'm glad she and the baby are okay. You must have been worried sick."

"Concerned, yes," he said. "I wouldn't say worried."

I watched him walk off and snorted quietly. Maybe he didn't want to admit it to his assistant director, but whatever had been wrong with his sister and her baby, it had been so serious that he'd worried himself almost to the point of illness.

He headed out through the front door and I heard what might have been him singing, and words that might have been a chorus of "Oh, What a Beautiful Mornin'."

And my teeny tiny worry that Stephen might have been involved in Stan's death, that he'd been a mess the last few weeks over guilt and fear of getting caught, puffed away into the air and disappeared forever.

The phone rang. "Good morning, Chilson District Library," I said. "How may I—"

"Yo, Min," Kristen said. "Got a question for you."

It had been a while since Kristen had called with a job for her personal search engine. I pulled the computer keyboard toward me. "Ready and waiting, ma'am."

"Kyle says Onaway potatoes are named for Onaway, Michigan, and I say they came from Maine. Who's right?"

"Hang on." In a few seconds I found the answer. "You both are. The first seedling came from Maine, but it was sent to Michigan for research and development and named the Onaway potato. Don't ask me why it was sent here because I don't know. And who's Kyle?"

"What? He works here. You've met him a zillion times."

I frowned. "There's no Kyle at the Three Seasons."

"Sure there is," she said. "You know. Larry Sutton."

Either Kristen was suffering from serious sleep deprivation or something very strange was going on. "What are you talking about?"

"Oh, right," she said. "I guess you wouldn't know. Back in high school, Kyle played basketball and the story is, the coach kept calling him Larry because he looked like his uncle Larry, a guy the coach grew up with." She paused. "He looks like a Larry, I guess, so the name stuck. But it's just a nickname."

She chattered on about the new potato dish she was making up, but I didn't hear much of what she said. Any of it, really, because I was suddenly back on Audry's front porch, drinking her lemonade, and hearing her say, "And one of them used names that started with *K*. Kevin, Kyle, Karla, and Kendra."

Late in the morning, the sky clouded up. The rain held off, but started to spatter down as I locked the building at four o'clock. Josh had been right, or at least right about the weather. When I got home, I found Eddie sleeping in a new spot. The seat of the shower stall.

"Why?" I asked him. "You don't look at all comfortable."

He blinked at me and didn't say anything.

"Okay, sure, I must not have latched the door all the way and this was a brand-new place for you, but still. It's fiberglass. And it was probably wet."

He stood, stretched, and jumped down. "Mrr," he said, and stalked off.

"Yeah, well, don't come crying to me if you wind up with a . . . with a stiff neck." Did cats get stiff necks? I watched him trot down the steps to the bedroom. He didn't look as if he had one, but if he did, how would I know?

I tossed together a fast dinner of grilled cheese and a broccoli/cauliflower mix steamed in the microwave. ("Of course I'm eating my vegetables, Mom.") I ate sitting at the dining table with the company of Eddie and my laptop, which was displaying the local weather. More specifically, the radar.

"Lots of yellow coming across Lake Michigan," I told Eddie. "Quite a bit of red, too. You know what that means."

He sniffed at my sandwich.

I used my forearm to push him away. Like a boomerang, he came right back. "It means a lot of rain. Hard rain that could wash away any of those quad tracks out by the farmhouse." There'd been rain since Stan's death, but not the heavy, driving stuff that was coming. "I should get out there," I murmured. "See if there are any tracks. I'm sure the detectives haven't been out there."

Eddie's sniff stopped abruptly.

"Could have told you you wouldn't like broccoli," I said. "Cats don't do vegetables. Your pointy teeth don't chew them up right."

When the kitchen was tidied, I dumped the contents of my backpack out on the bed and repacked with new items. "Flashlight, check. Bottle of water, check. Cell phone with charged-up battery, check. Map, pen, granola bar, all check. Am I forgetting anything?"

Eddie, who'd been supervising my efforts, said, "Mrr."

"Right." I snapped my fingers. "A book. Good idea." I picked through my To Be Read stack and selected a Frost mystery by R. D. Wingfield.

When I turned around, Eddie was slithering into the backpack.

"Hey!" I grasped him around the middle and pulled him out. "This isn't a cat carrier. At least not today."

"MMrrrrRR!"

I blinked. "That was quite a howl. Did I hurt you?" He squirmed out of my arms, thumped to the bed, and said, "MRR!"

The guilt that had been advancing retreated fast. "Well, sorry if I injured your feline dignity, but you can't go with me. I'm going to be tromping around the woods and going up and down hills, and that's just not your style."

He hurled himself into the backpack.

I pulled him out.

He gave a little growl.

"Eddie!" I held him up and stared. "What's gotten into you?"

"MMMRRR!" he said, three inches from my nose.

I winced at the cat breath and tried to give him a good snuggle. Nothing doing. He struggled away, jumped to the floor, and ran down the short hall and up the steps.

Fine. After I made a note on the whiteboard, I put on my rain gear and slung the backpack over a shoulder. "Hey, pal. I'm headed out and—"

And there was Edward, sitting on the boat's dashboard, poised to jump out the door as soon as I pushed it open half an inch.

"Not a chance," I told him. I stood in front of the door and turned my back to the dashboard. Slowly and carefully, I pushed the door open and slid one foot outside, then eased my body out, too, using the other foot and the backpack as a cat barrier.

Eddie thudded to the floor. Tried to jump over the backpack. "MRR!" His claws slid off the nylon.

I shut the door before he could gather himself for another effort.

"MMRRR!!" He stood on his hind legs and scratched at the glass door. *"MRR!!!"*

I was a horrible kitty mother. Clearly, he needed to get outside more. Maybe I'd get a cat harness and take him for walks. We could walk to get the mail, or down to the ice-cream shop for double dips of black cherry.

"See you, Eddie." I waved at him. "I'll be back before you know it. We'll go harness shopping tomorrow."

"Mrr!" He was sounding less like he was complaining and more like he was crying out a question. He kept crying as I walked off the dock and across the parking lot, and I almost thought I could still hear him as I drove out of town, the windshield wipers keeping time with his cries.

The farmhouse didn't look any different than it had the last time I'd seen it. I tromped up the driveway, following the path the emergency vehicles had created, and kept my gaze high. The last thing I wanted was to catch even a small glimpse of what was still on the ground. Even if rain had fallen for forty days and forty nights, I'd be able to see the red stains.

I stood near the back porch and looked out at the tall grass. Looked hard. Squinted and looked some more and saw nothing but grass waving in the light breeze. If there had been a path, I couldn't see it.

"A tracker I'm not," I murmured, and cautiously climbed up onto the far corner of the porch. Maybe an elevated view would help.

And, oddly, it did. Or something did. I closed my eyes, not seeing anything, trying to think of blank slates and flat lakes and smooth expanses of snow. When I opened my eyes and saw the hills rising up behind the house, I immediately saw the grassy trail. Not a very distinct trail, and maybe not even a trail at all, but maybe, just maybe, it was something to follow.

"Hey, Eddie, check it out!" I looked around my feet, all excited to share, then remembered that I'd left him home.

That's what happens when you start talking to cats. You think they actually understand what you're saying. And sometimes you even think they might be contributing to the conversation when, in reality, what they're saying is "Mrrr."

I adjusted my backpack's straps and started trudging across the open field. It was dotted with the scrub trees that grow up after a farm field lies fallow for even a few years. I tried to picture the young Stan of the high school photo driving a tractor up and down, up and down. Couldn't quite do it.

Through the wet field I went, heading for the trail I might—or might not—have seen. At the edge of the field, which was the bottom of the hill, there were rocks. Lots of rocks. Whoever had cleared the field had tossed all the fieldstones into a large heap exactly where the hill had started turning a serious slope. Not so dumb.

I took a look up at the steepness, wished I hadn't, and started climbing through the drippy rain.

Halfway up, I stopped to rest. While Josh's weather forecast might have been right about the rain, the temperature part was way off. The cool he'd promised was instead a hot heavy humidity that made it hard to breathe.

On up I climbed. And climbed. Slipping on the wet grass, clutching to it to keep from skidding back downhill, wishing Eddie had suggested I bring cleats instead of a book, climbing, climbing, head down and feet moving, thighs aching, lungs working hard.

At long last, the burning in my legs fell from a hot fire to a slow ache. I looked around and found I'd reached the edge of the hill's top. Not the tippy-top, but close.

I squinted into the deep, dark forest. The thick

cloud cover was making night fall before its time, and up ahead, thick canopies of maple leaves blocked out even that dusky light.

Well.

I looked back and saw the wet trail I'd just laid. Looked ahead to the murky forest. Shivered, then extracted the flashlight from my backpack. My dad had given me this LED light when I'd bought the houseboat, gravely telling me that no homeowner should be without one.

With a push of the thumb it went on, and I flinched as the bright light turned the night practically to day. Since I'd never used the flashlight before, its range amazed me. I danced the beam up the trees, down on the ground, and all around in a giant circle. "Wow," I murmured, "this thing is awesome. Thanks, Dad."

I aimed the light forward. Maple tree trunks a foot and a half in diameter. A few scattered bushes. The occasional tuft of grass. A thin carpet of leaves from last autumn. Moss. Not much else. Following a weeks-old quad trail through the woods wasn't going to be easy. Or . . . was it?

Bouncing the light off the ground, I saw some rips in the pea green moss. Long rips that were in a direct line with the trail behind me. The rips curved, then faded to dents.

Well, there you go. Tracking wasn't so hard; all you had to do was pay attention.

I took out my cell. Using one hand to shield it

from the rain, I clicked off a few pictures, then followed the mossy trail to the very top of the hill. From here, I could see nothing at all except more trees. When the leaves were down, the view must be stupendous, but now there was nothing but green.

The trail wound around the trees, zigging for an occasional monstrous maple, zagging every so often for a large rock, zigging again for a fallen tree, but always trending in the same direction. South, I was pretty sure. Another thing Eddie should have suggested was to bring a compass. Not that I owned one, but I could have down-loaded a compass app to my cell.

On through the greenish murk I went. Every so often I lost the trail and had to circle around to find it. Every so often I'd be fooled into following a deer path that would peter out to nothing, and back I'd go until I again found the moss dents.

At one point I stopped to drink some water and glugged down half of it before sense came into my brain. I didn't know how much farther there was to go; drinking all the water now would be worse than dumb.

I capped the bottle and started walking again. Intent as I was on following the moss trail, I didn't notice the bush with the very sharp thorns until I was in the middle of it.

"Ow!" The stinging pain flared up hot. Muttering to myself about the stupidity of city folk who like to pretend they know what they're doing out in the woods, I used the flashlight to push the branch this way and that, trying to loosen its thorny grip. I stepped back, oh so carefully, gritting my teeth at the scratches, then came to a sudden stop.

There, right in front of my eyeballs, was a cluster of long threads. "Huh," I said. Someone else had been caught by the clutching bush. And there, down at my feet, was another denting impression of quad tires.

A clue!

I wiggled my way out of the bush, then tucked the flashlight into my armpit, unzipped the backpack, and took out my cell phone.

Tempting though it was to pull off the threads and take them with me to dangle in front of the detectives, I didn't want to mess with the chain-of-evidence thing. So I clicked off a few pictures, the phone's flash lighting up the trees and sucking up battery power. E-mailing pictures to the detectives wasn't as good as dangling, but it would have to do.

Pictures taken, I reshouldered the backpack and went back to following the trail.

How far I walked, I wasn't sure. My normal walking pace (3.4 miles an hour, according to the last treadmill I'd been on, back in graduate school) was worth nothing in this situation. I wasn't even sure how long I'd been walking—the sky gave no hints and my cell was on my back.

Flashlight searching, feet moving, I made my way

across the forest floor. The sky was so dark that when I at last emerged into open ground, I almost didn't notice. What tipped me off was the moss fading away to nothing and the grass coming back.

I looked up, and out. Far, far out and away. Miles of river valley to the left of me, miles to the right, and straight ahead, distant over the wide valley, was another rise of hills.

A USGS quadrangle map was in my back pocket, but I didn't need to pull it out to know where I was. This was the Mitchell River Valley, hundreds of acres of state land dotted with the occasional private property. There wasn't a paved road inside the entire valley, just gravel roads and an extensive trail system.

Plus the new little trail I was following, now twin paths of bent grass going down down down the hill.

I stared at it, then hitched up the backpack. Well. This was what I'd come out here for. Not much point in turning back now.

Down I went, following the curving trail around the side of the hill, picking my way across the wet grass, trying not to fall on my behind, trying not to think how I'd get back to my car in the dark.

The farther down the hill I went, the quieter I tried to move. Somewhere up ahead there was a house or a barn or a something that the quad had come from. I was pretty sure that ownership of a quad could be traced. The police would find out if the owner had a connection to Stan. Would find out if the owner had a reason for murder. Then, Stan's voice would stop whispering in my ear, Holly could get some sleep, and Aunt Frances would stop eating herself up with guilt.

Down and down the hill. My ears strained to hear a car, the voices of strangers, anything, but the only thing I heard was my own footsteps.

Then, finally, around another curve and down a little more, there was a small house tucked into the side of the hill. The slope was so steep that the uphill roof almost touched the ground. A storybook house, if it weren't for the decaying shingles and peeling paint. If this was Gunnar's hunting cabin from the days of yore, it had become something else in the interim.

I turned off the flashlight. No lights were on in the house. And no lights on in the large weather-beaten barn standing to the side and slightly behind the house. The tracks led to a door in the side of the barn. I took one step forward. Stopped.

Should I?

*Could* I?

The needle of my moral compass bounced between GO AHEAD and GO HOME, spent a lot of time on GO HOME, then swung firmly to GO AHEAD.

I edged close to the house and peeked in through a kitchen window. No one was in sight. Excellent. I tiptoed to the barn, one eye on the house, one eye on the steep and rocky driveway. The light breeze I'd felt up on the ridge's top was nonexistent down here and my forehead beaded with rain and humid summer sweat. I got the sudden urge to use the bathroom.

No noise, no lights, no nothing. I made it to the barn undetected by anyone save a grasshopper or two, grasped the door handle, and pulled.

Nothing happened. I gaped. Locked? People locked their barn doors? A wave of complete defeat drained all the energy from my body. I'd come so far. . . .

No. There had to be a way in. I took a closer look at the door. No hinges. Duh. I pushed instead of pulled, and it creaked open.

A musty smell rushed out to greet me. I stepped inside quickly and shut the door.

Complete darkness.

I reopened the door a crack and let in enough light that I was able to spot the quad parked in the middle of the large space. Shadows all around suggested smaller rooms and old animal stalls, but I didn't bother poking around. I wanted to get back over the hill to my car and home.

Dumping my pack on the ground, I unzipped it and hunted around for my cell. I walked fast around the quad, snapping a few flash pictures, zooming in on the Off-Road Vehicle tag slapped on the front fender.

Done. Time to skedaddle. If this wasn't enough proof for the detectives, I'd have to keep my promise to Holly some other way.

I squatted down to put the cell back into my backpack. Just as the zipper hummed shut, complete darkness descended in front of my eyes.

"What . . . ?" My hands went up. Found cloth. "Hey!"

An unforgiving grip grabbed at my wrists and pulled them back behind me, one, then the other.

"What are you doing? I was hiking up in the hills and got lost. I thought maybe—"

My spur-of-the-moment lie was cut short when I felt my wrists being bound with something strong and sticky. Tape of some kind. Duct tape, or, even worse, the Gorilla Tape that Rafe always went on about. "Strongest tape ever made," he'd bragged, brandishing a roll. "This stuff won't ever come off."

"Listen," I said, "whatever you're doing, there's no harm done at this point, right? Cut me loose and I'll leave. Maybe spend a night in the woods, which will be unpleasant, but I'll live, and in the morning I'll find where I parked my car and no one will have to know anything about this and—"

I felt a small rush of air on my face. He was lifting whatever it was that he'd used to cover my head. "Thanks," I said gratefully, even though he hadn't lifted it very far. I still couldn't see, but it'd be okay in a minute. "It was getting a little stuffy in there." I gave a weak chuckle. "If you—"

He pushed my jaw shut and slapped tape over my mouth. My yell of protest got as far as my teeth and went no farther. The bag came back over my head and was tied down. I kicked, and hit only air. I tried to pull away, but his grip held me fast. I turned into a kicking, yelling, pulling, shoving, screaming, panicking, sweating mess of a human being. And nothing I did made any difference.

He grabbed my wrists, and pulled them up behind me. Pain shot through my arms, my shoulders, my back. Nothing existed but the agony being inflicted on me; nothing mattered so much as that it end.

Which it did when I started walking. He gave me a shove, I took a stumbling step. Another shove, another step. I couldn't see anything—for all I knew, he'd dug a hole and was going to push me into it and bury me alive. As the idea occurred to me, I slowed. Immediately, he grabbed my wrists again and yanked them high.

I quick-stepped forward. If he wanted me in a pit, I was going in a pit and there was nothing I could do about it.

Fury sang through my veins. Frustration came next, with a solid determination following close behind. I was going to get out of this. If he shoved me into a pit, I was going to climb out. If he tried to bury me alive, I'd hold my breath until he left and then climb out. He was not going to beat me. He. Was. *Not*.

My anger sustained me during the interminable walk across the barn. Shove, stumble. Shove, stumble. The barn hadn't seemed nearly this large when I'd walked into it. I spent half a second wanting this horrendous journey to end, then spent a much longer time not wanting it to end. Whatever was waiting for me couldn't be better than this. Stumbling around in the dark wasn't so bad when you considered possible alternatives.

Shove. Stumble. Shove. Stumble. Then a very, very hard shove.

I ran forward one, two, three steps, almost falling, sinking low to avoid falling because there's not much worse than falling with your hands tied behind your back. Then, breathing hard, I stood straight, anticipating his next shove.

It never came.

Instead, a door banged shut and a bolt slammed home. The door rattled a few times and I heard a grunt. Heavy footsteps crossed the barn. Another door slammed shut. Then nothing.

He was leaving.

I was alone. And not dead.

Two big pluses. Two extremely big pluses. And if I wanted to add more items to the positive side of the column, I wasn't in a pit, buried alive, or even injured if you didn't count the bruises I was sure were forming on my back.

So . . . now what?

Much depended on what he was going to do. If he was headed for the house to find his killing weapon of choice, I was pretty much out of luck.

Maybe I'd be able to work my way out of my bonds, get out of whatever room I was in, and run for help, but each of those things could take hours and he might be back in minutes. If that was his plan, the best I could do was to . . . to what? Make my death as hard for him as possible? Wouldn't that mean I'd be inflicting even more pain on myself, with the same eventual result?

I debated the point with myself, then decided that since the thought of giving in was making me angry all over again, one issue was resolved.

Of course, I still had no idea who this guy was. I knew it was a guy, because when he'd been pushing me around, I'd felt arms too hairy to belong to a female. So Caroline Grice was out, unless she'd hired her gardener to follow me. Was it Gunnar? Was it Larry, aka Kyle? Was it another of the Larabee relatives? I still didn't know.

The rumble of a engine starting made me blink. I hadn't seen a vehicle; it must have been parked on the other side of the barn. One point off Minnie's score for a poor job of reconnoitering.

I tilted my head, listening, trying to ignore the fear that was growing and spreading fast.

The car made its way down the gravel drive and onto the narrow gravel road I'd seen coming down the hill. It didn't take long for the noise of the car to fade away completely.

It took a lot longer for my sobs to stop.

# Chapter 19

When I ran out of tears, I started thinking. That didn't work very well at first, because I kept thinking that the most likely possibility for my future was one of two options. Either the bad guy would come back and finish me off, or I'd die from dehydration and starvation. Years from now, someone would come across my desiccated body. Dental records would eventually reveal my identity, my parents would get a chance to say good-bye, Tucker might see my name in the paper and spare a thought for a woman he barely remembered, and the mystery of how I'd come to die in a barn would go forever unsolved.

Unsolved? The thought brought me to some semblance of sense. The mystery of my death wouldn't go unsolved, not if I could help it. I had too much to do before I could even consider dying. I wanted to see the house of Green Gables, to track down the equivalent of St. Mary Mead, to find out if there really was a Zebra Drive in Botswana. Besides, if I died now, I'd never find out how the tangled love lines in the boarding-house got untangled.

Time to stop thinking and start doing.

I shuffled over to a wall and put my back up against it, then slid down its rough surface until I hit the floor. Relax, I told myself. The only way you're going to get out of this is to stay calm and loosen those muscles. Breathe deep. Center yourself.

My wish to relax was complicated by the fact that I could die soon, but I did my best to forget that singular item.

I rolled onto my side, my arms behind my back, arms that desperately wanted to be in front of me.

Loosen. Relax. Lengthen.

Don't think about the odds of getting free, don't think that he might come back any second, don't think about the strong, sticky tape around your wrists, don't think about the bag over your head—which smells as if it has been sitting on the floor of a barn for fifty years—and don't think about how thirsty you are. Definitely don't think about that.

Relax. Loosen. Lengthen.

The words of that long-ago ballet teacher came back to me. Long line, Minnie. Make yourself into a long line. Don't you see?

Finally, I did.

I let my arms lengthen into a line of the longest kind. Let my spine grow long. Made it into an arch. And, just like that, the twin changes in my body let my wrists slip around my hind end and up under my knees.

Gasping, sobbing a little again, I rolled to the

floor. Managed to pull one leg through, then the other.

I tucked my hands under my chin and held them there, relief singing in my ears. My hands weren't behind my back anymore! I'd won! A battle, not the war, but the small victory thrilled me more than all my Christmas and birthday presents put together.

Then I got over it.

Hands in front of me were well and good, but I still couldn't see, my hands were still tied together, and I was still trapped in a barn.

But though my wrists were strapped together tight, my fingers were free. I felt the bag that covered my head. Burlap, judging from the thick weave of the fabric. I felt around some more. A lined burlap bag, cotton on the inside, with a long length of twine sewn into the edge as a drawstring.

Twine that was tied tight with multiple knots.

I pictured a farm wife cutting a piece of cotton from an old shirt or dress, sewing it into the bag, cutting a length of twine for the drawstring, and giving it to her husband to use for carrying his . . . lunch? His spare socks? City girls don't spend enough time on farms to know these things. What I did know was that small fingers are good at picking out knots.

Shifting around a little, I sat up and used my heels to push myself over to the wall. I was good at picking out knots, but it was a slow business.

It'd be even slower because even if it were full daylight, I couldn't see anything except the inside of the bag, but perseverance was my middle name.

Well, my middle name was actually Joy, but that wasn't the point.

I don't know how long I spent poking and picking at those knots. It could have been twenty minutes; it could have been four hours. Every so often, my hands would start tingling from a lack of blood flow and I'd have to let them rest.

Break periods I spent breathing lightly, trying to hear for car noises, for footsteps, for voices, for anything. When my fingers stopped tingling, I started in again.

The last knot was the tightest. Two, three, four, five times I had to rest my hands. Each time I rested, I wondered if I'd ever get out of there, wondered if I was wasting my time. Then I'd take a deep breath and start in again.

There wasn't much choice. No one knew where I was. If I wanted to get out of here, I'd have to get myself out.

Fatigue was seeping into my bones when that horrible tight knot released. In a flash, my fatigue vanished. I ripped the bag off my head—and saw nothing. Panic flared hot. I shot to my feet and spun in a circle, searching for light. Any light, it didn't matter, the merest speck would be fine, please, just let me see something, I can't be blind, please . . .

I turned in a circle, starved for sight, scared beyond measure . . . and then I saw the merest speck of brightness. High up on the wall, through a gap in the siding, I spotted a star. I froze, staring at it, drinking it in, loving it.

"Thank you," I whispered.

At least that's what I tried to do. In my happiness at being unbagged, I'd forgotten that he'd taped my mouth shut.

With my hands in front of me and my vision assured, I was feeling strong and very, very angry. Fiercely, I worked at the tape. Hooked my thumbnails under the tight edge, pushed, didn't get anywhere, used my fingernails, thumbnails again, pushed, felt a searing pull and clean air on an infinitesimally small portion of my face, felt exhilaration, scrabbled frantically at the tape, pulled, pushed, pulled . . . got a good grip a very good grip *PULL!*

The hot rush of pain was eclipsed by my gasp of relief. "Off," I said, putting my head on my knees and panting. "It's off."

I sat a moment, then let the tape drop to the ground. It was tempting to ball it up and hurl it hard as I could, but I was too tired.

Tired, but not dead.

Which was good, but now what? As far as I knew, my cell phone was still in my backpack, far out of reach. If my bad guy had been smart, he'd have smashed it to bits, on the off chance I'd get out of my prison cell. Speaking of which . . .

I put my hands on the floor and pushed my awkward self to my feet. Time to explore.

It didn't take long. After I'd felt my way around the room once, I went toe to heel with my feet, rounding up since my shoes were maybe ten inches long. My prison was rectangular, eight feet wide on the short side, ten feet deep. The door was solid and its hinges were on the other side. I'd felt a window frame on the wall opposite the door, but it was boarded up.

There were no other openings. There was nothing in the room. I felt every inch of the walls up as high as I could reach and down all the way to the wooden floor. No hooks, no nails, no nothing.

I jumped, reaching high with my tied hands, trying to touch the ceiling, trying to find chain, a rope, anything.

Instead, I grasped a lot of empty air.

I stood in the middle of the room, gasping for breath, trying not to think too much about reality, because it wasn't that great. In spite of partially freeing myself, I was still locked in an empty windowless room with no tools and no weapons. If the guy came back, there was little I could do to stop him doing whatever he wanted to do to me.

The guy. I stood straight and stared into the dark at the door. For a while I kicked at it and when I stopped from fear of breaking bones in my feet, it was just as solid as when I'd started my assault.

Then for a while I banged on the boards covering up the empty window frame. They were attached from the outside, so maybe I could knock one loose. The boards were wide and I was small and desperate—if I could make a gap, surely I could squiggle through.

But the boards must have been screwed in, not nailed. All my thumping and banging didn't do a thing. Not one single thing.

Finally exhaustion took over, yelling at me that it was time to quit, that I should wait until morning, wait until it got light.

I sat next to the door, positioning myself for a quick jump up and a fast run should it happen to open.

I laid my arms on my knees, put my head on my arms, and slept.

My dreams were filled with the growls of animals in the dark and threats that I couldn't quite hear. At some point, I twitched awake into the barn's dim light. I'd heard something. . . .

The whooshing of bird wings flew past. "Caw caw!"

Blue jay? Crow? Maybe a robin? Bird identification was another skill I should work on.

I rubbed my face, felt the sticky leftover from

the tape, felt the yuck on my unbrushed teeth, felt the dirt and sweat and general ick all over my body and in my hair. When I got out of here, a hot shower was the first order of business.

*When* I got out?

Smiling, I mentally patted myself on the back for having such a cheery thought first thing after sleeping in the locked-up corner of a barn with my wrists tied together. Good for me. My self-esteem, which should have been at rock bottom, was, due to some miracle, doing okay. Now for the rest of me.

I pushed myself to my feet and looked at my surroundings. The morning sun didn't exactly flood the place, but enough light was filtering in through gaps in the wood that I could see well enough. The door was indeed solid, the boards over the window were indeed stuck on tight, and the ceiling was indubitably out of reach. The only opening I could see anywhere was a gap between the ceiling and the top of the inside wall.

Hmm.

If I could get up there, I might be able to wriggle through, but since there was no way I could scale a ten-foot-high smooth wall, there wasn't much point in . . . wait a minute.

The window. It was close to that inside wall.

If I could get my hands free, I could use the thin boards that framed the window as a sort of ladder. I could climb to the top of the window, lever myself up and out over the wall. An average-sized man would never be able to do that—the half-inch wood around the window would surely collapse under his weight—but this compact woman could.

The first part of the plan, however, might be the hardest of all.

I looked at my bound wrists. Thick black tape encircled each one, then wrapped around them both. Twice. It was thicker than normal duct tape, and it felt stickier. Duct tape on steroids, Rafe had called it. It'll stick to brick, stone, stucco, or plaster, he'd said, and it was doing a fantastic job of holding my wrists together.

The result of last night's inspection-by-feel of the walls matched what I saw now. No nails hanging anywhere to help me out, no screws, no hooks, no nothing. I couldn't even find a good sharp splinter to help me puncture the tape. My bad luck I got imprisoned in a barn built to last.

I sat down and studied the stupid tape. It was just tape, after all. There had to be two ends, and one of them had to be on the outside. All I had to do was find the end, peel up one corner, and unwrap the whole thing. Easy.

Unfortunately, the outside end was on the far side of my wrists, making it the worst location possible for unwrapping. I could hardly see it, could barely even feel it.

I picked at the unmoving end and got nowhere.

A tool. My kingdom for a tool. My grandfather

had always carried a penknife. My dad carried a money clip that had a bottle opener. All I had was me and the clothes I wore; shorts, T-shirt, underwear, socks, and shoes.

I smiled a wide, happy smile. Shoes. I was wearing shoes. With laces.

Bending forward, I untied my left shoe and pulled the lace through the eyelets. I grabbed the aglet at one end of the lace and pushed it up against the end of the tape.

Nothing.

Push. Push again. Push again.

Nothing.

Despair leaked into my formerly almost-perky attitude. The perkiness must have come from the unrealistic expectation that formulating a plan was as good as having it come to fruition. Sometimes I hated real life.

Push. Push-at-this-freaking-strong-tape! *Move!*

Nothing.

I took a deep breath, trying to stop the tears, trying to keep on trying to get free. It wasn't easy. I couldn't think of any other way to get loose, so I had to go on trying. Because the only other choice was to sit in the corner and wait to die. And that wasn't a true choice, not really.

Push. Push. Push.

Time passed.

Slowly.

The room heated up. Yesterday's humidity

lingered on. The sunlight shifted around, slanting now from the left instead of the right. There wasn't a breath of air. Sweat stuck to my fingers, rolled down my face, pooled in places I didn't want to think about. At least my status of dehydration meant I didn't have any full-bladder issues.

Push. Push. Push.

I rested. Maybe slept a little.

Push. Push . . .

And then the tape moved. Just a teensy bit, but it moved.

I sucked in a breath. Maybe I'd imagined it. Maybe I was hallucinating. Maybe . . .

Holding that breath, I lifted my wrists to see. I hadn't imagined it. I'd actually, finally, made the end of this insanely strong tape move a little.

I would have cheered, but a sudden urgency overcame me. The guy could be coming back even now. Just because he'd been gone a long time didn't mean he wouldn't come back. If he came back now, right before I escaped . . . if he found me . . .

No. That wouldn't happen. I wouldn't let it happen.

Fighting panic, I jabbed at the end of the tape.

Just a little more, a little more, *there!*

I'd pulled off an inch of tape. Hallelujah! I rolled the shoelace aglet up inside the sticky stuff, used my hot, swollen fingers to tie the other end of lace through an eyelet of the shoe, stretched my leg out, and pulled.

The ripping sound of the tape unfurling was the sweetest sound I'd ever heard.

I kept rolling the unstuck tape into a larger and larger sticky ball, kept using the leverage of my leg to pull off more tape, rolling, pulling, rolling, pulling. . . . *Free!*

Of their own volition, my hands moved apart as far as they could go, as if they wanted nothing to do with each other. A hiccuping sob bubbled up out of me. Silly old hands. You'd have thought they'd have gotten used to each other, tied together like that for so long.

How long, in fact, had it been? I had no idea.

The urgency came back with a vengeance. I untied the one end of the shoelace and relaced it through the shoe. I yanked at the big ball of tape, but couldn't get the other end free of the sticky mess. Cursing, I was forced to leave the tape attached to the lace, and tied a bad and very lumpy knot.

I scrambled to my feet and ran across the small room. Hand there, foot there, and I was balancing on the bottom of the window frame. Hand up, foot up, hand up higher into a cobwebby darkness, foot up on the window frame's top, other foot beside it.

Gingerly, I stood up straight, doing my best not to look down. I didn't think I was afraid of heights, but I'd never been standing on a board not even an inch wide with my head at least ten feet off the ground before, either.

I poked my head over the top of the wall. Please, let there be a way out. Please . . .

The darkness on the other side was deep. But that didn't mean there wasn't an unlocked door through which I could escape. All I had to do was figure out a way to get over the wall and drop down on the other side without getting stuck in the ceiling or breaking a leg on the way down.

I stood there, my legs starting to quiver, waiting for my eyes to adjust to the dark. Was that a shelf down there? Maybe it would hold me. Maybe . . .

The sound of gravel crunching changed everything.

Without thought, I jumped high and shoved myself into the small space at the top of the wall. I didn't fit, didn't fit, had to fit, had to get through and out and away before he got here, had to go out, and then my head and shoulders were through and—

Voices. Footsteps. Car doors opening and closing.

I grabbed the top of the wall, pulled, couldn't get my big fat butt through the gap, wiggled, squirmed, pulled the rest of me over to the other side, slithered down the wall, hung on as my feet scrabbled for the shelf.

Where was it? I had to find it couldn't risk landing on it had to run had to get away had to—

A hand clamped around my ankle.

*"NO!"* I yelled, screamed, shrieked. I kicked, I kicked again, I was not going without a fight, he'd have to kill me in order to kill me he'd have to—

"Ms. Hamilton," said a male voice, "this is Detective Inwood. You can come down. Don't worry. You're safe now. It's okay."

But I was frozen in place. I couldn't move, couldn't make a sound, couldn't even nod my head. Strong hands encircled me, helped me down, away out of that barn, and into the sunlight of early evening.

Evening. I'd been in that barn a full day.

"You're shivering," Detective Devereaux said. "Let me get you a blanket." Two police cars were in the driveway, one unmarked vehicle and one patrol car with someone, I couldn't make out who, sitting in the backseat. Devereaux sat me in the unmarked and brought me a fuzzy blanket. I saw real concern in his eyes.

I tried to thank him, but it came out as a froggy croak.

"What was that?" the detective asked. "Your voice is pretty hoarse. Bet you're dry as a bone after spending, what, almost twenty-four hours in that barn. I'm so sorry we didn't get to you sooner." He looked over his shoulder. "Deputy, get the lady some water, will you?"

A uniformed officer, whom I recognized as

Deputy Wolverson, ran over with a water bottle. He cracked the top off the bottle, and held it out to me.

Water. I stared at it. At him. My mouth moved, but nothing came out.

"Go on," Detective Devereaux said. "It's all yours. There's more, if you want."

I did my best to smile at the deputy, then took the bottle and drank greedily, slugging it all down, not wasting a single precious drop. Nothing had ever tasted so good. The detectives let me drink, then asked if I needed an ambulance. I shook my head. All I needed was water and, after a gallon or so of that, a hot shower and whatever dinner Kristen wanted to cook for me.

"You sure?" Devereaux asked. "We can have one here in no time."

I shook my head again and drank water until I couldn't drink any more. When I lowered the bottle, I wiped my mouth with the back of my hand and envisioned dinner. Prime rib or whitefish, that was the question.

"Okay, then," Devereaux said. "What was that you were saying before?"

". . . Thanks. Just . . . thanks."

He studied me. "You know, we were listening to you all along."

Either my time in the barn had done something to my hearing or I hadn't gotten the memo about you-know-where freezing over. I looked at him.

He didn't appear to be playing a practical joke on me. "It didn't seem like it," I said.

"Yeah, I know."

I finished off the water bottle and he handed me a full one. When I'd poured it down my throat, I said, "If that was an apology, it wasn't a very good one."

"How about if I say I'm sorry you were locked in a barn all night?"

I shook my head.

He looked around. "Hey, Woody! She wants me to apologize for you being such a jerk."

Detective Inwood came over. "Ms. Hamilton, I'm deeply sorry."

I eyed him. "For what?"

Inwood sighed. "Ms. Hamilton, we seem to have gotten off on the wrong foot. Please accept my apologies for not seeming to take you seriously. But we were, and it was your tip about the quad that got us looking in the right place."

"Okay," I said. "Apology accepted. And I'm sorry, too. I should have had more patience and I really shouldn't have lost my temper yesterday."

The detectives nodded, and, for the first time, we were friends. But . . . "How did you know I was out here?"

They exchanged a glance I couldn't interpret at all. "You can thank your cat," Inwood said. "He was howling and making such a racket this morning that your neighbor, Louisa Axford, came to see what the problem was. When you weren't there, she used the key she said you gave her"—he looked at me with his eyebrows raised and I nodded—"to get in. She was worried you might have been sick and went in to check. That's when she saw the note you'd written. The one that said you'd expected to be back by dark yesterday. Good idea, leaving that."

*Bless you, Mom,* I thought. *You were right all along and I will forever do whatever you say without question.*

"The note also said where you were and what you were doing," Devereaux said. "We've been searching for you for some time. Nice to find you all in one piece."

I agreed wholeheartedly, and I told him how much I appreciated their efforts, but . . . "Who's in the backseat?" I gestured to the other vehicle.

"Oh, yeah." Detective Devereaux smiled. "That is a gentleman who was found driving down this road. After a short chase he obligingly stopped. Since the only place the road leads is this house, what do you bet we'll find his fingerprints all over this barn and that nice quad parked inside?"

"A quad with an ORV license issued to one Kyle Sutton." Inwood raised his eyebrows. "And I'm willing to bet that Mr. Sutton here owns the exact type of rifle that was used to murder Stan Larabee. What do you think, Don?"

What I thought was that it was over, and that I

wasn't surprised at the ending. So it had been Kyle Sutton. He was the one who put me in the barn. Afterward, he'd probably left for his shift at the restaurant. Some of those growling noises in my dreams had probably been his car returning.

The knowledge that he'd been sleeping in the house while I'd been trying to escape gave me the creeps. And the knowledge that I must have been making too much noise to hear the noise of his recent leave-taking was even creepier.

But at least it was over. I wasn't dead from dehydration or any other means, and Stan's killer was in police custody.

"Sorry this took so long, Stan," I murmured, and in a quiet part of my thoughts, I heard his reply.

*Remember what I told you about reputations, Minnie. And thanks.*

"Thanks for what?" Devereaux asked.

I shook my head. "Could I get a ride back to my car?" There was a cat waiting for me, and I had a lot to tell him.

# Chapter 20

The next evening, Kristen and I sat out on the marina's patio. My best friend was smart, brave, strong, and able to cook soufflés without a recipe, but she hated boats with a passion. Wouldn't have anything to do with them. Wouldn't even sit on the houseboat's deck while tied up to the dock. I'd long since given up trying to jolly her out of her fears and had brought out a freshly opened bottle of red adult beverage and a couple of glasses.

"When I hired Larry," she said, "I asked around about him. I knew him in high school, but hadn't seen him since. Everybody said he was a great chef, but that managing money was his weak point." She snorted. "I'm such an idiot. I remember thinking, well, gosh, I'm hiring a chef, not a manager. What do I care about his financial skills? But this was all about money, wasn't it?"

On the ride back to my car, Detective Devereaux had told me what they'd already found out through some fast investigating.

Larry, aka Kyle, and his wife had lost their house to foreclosure a few months ago. They'd rented that place in the valley because it was dirt cheap. His wife had hated it. Devereaux had already tracked down her phone number; she said she'd left Kyle and moved downstate to stay with friends while she was looking for a job.

The captured Kyle had told the detectives that he was headed south that morning to talk her into coming home, that he was going to call the police from a pay phone at a rest stop some-where and give an anonymous tip that I was locked in the barn.

Kristen rolled her eyes. "And they believed him?"

I shrugged. They hadn't, but I had. Or I'd wanted to. Thinking that he'd left me there to die wasn't going to improve my dreams any, and since I'd escaped, I'd decided to accept the explanation.

Kristen sipped her wine. "Man, this is good. Where did you get it?"

"You gave it to me for Christmas."

She nodded absently. "There's one thing I haven't been able to figure out. Why did Larry think he was going to inherit anything?"

I looked at the never-ending blue sky. "He thought Stan liked him." I remembered what Larry had said, the night Caroline and I had eaten dinner together. From Stan's undoubtedly offhand comment about money being easy to come by, Larry must have built up a fantasy of inheritances and money owed from long-ago wrongs. And I heard again what Larry had said, the first time I'd met him, about his dreams of building a restaurant.

Had it really been all about money?

I'd had a lot of time to think about Kristen's question, out there in the barn, and I still didn't know. I'd had time to think about the farmhouse, about Stan, about his shady business practices, and about his six sisters. I'd thought about genealogy and how the sting of injustice can survive through generations. I'd thought about how Stan's sale of the farmhouse had started his empire, and how it had ruined his relationship with his sisters forever. I'd thought about families and money and motivations and hatred, and standing there in the warm sunshine outside the barn, I'd asked the detectives if they knew the maiden name of Kyle's grandmother.

They'd looked at each other. "No idea," Inwood said. "Why?"

When I suggested that it might be Larabee, they both gave slow nods and pulled out their cell phones. Devereaux got the answer first, from his sister-in-law who'd grown up in that part of the county.

He'd nodded. "Larabee. How'd you know?"

I didn't say anything, but watched as Deputy Wolverson got into the patrol car, started it up, and drove off, taking Larry away.

"Say, I forgot to tell you, Ms. Hamilton," Detective Devereaux had said. "We recovered a bullet from one of the bookmobile tires. What do you bet the bullet was fired from a gun Mr.

Sutton owns? And it'll be easy enough to get witnesses to testify that Mr. Sutton knew the bookmobile lady was trying to find Stan's killer."

I'd frowned. "It will?"

Devereaux had chuckled. "Sure. Everybody knew."

When I was relating this part of the story to Kristen, she sat up so suddenly that wine slopped over the side of her glass. "Shot?!" she yelled. "Larry shot at you?"

Oops. "I never told you about that? Well, it was only a few days ago. And nothing happened, so—"

"Nothing happened?" She sent me her fierce I-could-make-life-miserable-for-you-if-I-wanted-to look. "My best friend gets shot at by one of my employees—*shot* at!—and she doesn't think I might want to know?"

"It wasn't me, it was the tires. And at the time I didn't know it was Larry."

"Kyle," she muttered. "Should have known from the beginning that guy was trouble. Anybody named Kyle who'd rather go by Larry is bound to have a screw loose." She squinted a little. "Of course, he looks like a Larry, doesn't he?"

"If you live in the town where you grew up, it can be hard to get rid of a nickname." Or a reputation.

When I'd called Aunt Frances last night, I'd told her that not only was Stan's killer in jail, but none of it had been her fault. Not in the least. She hadn't believed me at first, but I'd eventually convinced her. After her tears had stopped, we'd made a pact to rehabilitate Stan's reputation. It would take time, but with two determined women on the job, maybe it wouldn't take so very long.

"Yeah, well." Kristen sipped her wine. "I just hope when he gets out of jail, he comes to me looking for work."

"Why's that?"

"So I can beat him over the head, of course." One-handed, she used an imaginary bat to do the job. "By the way, what's going on with that hot doctor of yours?"

I looked at her sideways. "You were there our whole first date. What don't you already know?"

"Oh, come on, it was funny. Yeah, I see you trying not to laugh. Don't laugh, Minnie, don't laugh. . . ."

I swiped off my smile with the back of my hand. "So how about a double date, me and Tucker, you and Mitchell Koyne?"

She nodded. "Good idea. How about Friday?"

My jaw dropped. "You . . . you're going out with Mitchell?"

"Why not?" She shrugged. "He's about our age, can almost speak a complete sentence, sometimes has a job, and of course I'm not going out with him, you goofus." She laughed. "Had you going there, didn't I?"

I rested my head against the chair's back and blew out a huge breath. "For a second I thought I'd created a monster."

"The only monster around here is in jail," she said. "And now I'm short a chef three days before the Fourth of July. You know, if you'd been more considerate of your friends, you would have waited until after the holiday to get tossed in that barn."

"I'll try to do better next time."

She grinned. "Good. So, now that we know what happened, who's going to get Stan's money? Is the library going to make out like a bandit?"

"From the number of attorney letters I've seen on Stephen's desk, I'd guess it'll be tied up in courts for months, if not years."

Kristen snorted. She wasn't a big fan of the lawyer breed.

"On the other hand," I said, "both Caroline Grice and Gunnar Olson have sent nice donation checks."

"Hey, congratulations!" Kristen held out her glass to tink with mine, but before the glasses clinked, she looked down. "Hmm. Minnie, methinks you might have an escapee."

"Mrr."

Sure enough, it was my rotten cat. "Eddie, what are you doing out here?" I'd left him inside the boat with the windows shut and the door . . . The door. I'd left the solid door open, leaving only the screen door latched. Wonderful. Eddie had learned how to open the screen door. Simply outstanding.

He bumped my shin with the top of his head, jumped up onto my lap, and turned around one, two, three times. When he finally settled down, he was facing Kristen. "Mrr," he said to her, dipping his head.

She laughed. "And to you, Mr. Bookmobile Cat."

I petted his thick fur. Eddie, the bookmobile cat. Eddie, the cat who had found Stan. Eddie, the cat who'd ripped up the Grice genealogy research that had been a waste of time. Eddie, who'd gone ballistic when he'd seen Audry. Eddie, who had nearly scratched a hole in the door when I'd left for the farmhouse.

I stared at him. Had he actually guided me toward the answers? Pushed me in the right direction when I was taking the wrong path? Tried to warn me of danger?

My hand stilled and I looked down at him. He looked up at me and our gazes met, my brown eyes staring into his yellow ones.

Nah. It was my imagination. Had to be. Eddie might be smart, but he wasn't that smart. No cat was.

He shut one eye, then opened it again.

"Did he just wink at you?" Kristen asked. "He did! He winked at you!"

"I hope not," I said slowly. "I really, truly hope not."

Eddie shut both of his eyes.

And purred.

**Center Point Large Print**
600 Brooks Road / PO Box 1
Thorndike, ME 04986-0001 USA

**(207) 568-3717**

**US & Canada:**
**1 800 929-9108**
www.centerpointlargeprint.com